Stephen was  **lt his**
contentn̶̶̶̶̶̶̶̶̶̶ming
her bloo̶̶̶̶̶̶̶̶̶̶made
her *feel* b̶̶̶̶̶̶

Her eyes slid closed. For long minutes she
lost herself to the glory of the music and the
moment. Stephen gave in to it as well; she could
feel his surrender in the grip of his hands, in
the intimate press of his legs to hers, and in the
graceful, floating ease with which he guided
them about the dance floor.

And that was when she knew she'd come full
circle. Her campaign was forgotten, her plans
and strategies left behind. Here she was, right
back where she'd started two years ago, wanting
Stephen Manning with all of her heart.

Perhaps she needed a new campaign, with new
strategies designed to win his heart. Because she
longed for it, and for his unfathomable blue eyes
and his maddening imperious ways and his warm
acceptance and his heated kisses.

But there was one other thing that was different
now, too. She wasn't that young girl any more,
happy to accept whatever part of himself Stephen
was willing or able to give. She wanted all of
him. And no campaign of hers was going to be
successful in flushing it out. She sighed. He had
to choose to give it.

AUTHOR NOTE

Horse racing was a popular pastime in the Georgian and Regency periods, and quite a different spectacle from what it is today. Imagine the ruckus that might happen if enthusiastic spectators joined in the last leg and rode along with the finishers in a modern race! I loved dipping into racing's illustrious history, and hope you will enjoy a glimpse of historic Newmarket and this exciting sport.

Neither Pratchett nor Ornithopter were real horses, but the gambling 'legs' and 'black legs' truly existed, and poisoned water troughs, opium balls and laming were a few of the terrible methods that were used to influence the outcome of races. I admit to shifting the order of the races that would have taken place in Newmarket at the time, but as it was done for Stephen and Mae's sake I hope you will forgive me.

HOW TO MARRY
A RAKE

Deb Marlowe

All Best
Wishes,
Deb
Marlowe

MILLS
BOON

All the characters in this book have no existence outside the imagination of the author, and have no relation whatsoever to anyone bearing the same name or names. They are not even distantly inspired by any individual known or unknown to the author, and all the incidents are pure invention.

First published in Great Britain 2011
Harlequin Mills & Boon Limited,
Eton House, 18-24 Paradise Road, Richmond, Surrey TW9 1SR

© Deb Marlowe 2011

ISBN: 978 0 263 88244 5

Harlequin Mills & Boon policy is to use papers that are natural, renewable and recyclable products and made from wood grown in sustainable forests. The logging and manufacturing process conform to the legal environmental regulations of the country of origin.

Printed and bound in Spain
by Litografia Rosés, S.A., Barcelona

Deb Marlowe grew up in Pennsylvania with her nose in a book. Luckily, she'd read enough romances to recognise the true modern hero she met at a college Halloween party—even though he wore a tuxedo T-shirt instead of breeches and tall boots. They married, settled in North Carolina, and produced two handsome, intelligent and genuinely amusing boys.

Though she now spends much of her time with her nose in her laptop, for the sake of her family she does occasionally abandon her inner world for the domestic adventure of laundry, dinner and carpool. Despite her sacrifice, not one of the men in her family is yet willing to don breeches or tall boots. She's working on it. Deb would love to hear from readers! You can contact her at debmarlowe@debmarlowe.com

Previous novels by Deb Marlowe:

SCANDALOUS LORD, REBELLIOUS MISS
AN IMPROPER ARISTOCRAT
HER CINDERELLA SEASON
ANNALISE AND THE SCANDALOUS RAKE
    (part of *Regency Summer Scandals*)
TALL, DARK AND DISREPUTABLE

For Darlene—the only true Super Mom
that I've known. You are an inspiration.
I want to be just like you when I grow up.

Chapter One

~~~~~~~~~~~~~~~~~~~~~~~~~

Newmarket, Suffolk, England

A great swell of music rose from below, bursting over Lord Stephen Manning like a bubble and causing him to lengthen his stride.

He was late.

This is what came of dawdling in Newmarket all afternoon. Titchley Hall lay just outside the famous racing town, and Stephen had passed through on his way to the Earl of Toswick's house party. He'd attended the spring meetings before, of course, but today he'd been unable to resist stopping to see the courses, clipped and ready, and the Heath, lush, green and quiet after all those gorgeous thoroughbreds had finished exercising for the day.

Everything had looked the same, and yet it all *felt* very different. Stephen had wandered the long, familiar stretch of High Street, trying to unearth a reason for his sense of displacement. Not until he found himself back on the Rowley Mile, mentally measuring the padding on a course post, did the realisation strike—Newmarket was the same. It was he who had changed.

He had been discerning details and noticing incidentals that he never had before—because today he looked through new eyes. No longer was he just a spectator, another young blood of the *ton* seeking the excitement of the races and the thrill of risking his quarterly allowance. He was older now, and hopefully wiser, and, most importantly—he was a man with all the burdens and responsibilities that came with owning his own racecourse.

All the warmth of pride and accomplishment swept over him again as he reached Titchley's grand stairway. After two long years of work and sweat and sacrifice, he'd done it. He'd taken a neglected and broken-down estate and literally transformed it. Fincote Park lay waiting, pristine and challenging and bristling with potential.

And empty.

Impatient, Stephen brushed the thought away. He banished, too, the wispy, haunting image of his forlorn mother. Shame and despair had once been Fincote's main commodities, but those days were over now. That's exactly what all those months of labour had been about. He summoned instead the picture of Fincote's people, all the eager and hopeful faces that had seen him off. They were why he had come here. They were what made this house party the most important social event of his life.

The marbled hall at the bottom of the stairs had emptied already. To the right echoed the clink of porcelain and the clatter of furniture as servants transformed a long parlour into a dining area. Stephen rounded the turn in a hurry and headed left instead, toward the brightly lit passage leading towards the ballroom. If luck was with him, then he'd only missed the opening set.

'*Manning?*'

The call came from the door behind him, accompanied by a gust of cool, evening air. Stephen turned.

'Devil take me! It *is* you!'

A reluctant smile turned abruptly into a wince as George Dunn, Viscount Landry, crossed the hall to pound him enthusiastically on the shoulder.

'By God—but it is good to see you! How long has it been? I never thought you would stay away from London—and yet it's been months and months.'

'Too long,' Stephen agreed. 'Damned if it's not good to see you, too.'

'Lord, but haven't we missed you? Town has been as dull as ditchwater without you to liven things up!'

Stephen laughed. 'As dull as that? Not that I believe it for a second, old man. Not with you about. You always dreamt up more mischief in a day than I ever could in a month.' He pulled his hand away before the viscount could wring it from his arm.

'Well, that goes without saying,' retorted Landry with a grin. 'But there's never been another that could claim half your style.'

Stephen sketched an ironic bow.

'Do you know that they still talk in the clubs about how you convinced your brother's ladybird that she

needed some sort of gambit to truly stand out from the
rest of the *demi-monde*?'

He could not hold back a reminiscent snort. 'I didn't
suggest the Bird of Paradise theme—she thought that
one up all on her own.'

Landry laughed out loud. 'Garish feathers attached
to every gown and bonnet—and even her shoes. The
daft girl had feathers braided into her mount's mane
and entwined through the spokes of the wheels on her
gig.' He laughed harder. 'And your brother sneezed
every time he got within a yard of her!'

Stephen's smile grew wry. 'Which is only one reason
why Nicholas, at least, has been happy to have me
tucked away in Sussex.'

'Ah, yes, I recollect it now. The estate you inherited
from your mother is out there, is it not? But Good God,
man! Surely there was no need to cloister yourself away
like a novice in a nunnery!'

Good humour swiftly abandoned him. 'I'm afraid it
was necessary. The estate needed…attention.'

'Attention?' The viscount gaped. 'I'm sensing one of
your infamous understatements. I shudder to imagine
what sort of shape the place must have been in to have
required nearly two years worth of *attention*.'

Stephen stiffened. Deliberately, he forced his muscles to relax and reached for a quip to turn the growing
intrusiveness of the conversation, but Landry beat him
to it.

'No, please.' The viscount held out a staying hand.
'None of your witticisms right now. And do spare me
the details. The heavy yoke of my own responsibility
is weighing me down. I've no need to add yours to the

mix.' He shook his head, his movements gone slow
and heavy as if the weight of the world did indeed rest
on his shoulders. 'I never thought it would all come
so soon. But look to your family—you, farming out
in Sussex, Nicholas happy with his duchess, and your
sisters all married and spitting out brats as prodigiously
as they used to stir up scandal.' He sighed heavily. 'If
the notorious Fitzmanning Miscellany has bowed to
convention, then who am I to resist?'

The music drifting from the ballroom ended with a
flourish. As if it had been the signal he'd been waiting
for, Landry straightened and adjusted his neckcloth.
'Well, let's to it then, shall we?' He set off, but had
only taken a step or two towards the ballroom before he
stopped abruptly. 'I say, Manning.' Tension hardened
his face as he turned back towards Stephen. 'You're not
here after the new heiress as well, are you?'

Startled, Stephen laughed. 'God, no.'

Landry relaxed. 'Ah. Good, then.' He bit his lip, considering. 'Not that it's a bad idea, particularly if your
estate's coffers are poorly. But I've got first crack at this
new girl, I say. She's just back in England.'

'And thus unlikely to have heard anything untow-
ard about you?' Stephen asked with a grin. 'Have at
it, man.' He rolled his eyes. 'If you stopped to think a
minute, you'd recall just how we Mannings and Fitzmannings came by our epithet. My father married
an heiress, did he not? And considering how that all
turned out, do you think I would be so eager to repeat
his mistakes?'

'Hmm. I hadn't considered it from that angle.'

Stephen gave a shudder. 'You're looking for a leg-shackle? Consider the field open, man. I've far too many irons in the fire to even contemplate such a thing.' Fincote was his priority and deserved all of his focus.

Landry brightened. 'But your father did have the right idea about one thing, at least. Marriage needn't make a monk of me.'

They had nearly reached the ballroom. Groups of guests had spilled out and gathered in the passageway here. Landry nodded at an acquaintance, still musing. 'Of course, I cannot see that I would abandon my heiress to live out my days with my mistress, as he did.' He cast a hurried glance in Stephen's direction. 'Not that any man could blame your father. Catherine Ramsey… that is, your stepmother…the duchess, eventually… Well, there will never be another like her, will there? Women like that come as rare as hen's teeth.'

Stephen didn't respond. It wasn't much of a struggle, really, to keep his face carefully blank. Someone like Landry could never understand the wealth of conflicted emotions he held towards his father, his mother and the woman who had split them apart, but still welcomed him into her chaotic home and happy family. He'd become accustomed to this sort of awkward commentary—just as he'd become accustomed to deflecting it with a jibe.

Scandalous parents and an unconventional upbringing were burdens that Stephen shared with all of his siblings and half-siblings—and each of them had developed their own tactics to endure them. Redirect, reflect, sidetrack—it was a bag of tricks that worked for Stephen as a child. As a course of action it had proven ever more valuable as he grew and had to face even more difficult challenges.

One of which waited within. He and Landry had come to a stop just outside the wide, sweeping doors into the ballroom. Light, heat, noise and the chatter of many voices emanated from within. It might only be the diehard members of the racing community here in Newmarket nearly a week ahead of the start of racing, but it appeared that Toswick had encountered no difficulty filling his guest list.

Landry hung back, obvious reluctance in his eye as he faced the glittering assembly. 'Damn if I'm not envious of you, Manning. You are free to enjoy the evening as it comes, while I must assemble my weapons and enter the hunt.'

'Well, there you are wrong. There's more than one sort of hunt afoot at an event like this. And more prizes to be had than just heiresses.' In fact, the thought of chasing down a woman and her money to solve his problems sent his every feeling into revolt, and not only because of his parents and the mess that they had made of their relationship.

He'd come so far in the last gruelling and backbreaking months—a thousand leagues beyond the attention-hungry young man that Landry had known. And he had done it on his own. He wanted to see this through, *must* see it through, to prove to himself, and to the people at Fincote, that he could.

Interest, spiked with a bit of mischief, lifted Landry's brow. 'Oh? On the hunt, but not in the petticoat line? What is it then? Shall you rescue your fortune and your estate at the card table?' The viscount looked wistful. 'Perhaps I will join you there, later.'

'No, not cards,' corrected Stephen. 'Something entirely different.' He grew exasperated at his friend's lifted eyebrows. 'It's not farming that I've been up to in Sussex. I've been breaking my back—and my bank account—turning Fincote into a world-class racecourse.'

Only Landry could convey so much scepticism with a blink.

Stephen shrugged. 'It's true, old man. Ah, but I wish you could see it.' His heart thumped. With calculation, he allowed his enthusiasm to leak into his words. 'Two courses, both smooth and done up to every modern standard. One with a climbing start and a section along the Downs where you can feel the sea wind in your face. The other a demanding track through the woods with an uphill finish. New stables, accommodations, everything.'

'By God, you're serious!'

'I am. The town's merchants put together a cup and we held a local meet to test the waters. It went off smooth as silk. Fincote is ready and waiting, and now I need to catch the attention of the racing world. It's why I'm here.'

Landry stared as if he'd never seen him before. 'Passion, purpose and planning. My God, it truly is the end of an era.' His mouth twisted into a grin. 'But what do the signs tell you?'

Stephen laughed. 'Rest easy—I haven't changed that much. I kept my eye open for portents every step of the way here—you'll be happy to know that they were all favourable.'

'Well, that is a relief. I confess I would have been distraught had you given up your superstitions entirely.' Landry chuckled. 'And gaining attention was always your strong suit. Have you a plan?'

Stephen lowered his voice. 'What I need is to arrange a truly remarkable private match. A spectacular race that will launch Fincote with a noise heard throughout racing, gain the attention of the Jockey Club and bring every owner, trainer, spectator and stable boy flocking to our doors.' He ran an eye over the shifting crowd before them. 'That's why, even as you are angling after your heiress, I will be angling after an introduction to the Earl of Ryeton.'

Landry's mobile face went perilously still. 'Ryeton?'

'Yes. Do you know him?'

'Enough to warn you away from the man.' Even Landry's voice had gone cold and flat.

Stephen stared at his friend. 'Why?'

Landry shook his head. 'I cannot elaborate. Only believe that I mean this as a friend—you'd do best to stay far away from the man.'

'That's not an option.' He frowned. 'The earl is the reigning king of the turf. His string of winning horses is a mile long. The depth of his stables is amazing. But, most importantly—he owns the most talked-about racehorse since Eclipse.'

'Pratchett.' Landry nearly chocked on the horse's name.

'Yes, Pratchett. That horse is why I'm here. He's incredible. If I can convince Ryeton to race him at

Fincote, our success will be assured. People will flock from every corner of the kingdom to see that thoroughbred run, no matter who he's matched against.'

Landry snorted. 'It's a sound enough idea. Unfortunately, Ryeton's not likely to go along with it.'

Stephen bristled. 'Why not?'

'The man's an elitist. A racing snob. Some of the old guard is like that, you know—if you haven't been breeding and racing since the time of Charles II, then you are nothing. And Ryeton's the worst. He decries the entrance of the *nouveau riche* or even the newly interested into his snug little world.' He made another dismissive sound. 'Although he's not above taking their money.'

Stephen's jaw tightened in determination. 'I have to try. This plan is the best and quickest way to Fincote's success.'

'Try, then.' Landry sighed. 'But you would do best not to hint at an association with me. It won't do you any good in Ryeton's eyes.'

'It's as bad as that?'

'Don't say I didn't warn you.' The viscount stood tall and smoothed his coat. A footman sidled by, heading into the ballroom with a full tray of champagne flutes, and Landry reached out and snagged two as he passed. He handed one to Stephen and held his aloft. 'Success to us both,' he toasted.

'And my thanks for the advice.' Stephen took a sip and watched as Landry drained his in one long drink.

'Ah, the music begins again.' Landry handed his empty glass to a footman positioned just outside the ballroom door. The poor man looked at him and at it in bemusement. 'It is our call to the start, Manning.' He tossed a last cheeky grin as he moved forwards to melt into the crowd. 'And we're off.'

Stephen laughed, then he squared his shoulders and slid into the crowd in another direction. The race had indeed begun. And he did not mean to lose.

Miss Mae Halford hovered at the entrance to Lord Toswick's ballroom, a smile quirking at the corners of her mouth, a sense of anticipatory excitement swelling in her breast. Tension stretched tight across her shoulders and settled into the valley between, but she welcomed it. She was a soldier, and the glittering battlefield lay before her.

'Don't worry, dear,' her mother said at her elbow. 'Your father has *promised* not to abandon us until we've mingled a bit and made the acquaintance of the right sort of people.'

Mae patted her mother's hand. 'I'm not worried a bit, Mama,' she said reassuringly. But she couldn't fault her mother's anxiety. Anyone looking from the outside would judge that the pair had plenty to worry about.

Despite his promises, her father had already spotted his cronies and surged ahead. In less than thirty seconds they'd all be up to their haunches in horse talk. He'd be useless this evening, even as Mae prepared to attempt the impossible.

After a rocky entry into young womanhood and a subsequent two years abroad, Mae Halford was about to worm her way back into the stifling and rarified atmosphere of English society. And she was going to do it without the benefit of a title or family connections.

Her father was a vastly successful businessman, a man whose two abiding passions—making money and spending it on thoroughbred racing horses—left precious little time or attention for aught else. Her mother, the daughter of a shopkeeper, had caught Barty Halford before he became richer than Croesus. Even after all these years she still had not reconciled herself to her role as a wealthy man's wife, or become comfortable socialising with those she still considered her betters.

But all was not doom and dire gloom. After all, Mae's father was not just wealthy, he was *obscenely* wealthy, and that fact was bound to open a door or two. Her personal assets were not totally lacking either. Wit came easily to her and immersion in European salons had taught her how to temper it into charm. She had her mother's pretty blue eyes, blond hair with a hint of a strawberry tint and a bosom that her knowing French maid assured her was just large enough without straying into vulgarity.

Without a doubt, though, Mae knew that her biggest asset lay between her ears, not inside her bodice. Her father called her a *thinker* and bemoaned the fact that she had not been born a son. She *had* been born a planner, an organiser and a strategist. They were characteristics that would indeed have been ideally suited to her father's son, but which had so far proven largely lamentable in a daughter. She meant to put them to good use now. For she stood on the verge of her greatest project, her most important scheme—her Marriage Campaign.

'Mrs Halford, I'm so glad you decided to come down and join us.' Their hostess approached with a smile.

'You can hardly have recovered your land legs, so soon from your voyage, but I promise that you shall enjoy yourself. I know several ladies who are interested in hearing about your travels.'

'Thank you, my lady.' Mae's mother relaxed a bit under the countess's kind attention.

'I see your husband is as well occupied as mine.' Lady Toswick rolled her eyes at the knot of gentlemen gathered in a corner. She turned a smile upon Mae. 'But I hope your daughter will be happy to learn that she has an acquaintance among my house guests.'

'I'm thrilled to hear it, Lady Toswick,' Mae answered with a smile. 'And curious, too.'

'Yes, as am I,' her mother agreed. Her eyes darted nervously around the room. 'We've been abroad so long and this is our first social engagement since we've been back in England. Who could it be?'

'A school friend, I understand. Lady Corbet. Although as she is newly married, I'm sure you'll remember her as Miss Adelaide Ward.'

'Oh, Addy! Yes, of course. I remember her fondly.'

'Well, you'll find her at the dancing, I'm sure.' Lady Toswick was searching the ballroom with a practised eye. 'Yes, there, she's just ending a set. Oh, and she's spotted us!' The countess tucked her mother's arm firmly through her own. 'Go and enjoy your reunion, Miss Halford. My friends and I are all agog to tease your mother until she tells us where she purchased the gorgeous silk for her gown.'

Mae smiled encouragement and watched her mother follow alongside the countess before turning to meet Lady Corbet—Addy. She grinned at the spectacle her old friend made as she squealed her way across the ballroom, flapping her hands as she came. Miss Trippet of The Select School for Young Girls had not succeeded in squelching Addy's vivaciousness any more than she'd cured Mae's tendency to organise her schoolgirls into trouble.

'Oh, Mae, it is you!' Addy clasped her by the hands and squeezed. 'How elegant you are! Is that waistline the latest Paris fashion?' She stood back and examined Mae from head to toe. 'You are going to put every girl in London to shame.' She grinned. 'I'm so glad you are back!'

'Addy,' Mae said warmly. 'How glad I am to see you.' She pulled her old friend in for a quick embrace. 'You are practically the first person I've seen since we docked!' She raised a brow. 'And Lady Toswick says that you are newly married? Congratulations!'

'Yes, I am a wife now—can you believe it? To Lord Corbet. He's only a baron, which disappointed Papa, of course.' Addy's father was a wealthy cit like Mae's, as were so many fathers of the girls at Miss Trippet's school. 'He can be the greatest dunderhead at times,' she continued, 'but he's *my* dunderhead.' The smile that crossed her face was tender. 'Just as I am his addlepate. I confess, I am quite fond of him.'

'Then I am supremely happy for you.' And a tad envious, too. Mae could only hope that she found someone as willing to overlook her own flaws. 'Is your husband here tonight? I should love to meet him.'

'Oh, yes. He's likely slunk off to the card room. We'll go and drag him out of there in a moment.' She frowned. The surrounding crowd had grown steadily larger and was pressing ever closer. 'But first, I have to hear everything. There were rumours, you know, about you and a young man, but no one seemed to know who he might be—and then you were gone! Come. Let's go sit in the chaperons' chairs. We can put our heads together and gossip like a couple of old biddies.'

She pulled Mae through the glittering spectacle and over to a row of straight-backed chairs. She chose a pair well away from the closest, capped matrons. 'Were the whispers true, then?' Addy leaned in close. 'Was there a completely ineligible young man ready to cart you away to Gretna Green? Did your parents whisk you to Europe in order to keep you from his clutches?'

'Of course not!' There had been nothing ineligible about the young man in question. And while Mae would gladly have travelled with him to the ends of the earth, he hadn't been interested enough to walk her in to dinner, let alone willing to run off to get married.

'Oh.' Addy sounded vastly disappointed. 'Well, it was a long time ago, in any case.' She cocked her head. 'How long *have* you been abroad?'

'Nearly two years.'

'So long? You must have been pining to come home.'

Mae laughed. 'Not at all, actually.' She smiled in reminiscence. 'I had the making of all the travel arrangements to myself. My father cared not where we went, as long as there was an opportunity for business or a reputable horse breeder nearby. My mother only worried over the comfort of our rooms. So I was free to indulge myself.' She shot a conspirator's grin at her friend. 'And I did. I simply wallowed in great churches and grand palaces and large estates. I explored battle-fields and boated in lakes and rivers all over Europe. I attended theatres and salons in every great city and met scores of interesting people.'

None, however, who could completely erase the image of the man she'd left behind. Such a man did exist, however. He was out there—and Mae fully intended to find him.

'But now you are back,' Addy said with satisfaction. A crafty look descended over her pretty face. 'And I'd wager you're here because your father decided it was time to find you a husband.' Her eyes rounded suddenly in horror. 'But the Season is nearly half over! There's no time to waste! You should have gone straight to London! Whatever are you doing in Newmarket, when there are husbands to be hunted?'

Laughing, Mae agreed. 'We have left it a bit late, haven't we?' She leaned in, as Addy had done before. 'We are in Newmarket, dear, because my father has brought home a most promising new filly. He means to race her in the Guineas—and he expects her to make a name for herself. He has grand plans to let her win a few important races and then pull in a fortune breeding future champions off of her.' She lowered her voice. 'Truthfully, although Father says it's time I had a hus-band, I believe he is at least as concerned about search-ing out a stud to cover that filly as he is about finding one for me.'

Addy gasped. Then she let out a peal of shocked laughter. 'You haven't changed a bit, Mae Halford!'

'Oh, but I have. I've grown up—and I've had the value of being circumspect forced down my gullet.'

She smirked. 'I'm still me. I still analyse and organise and plan, but now I know how to make it look socially acceptable.'

Addy stared. 'Oh! I know that look. You had the exact same gleam in your eye when you organised Miss Trippet's girls to boycott the painting master.'

'Something had to be done,' Mae protested. 'He was beyond appalling—coming in from behind to critique our work and sneaking unnecessary touches. The last straw was when he tried to convince poor Esther that posing nude was the only way to prove her dedication to art.'

'And now you are trying to distract me! You *are* scheming something.' Addy nearly glowed with mischief. 'You must allow me to help. It'll be as if we were girls again.'

'This is no girl's crusade. It's far more important.' Mae knew enough now to tamp down the enthusiasm in her voice. 'I'm just as happy to be in Newmarket, for while my father is distracted with his horses, I intend to map out a plan for my future.' She cocked her head at Addy's surprised expression. 'And why should I not? Should I leave it to my father? He used to say he wished me to be a lady, but I think he's given it up. He's determined to fire me off, and of course, he's correct—if I were a man I would be using my talents learning the family business.' She sighed. 'Such is not my fate—and as marriage is, then I'm determined to have a say in it.'

Addy nodded, impressed.

'What frightens me is that Papa spends more time poring over the Stud Book than his Debrett's. I'm afraid he'll hand me right over to the first man to come along and offer land with a good ore vein or a favourable shipping contract.'

'Or the owner of the best-blooded stallion.' Addy giggled.

'Exactly.' Except that this was no laughing matter. This was Mae's life's happiness at stake. She had to at least try to find someone who could accept her as she was. She'd been battling her whole life, fighting to keep from being squeezed into a stultifying society mould. She didn't want to spend a lifetime fighting her husband as well.

There must be at least one gentleman in England who would not be offended or threatened by her…abilities. Mae was determined to find him.

'What do you mean to do?'

'What I do best. Careful planning and brilliant manoeuvring.'

'You sound like a general.' Addy sounded awed.

'I *am* a general. Make no mistake, Addy. This is war. And this…' she gestured to the brilliant, seething scene in front of them '…this is merely the first skirmish. Tonight I begin to gather intelligence. There can be no strategy without sufficient information.'

'I never thought I would feel sorry for society's single gentlemen. They can have no idea what is about to hit them.' Abruptly Addy reached out and grasped her hand. 'You'll do brilliantly.' The warmth and reassurance in her voice touched Mae. 'You've never failed to accomplish what you set out to do.' She stood. 'You shall command the campaign and I will be your loyal assistant.' Her eyes sparkled. 'Now, let's go and find my husband. He can be our first source of information.'

Willingly, Mae followed, glad that Addy had turned away to search out a path through the crowd. For she was wrong. Mae had indeed known failure—and in the one chase that had meant more than all the others together.

Unbidden, her mind's eye turned inwards, to where she'd locked away her remembrances like a horde of treasure. Laughing blue eyes slipped out. A heated embrace, incredibly soft lips. She made a small sound and gathered her determination, closing her eyes against a flood of similarly wistful recollections. Stephen Manning hadn't wanted her. He was her past. And tonight was only about her future.

'This way,' Addy called. Smiling over her shoulder, she added, 'Corbet has a great many friends that he rides and drinks and plays cards with. We'll convince him to take you out for a dance and then they will all have the chance to become intrigued.' She paused to wait for Mae to catch up. 'We'll have you in the first stare of fashion before you can blink!'

'I admit, I'm anxious to meet your new husband, but I don't wish to be a bother.'

'Oh—not to worry! Corbet won't mind. He's a darling, that way.'

The baron was, in fact, a darling. He greeted his wife with a kiss and made Mae's acquaintance with every evidence of pleasure. Immediately, Lord Corbet introduced her to a card table full of his friends, and with only the smallest nudge from Addy he begged for her hand in a dance.

Mae's estimation of Addy's husband only rose from there. She could only hope to be half so fortunate in her search for a mate. The baron danced with enthusiasm and when the country dance brought them together he had her chuckling at his self-deprecating humour. They were near the end of a line, the set nearly over, when he made a ludicrous comment about needing to lace his corset tighter in order to buckle his shoe. Mae choked as they circled. Lord Corbet handed her off to the next gentleman, and, still laughing, she looked up and into her new partner's face.

She stumbled to a stop.

Breathless laughter. Good-natured teasing. Longing. Admiration. Determination. Every one of them a sensation that collected into a cold knot at the base of her spine. She shivered as one by one they raced the message upwards to her brain.

Stephen.

Any connection between her head and her limbs had melted away. She'd lost her place in the dance. The couple behind them, oblivious to the earth-shattering nature of this moment, danced on. The lady backed into Mae, sending her stumbling. Her ankle wrenched. She bit back a cry of mingled shock and pain and started to fall.

Strong arms plucked her from the air before she could hit the floor. Stephen was frowning down at her. 'Good heavens, are you all right?'

She saw the moment that recognition forced its way into his consciousness. He faltered, too, his eyes bright and his colour high. Mae stared. His expression was the most fascinating mix of pleasure and horrified surprise she'd ever seen.

'Mae?' His voice had gone hoarse.

Dizziness swamped her. He stood so close—held her in his arms, even—and yet the distance between them was immense, in every way that counted.

She winced. 'Good evening, Stephen.'

Chapter Two

Irreconcilable events hit Stephen from opposite directions and from out of the blue. The incongruity of it set his brain box to rattling. He glanced about in an attempt to anchor himself once more. Newmarket, Lord Toswick's house party, fire in his belly and determination in his heart—to do whatever might be necessary to thrust Fincote into the collective awareness of the racing world. Yet one minute he'd been partnering his hostess in a dance, and the next he was holding Mae Halford pressed up tightly against him.

Impossible. Or at least highly unlikely. He would have pinched himself if his hands hadn't already been full.

Pleasurably full, too—filled with generous curves and sweetly yielding flesh. She realised it in the same instant and tried to back away, out of his embrace. But her ankle gave way and she started to go down again.

With a shake of his head he swooped her off her feet and into his arms. The entire dance had broken down and people had begun to gather around them. The music limped to a stop, leaving the air full of murmurs of concern, curious whispers and tittering laughter.

Stephen caught Lady Toswick's eye. 'Could you lead us to a private spot, my lady?' he asked his erstwhile dance partner. 'I believe the lady has injured herself.'

'Of course!' Lady Toswick, staring bemused at the wreck in the midst of her ball, gave a start. 'If you'll follow me, Lord Stephen?'

Mae twisted in his arms. Warm breath stirred over his ear and interesting bits of anatomy brushed against his chest as she spoke over his shoulder. 'Lord Corbet, would you be so good as to fetch Addy? And my mother!' she called as Stephen strode away.

A frazzled butterfly, Lady Toswick flitted her way through the crowd gathered on the dance floor. Casting false smiles and breathless reassurances, she led the way out and down the hall to a small antechamber.

Stephen followed, his jaw clenched in irritation as fans fluttered and tongues wagged in their wake. Two years ago he would have revelled in the attention, but circumstances had changed. *He* had changed. He was here to win the respect of these people, to prove himself as a knowledgeable racing man and a sound man of business, not to stir up old scandalbroth.

He'd entered the ballroom in a state of focused resolution. But now he'd been knocked off course. By Mae Halford. Again.

'Oh, dear,' the countess moaned. She'd opened the door onto an empty room. 'The chairs are gone. Likely the servants are using them as extra seating in the parlour. We need a bit more dining space for the late supper, you see.' She wrung her hands. 'Good heavens, I'll call a footman. Will you be all right, Lord Stephen? Can you hold her until I can have a chair fetched?'

'I'm perfectly fine, my lady,' replied Stephen. 'Perhaps you could send for two chairs? Or a *chaise,* perhaps. I believe Miss Halford should keep her foot elevated, if possible.'

'Oh. Yes, of course.' She eyed Mae with concern. 'I shall be gone but a moment and I'll be sure your mother is on her way, my dear.' Her gown fluttering behind her, the countess disappeared.

Which left Stephen and Mae nothing to do but stare at each other, their faces mere inches apart. Mae's eyes were huge, her expression wary. A soft, citrusy scent drifted up from her hair.

Hell and damnation, but Stephen did not want to be noticing the scent of her hair. Abruptly, the clatter in his head quieted enough for his brain to make a connection. 'Oh, Good Lord,' he said. '*You're* the heiress.'

Her face went blank. 'I beg your pardon?'

He glared at her. 'This had damned well better not be one of your tricks, Mae.'

He'd known from the moment that he took her hand in the dance that he'd encountered something different. He'd gone warm all over and his heart had begun to pound, even before he realised who she was. An example of his body being quicker than his brain, because once he had done so, his instinctive reaction had been a sharp, happy stab of recognition. An intimate friend of his half-sister Charlotte, Mae had been a constant fixture in his life for years. Practically a member of his already large and chaotic family, she was a part of many of his happiest memories.

But now nostalgia was quickly kicked aside by trepidation. For Mae featured at the centre of several of his most uncomfortable memories, too. Several years past, she'd made him the focus of her ardent schoolgirl fantasies. Stephen, a few years older, flush with the first freedoms of manhood, and having a grand time playing the young buck about town with his brothers, had been less than interested. Still, he had tried to tread carefully around her too-evident feelings, and at first he'd found the situation amusing, and more than a little flattering.

But Mae was…Mae. A veritable force of nature. She had pursued him with all the zeal and determination and inventiveness at her disposal—which was to say, more than many a grown man of Stephen's acquaintance. Hell, she had more grit than a platoon of men. For over a year he had stayed one step ahead of her in their awkward dance. Eventually, though, the state of affairs had deteriorated, leading to that last, explosive incident, and ultimately, to Mae's trip abroad.

She was back now, though, and his accusation had set her back up, if the flash of fire in her narrowed blue eyes was any indication.

'Yes, Stephen. Indeed, I had this all planned. I got off the boat, tracked you down and promptly crippled myself to gain your attention.'

He refused to back down. One didn't, when dealing with Mae Halford. His gut began to roil. Images of chaos and destruction danced in his head; all pictures of the special sort of havoc that only Mae could wreak with his plans.

'It sounds ridiculous, doesn't it?' he asked, his tone laced with sarcasm. 'Except that it does not—not to anyone with a close acquaintance with you. And especially not to me. I've been on the dangerous end of more than one of your schemes in the past, if you will recall.'

She stared at him, aghast, and then she began to struggle. 'You great, conceited lout,' she gasped. 'Do you think that I've been abroad *pining* for you all this time?'

'God, I hope not,' he muttered.

She pushed on his shoulder, straining to get away. Her squirming curves were becoming increasingly difficult to hold on to. 'Put me down!'

He had to obey, lest he drop her. She limped away from him, crossing to lean on the wall for support. His heart twisted a little, seeing her hurt. Despite his misgivings, he couldn't help raking a gaze over her, cataloguing each alteration, evaluating for changes and improvements.

They were all improvements. Sleek and stylish, she was dressed and coiffed in the sort of simple elegance that only pots of money could buy. She had grown taller. She'd also grown quite a luscious figure, and learned how to show it to her best advantage.

He wrenched his gaze back up to her obstinate expression. 'I'm sorry,' he said on a sigh. 'I should not have spoken so harshly.'

'Don't be sorry—for you give me the excuse to descend to the same level of bluntness.' Her pert nose was in the air and she looked at him as though he was something the cat had coughed up. 'You may stop flattering yourself right this minute, Stephen Manning. I had no idea you were here tonight and, frankly, I wish you were not. It's a long time since I've been that calf-love-stricken girl.'

He started to speak, but she stopped him with a wave of her hand. 'If I thought of you at all as we returned, it was only to hope that it might be months, perhaps *years,* before we met up again.' She looked away and cast beseeching eyes heavenwards. 'I certainly did not wish to bump into you—literally!—at my first entry back into English society.'

Stephen crossed his arms. 'I am sorry. It's just that I'm here on important business and I cannot have any… shenanigans…fouling it up.'

Voices sounded out in the passageway. She cocked her head, listening for a moment. 'Good,' she said in a hurry. 'We are agreed then. I have important matters at hand as well and your presence will *not* be helpful.' She pushed away from the wall and made shooing motions at him with her hands. 'It would be best if you go. *Now,*' she urged. 'I don't want to contemplate what my father would say, should he find us here like this.'

Tiny golden threads winked at him from amidst the amber embroidery on her bodice. He blinked back. For one wild moment he wondered if this was some sort of deep play she was engaging in. 'I was not aware that your father looked on me with ill will.' He shifted. 'Surely he does not blame me for…' *Damn.* 'For your travels,' he finished lamely.

'Of course he doesn't!' She gave a huff of exas-

peration and closed her eyes. She drew a calming breath
and her shoulders went back. The movement drew his
eye right back to her shimmering bodice and the curves
it contained.

'Papa doesn't blame anyone. It was merely a case of
him knowing how…determined…I can be—and wishing to give me something else on which to focus my
energies.'

A clatter sounded outside and a footman rushed in
with a chair. 'Your pardon, miss, but the countess is
having a more comfortable *chaise* brought along.' He
placed the chair at Mae's side and she sank down onto
it.

'Thank you,' she called as the servant hurried out
again.

She heaved a deep sigh of relief. It did wondrous
things for the décolletage of her gown. And though he
was only observing, somehow Stephen felt the rush of
all that oxygen hit *his* bloodstream.

Mae met his gaze again. 'If my father gets even a
hint of a suspicion that I, that we…' She allowed her
voice to trail away. 'Let me just say that it would be
better if he did not find us together. He's liable to sweep
us up and out of this house party so fast that my head
would spin. The consequences for me would likely be
unpleasant—and long lasting.'

Stephen stilled. His heart thumped at the frightening truth that lay hidden in her words. 'You are a guest
here? At the house party?'

She nodded, then abruptly froze. 'You are staying on
here as well?' She stared. 'You are not invited just for
the evening? For the opening ball?'

He shook his head.

With a cry of dismay, Mae's mother entered, hurrying to kneel at her daughter's side. Lady Corbet followed, and close on her heels came Lady Toswick with a brace of footmen and a large, cushioned *chaise*.

Stephen stood back as the women fussed over Mae. He noted the small frown creasing her brow as she answered her mother's enquiries, but she never looked his way. With interest, he watched as she kept calm in the face of her mother's alarm and Lady Toswick's disjointed attentions. It appeared that somehow she'd managed to tame all the raw, nervous energy that had marked her as an always unpredictable—and sometimes nerve-racking—companion.

He tore his gaze abruptly away. It didn't matter how many intriguing ways Mae had changed, or in how many irritating ways she had stayed the same. Her presence here could only be a distraction at best. It could prove to be an obstacle at worst, if she decided to make his life difficult—or if her father decided to take him into dislike. Barty Halford was a dedicated and influential racing man. Certainly he had the ability to crush Stephen's plans with only a few words into the right ears.

With a curse, he made his way to Mae's side. 'I can see that you are in capable hands now, Miss Halford,' he said formally. 'I'll just leave you to them. I beg your pardon if I somehow contributed to your accident.'

Mae glanced at her mother. She, in turn, exchanged speaking looks with the other women and stepped back a little, drawing the others with her and shooting nervous glances in Stephen's direction.

Mae leaned towards him. 'Let's just agree to stay out of each other's path? At least as much as possible?' She offered her hand.

He bent over it. His nose ended up mere inches from that sparkling bodice. Her new, supple form spread out before him like a Michaelmas feast, all slick curves and sharp indentations. All of his masculine bits took notice, stretching and stirring to life, to let him know that they were awake—and hungry.

Well, they could dance a metaphorical jig if they liked, but they were not going to dine here.

He pulled away. 'Agreed,' he barked.

Spinning on his heel, Stephen stalked from the room. *Wrong place, wrong time,* he told his protesting body parts.

And definitely the wrong woman.

Mae chewed her bottom lip as she watched Stephen stalk away. Two long years, she marvelled. Thousands of miles travelled. Countless new people met, more than a few flirtations engaged in and two sincere marriage proposals received. None of which she was to be given credit for. Stephen had treated her as if she were still the same over-eager, love-struck girl.

Well, she was not that girl any longer—she smiled at her mother and at Lady Toswick, assured them that, *yes,* she was fine and, *no,* she ought not dance any more this evening—and she set out to prove it.

It turned out not to be as difficult as she feared, thanks in large part to Addy and her husband. Mae returned to the ballroom and was enthroned upon a comfortable chair in the corner, with a padded ottoman upon which to prop her foot—decently covered with an embroidered shawl, of course. She suffered a moment's panic after settling in, envisioning herself an island of misery and loneliness in the midst of all the gaiety, but within moments Lord Corbet's friends were obligingly clustering about her.

At first they were all a bit stiff and formal in their enquiries, but Mae was so grateful she did not hesitate to turn the sharp edge of her wit onto her own clumsiness. She thought she showed remarkable restraint in only sacrificing Stephen upon a pointed barb or two, and soon enough the gentlemen were relaxed and chuckling and vying for the right to sit out a set at her side.

Mae relaxed, too, as the evening went on and she concluded that, despite the inauspicious beginning, this evening was proving to be a grand start to her campaign. She was meeting eligible gentlemen, gathering vital information and making excellent connections.

She slipped only once. A Mr Fatch had taken the seat beside her. An earnest young gentleman, he was thrilled with the opportunity to tell her—extensively—about his ancestral acres and the minerals that had recently been discovered there.

The whole thing was Stephen's fault, really. Mr Fatch rambled comfortably on about the canal he wished to build to transport his ores to market and Mae found she could not quite keep her gaze from straying in Stephen's direction.

She could hardly be blamed. It had ever been thus—Stephen was invariably and always the most *alive* person in the room. It was impossible not to sneak glances at him, and impossible not to feel lighter for doing so.

He had a thousand mercurial moods—and the gift of always donning the correct one for the occasion. Tonight he was polished, convivial and full of dry wit, judging from the outbursts of laughter from the group of gentlemen he'd joined.

And Mae was distracted, despite her intent not to be. And intensely annoyed with herself, too. Mr Fatch might be a perfectly lovely gentleman, might he not? She turned her attention firmly back to him and took up his chosen subject with interest and fervour.

Except that wasn't the right course either. Mae knew quite a bit about canals. Over the next few minutes she recalled her lessons on how the ancients had made use of them, talked of what she had learned in Paris, where Napoleon had attempted to use the idea to bring water to the city, and speculated that the use of steam-powered engines in boats was going to bring about an expansion of canal systems all over Europe.

She realised her mistake too late. Mr Fatch's expression transformed from content to bemused and on to faintly horrified.

She stopped talking and stifled a groan.

'Or so my papa believes,' she finished with a weak smile. And threw in a flutter of her eyelashes for good measure.

But there was no salvaging the situation.

'Indeed? Well, then, I thank you for sharing his views. And so thoroughly, too.' Mr Fatch stood and sketched a hasty bow. 'Do enjoy the rest of your evening.'

And he was gone. Mae bit back an eloquent curse she'd learned from her French maid.

She had not a moment to dwell on the setback, however, for her papa dropped into the empty seat with a grateful sigh. He glanced longingly at her stool, as if he'd like nothing better than to lean back and prop up his feet, as well.

'You promised me a dance,' he complained. 'And now I cannot collect.' He chucked her on the chin as if she was an infant. 'You know how I hate an unpaid debt. I shall have to charge you interest.'

'Then I shall be sure to dance with you twice at the next opportunity.' Despite herself, she grinned.

His mouth curled up at the edges, but he didn't say anything more. He just watched her with a brow raised and a patient look on his face, as though he had all the time in the world to wait for the answer to his unspoken question.

'What is it?' she asked.

He only continued to look at her.

'Papa?' Mae doubted this was about the hapless Mr Fatch. She raised a brow right back at him. 'I'll have you know that despite my inability to stun everyone with my graceful dancing, I am still counting this evening as a success.'

'Are you?' His tone was mild.

'Indeed. For I've kept my smile fixed and my conversation light.' No need to confess to sins he hadn't discovered. 'I did not speak to Lady Toswick about her grossly inefficient dinner seating. I also showed great restraint in not reorganising her servants, even though the savoury tarts were served cold and the champagne warm.'

That made him laugh. 'A success, indeed.'

'I've also made the acquaintance of several eligible gentlemen,' she said loftily.

'And become reacquainted with a certain one, or so I hear.'

She grimaced. 'To the detriment of my ankle,' she said wryly.

'As long as the damage is contained to your ankle…' He allowed the thought to trail away, but there was no need to continue. A wealth of warning conveyed in so few words.

Mae's mouth compressed. 'You are not being fair,' she accused.

Her father merely snorted.

Her chin lifted. 'You are as annoying as he is. All of that was a long time ago. It's time for you both to realise that I am not the same person.' She folded her arms and glared. 'That young and inexperienced girl is in my past. And so is Lord Stephen Manning.'

Silent again, he searched her face. Whatever he saw there must have satisfied him. He nodded and kissed her forehead. 'Look at your mother,' he said. 'Lady Toswick must be inordinately skilled. It's been a long time since I've seen her enjoy herself at an event like this.' He glanced back down at her. 'But she's drifted too far away. I'll send her back to you.'

Mae watched him go and step up behind her mother. She saw the hand he slipped across the small of her back and the pleasure, spiced with just a hint of heat, in the smile she cast up at him.

And her gaze slid right back to Stephen.

Curse him, he shone in this milieu. Dark evening clothes only emphasised the width of his shoulders and outlined the splendid leanness of his physique. Candle-light glowed in his short, golden hair and flashed from strong, white teeth. But it was his eyes—always his eyes—that captivated Mae.

Stephen Manning lived in the centre of attention, as the focus of every group he'd ever entered. He spent his life enticing the world to look at him, daring them not to—and denying them even a glimpse of his true self.

And Mae was the only one who had ever realised it.

The *ton*, even his family and friends, had always been content to watch him in fascination and accept the reflection that he cast back at them. Everyone believed in the shallow image he projected to the world.

It was all smoke and mirrors. Another person lived behind those eyes and only Mae knew the truth of it.

And if she wasn't careful then she might fall vic-tim—again—to the burning need, the consuming desire, to uncover him.

Except that she'd meant what she'd said to her father. It was those two stubborn men who were stuck in the past. She'd had plenty of time to think as she travelled with her family, plenty of time to recognise the mistakes in her past and to identify what she wanted for her future.

Mae wanted what everyone else appeared to take for granted. She wanted to be seen for what she was—and appreciated for it. More than anything, she longed for a man who could listen to her spout on about canals—and find it charming. Even better if he had the intelligence and the confidence to debate or discuss it with her.

Stephen looked at her and saw only what he expected to see. Mr Fatch and his kind only noticed the things they wished to change.

Mae set her shoulders. She would put her ankle to the test and take a stroll around the room. Surely, somewhere out there was a man who would find her idiosyncrasies to be delightful, who would view her capabilities as an asset, not as an obstacle. She fixed a smile on her face and set out to find him.

Chapter Three

~~~~~~

Mae Halford's laugh was a nearly palpable thing. It
was a bedroom laugh, intimate and husky. It belonged
in the dark, in moments of contented teasing and happy
repletion. Out of place in a ballroom, it kept catching
Stephen by surprise, destroying his concentration and
tempting him to turn his head.

The Earl of Ryeton, on the other hand, laughed like
a donkey.

Between the two of them, they had Stephen feeling
like a damned puppet on a string, his head bobbing
from one side of the room to the other, his attention
reluctantly bouncing between the man who could help
him achieve his dream and the woman he feared could
wreck it.

It was time to get stern with himself. He had to
focus on the task—or the man—at hand. He'd done
more than a bit of research on the earl. Ryeton was
practically a legend in racing, widely acknowledged to
own the deepest stables in the kingdom. But beyond his

racing credentials, Stephen had discovered only that the earl gambled at the drop of a hat, had a contentious relationship with his countess and kept a mistress of long standing here in Newmarket.

He hadn't heard of the braying laugh before tonight. Or that the man could be so damned elusive.

Perhaps it was Landry's assertion of snobbery that explained the earl's reticence. Perhaps he didn't approve of the Manning family's reputation or even of Stephen's own colourful past. Whatever the case, Stephen was drawing desperately close to the conclusion that the man was *trying* to avoid him.

The ballroom was crowded, but the two of them were moving in the same circles. Mae's father was here, too, and he was just one more object to throw into this delicate balancing act. This was more of a circus than a ball, what with Stephen subtly chasing Ryeton, delicately avoiding Barty Halford, and shivering each time Mae's throaty chuckle floated past.

If there was one bright spot in this difficult evening, it was the enjoyably single-minded nature of the conversations. In this end of the room, there was only one subject of interest. Horses and racing were what had brought them all together. The air was replete with references to bloodlines, time trials and handicaps. Pratchett's name was on everyone's lips and Stephen felt a stab of longing every time he heard it.

This was his chance. Not for nothing had Stephen lounged for hours with his brother Leo in Welbourne's stable offices. Just for this moment had he fought exhaustion and stayed awake after a long day's labour at Fincote, devouring the Racing Calendar and the Stud

Book. He entered into the debates with fervour, insight and authority and held his own with these men of the turf.

He saw surprise on some faces—and a grudging respect on others—and his spirits soared. That look meant everything to him. He craved it. He might be a man grown, with burdens and responsibilities and goals, but the shameful truth was that there was still a remnant of the young man he used to be inside him— the one always searching for an audience. Earning a bit of esteem from these men soothed that bit of his past and at the same time promised security to the people of Fincote who were his future.

Now if only he could find the chance to inspire it in the Earl of Ryeton. He made a surreptitious half-turn, trying to search out the earl's whereabouts, but his gaze fell on Mae Halford instead.

And held there.

She had left her chair and was moving gingerly about the ballroom. He seemed to have been almost unnaturally aware of her all evening. It felt ridiculous—as if time had somehow swapped their roles and now he was the one with the fixation. He told himself that he was only being wary. That it was only that laugh, so much more adult, more *aware* somehow, than the girlish giggle he remembered. But there was more to it than that.

At least fifty other ladies flitted throughout the ballroom; Mae managed to outshine them all. The others shone in the bright light of the chandeliers, their jewelled gowns and soft skin showing to advantage. But it was as if a thousand little lamps were lit *inside* Mae.

She glowed from within—and it took an extreme force of will to look away.

He expended the effort. Lord Toswick was calling him. His host clapped him on the shoulder as Stephen stepped over to join his group.

'We're discussing the growing difficulties with the legs,' Toswick informed him. 'Seems like more and more of them have gone crooked.'

A leg, or black leg, was a professional gambler, a man who 'made a book' by taking bets on all the horses in a race. Legs flocked to every major race, and racing men flocked to lay down their money with them.

'I heard the Blands were in town,' someone said in hushed tones. The Bland brothers, and a few others like them, had become notorious for interfering with horses in order to affect the outcome of a race. Laming, opium balls, even poison had been used to nobble a favourite and ensure the leg a hefty income.

'Lord Stephen has had some first-hand experience with just their sort,' Toswick said with a laugh. 'And he was barely out of leading strings.'

'I was fifteen,' protested Stephen. 'Hardly a babe.'

'Tell the story,' Toswick urged.

The other gentlemen urged him on, so Stephen told the tale of how, disappointed at being left behind when his parents travelled to see the St Leger, he had run away to Doncaster on his own. While hiding in the stables he had uncovered a plot to maim the race favourite. He'd foiled the plan, reported it, and then won a small fortune betting on another horse altogether.

As it was rather late, and the champagne had been flowing freely all evening, the gentlemen all found this to be uproariously funny. Stephen's hand was shook and he was congratulated all around, until a more officious voice broke in.

'That was extremely well done of you, and at such a young age, too.' It was the Earl of Ryeton, joining their group and shaking his head. 'Surely something must be done about these blasted legs.' He glanced down his nose. 'Young Manning, is it not?'

Lord Toswick stepped in to make the introductions. Stephen's heart accelerated and he sent the man a silent blessing for the opportunity.

'Of course, I don't mean to paint all the legs with the same brush,' he told Ryeton. 'Gambling has always been a large part of the sport.' He nodded to the company around them. 'Everyone here knows that racing would not be what it is today, if not for the betting.'

'Yes, yes, and of course there are plenty of honest men making books.' The earl appeared to be impatient with even a hint of disagreement. 'It's the crooked ones that are making things so damned difficult. Three separate incidents I've had in my stables over the past year. Two were caught in time, but I lost a very promising filly to poisoned feed.' Ryeton's colour had grown higher. 'It's a travesty, is what it is.' He tossed back his drink and waved for another.

'It does lend an ugly taint,' Stephen agreed. 'Cheating only breeds suspicion and distrust where we would hope for enthusiastic and healthy competition.'

'Something must be done before things get even more out of hand. I've called a gathering of the Jockey Club stewards to discuss the issue. We need swift justice—and stern consequences. A precedent must be established.' He gave a low laugh. 'We cannot expect these people to govern themselves. They are not *gentlemen.*'

He glanced askance at Stephen. 'The stewards meet early tomorrow. Perhaps if you are about…' He paused. 'Ah, but I'd forgotten. You are not a member of the Jockey Club, are you, Manning?'

'That honour has not been mine.' *Not yet.* 'But I am hoping to find sponsorship for admittance to the Coffee Rooms,' Stephen added smoothly. Acceptance as a member of the Jockey Club Rooms was the first step towards becoming a full member of racing's elite body.

Ryeton hesitated, then nodded towards their host. 'I'm assembling a group to ride out and watch the practice on the Heath tomorrow afternoon. I had just invited Toswick.'

Stephen grinned. 'There's scarcely a better moment, is there? To lean into the wind of a group of galloping thoroughbreds and feel the thunder of their passing beneath your feet?'

Ryeton nodded and triumph bloomed fiercely in Stephen's chest. This was it; the earl was going to invite him along. *Yes.* He needed this. Fincote needed this. It was a small step, but a first one towards a bright future. For him and for the people who depended on him.

'Perhaps you would care to—'

Something struck Stephen behind the knee and he stumbled forwards into Ryeton, cutting him off.

'Perhaps, Manning, all that thunder and wind comes from your flapping jaw,' someone said behind him.

'What?' Turning, Stephen suppressed a surge of

irritation and a vision of Mae Halford's mischievous grin. She always did have an exquisite sense of timing—and an uncanny ability to intervene in the most inopportune moments.

But of course it wasn't Mae interfering. Instead, he found a gentleman hovering close, his handsome visage blighted by rough scars that traced a path along his jaw and climbed the right side of his face. He leaned heavily on a cane with one hand, held the other outstretched and grinned widely all over his face.

'Grange?' Stephen's jaw dropped in shock. 'Matthew Grange! What in blazes are you doing here, man?' His eyes running over his friend, he reached out and grasped his hand.

'I thought to hire myself out as a jockey.' Matthew's mouth twisted. 'Idiot!' he said fondly. 'What do you think? I'm here for the races.'

Stephen still had not let go of his hand. 'Of course. Hanstead Hall is so close—I'd hoped to stop for a visit after the racing. I hadn't expected… It's just so damned good to see you out and about.' Recollecting himself, he pulled away. 'I'm sorry, you shocked the good manners right out of me. Matthew, do you know the Earl of Ryeton?' He turned. 'Ryeton, if I may present an old friend…'

But the earl had taken a step back and was already engaged in conversation with some others. 'Perhaps later,' Stephen said, swallowing a wave of disappointment. He stared at Matthew again and a slow smile broke out over his face. 'Damn, but you look a sight better than the last time I saw you.'

He'd met Matthew Grange on the first day of school,

when he'd punched him in the nose for calling his father's mistress a whore. Matthew had tripped him on his way down, and despite the fact that Grange had two years on him, they had been evenly matched. They'd beaten each other to a bloody pulp, Matthew had apologised and they'd been inseparable for years.

Until his friend bought a commission and went away to put Napoleon in his place. Matthew had barely got in on the end of the conflict, but he'd been at Waterloo. In fact, he'd been caught right next to a twelve-pounder when a mortar hit it. Burned by exploding gunpowder, scarred by molten metal, and with the addition of a load of shrapnel in his right leg, it had been nearly a year before he could be moved.

Matthew had continued to fight, struggling to heal at home, but heartbreakingly, had lost his leg last year.

'I dare say cadavers have looked better than I did when last I saw you.' Matthew laughed. 'But I feel a damned sight better, I don't mind telling you.'

'And glad I am to hear it.'

'What's that I heard about the Jockey Club? Hoping to wiggle your way in?'

'Hoping to *earn* my way in,' Stephen corrected. Matthew already knew about Fincote. He took a minute to explain his hopes regarding Pratchett. 'Ryeton's champion is my best hope for a spectacular launch, but barring that sort of instant notoriety and success, membership in the Jockey Club is the next best way for me to establish Fincote as a racecourse of repute.' He sighed. 'It's a significantly longer path, though.'

Matthew grinned. 'You're young yet, Manning.'

'Were it only me I had to worry about, I'd have the patience of Job.' Stephen had to work to hide his anxiety from his friend. 'I know I wrote to you about the conditions I found at Fincote.'

But he hadn't, really. Even if he'd been so inclined, there had been no way to put down on paper what he'd discovered or how it had made him feel. Why hadn't he checked in on the estate when he'd first inherited it? He knew why, but still he'd cursed himself a thousand times for allowing Fincote's people to become as help-less and hopeless as his mother had been.

'I convinced them to go along with my plans,' he continued. 'They deserve to finally see some returns for their labours.' He sighed. And then he returned Matthew's grin as he scrubbed a hand through his hair. 'But enough about me. This *is* a night for unexpected comings and goings.'

He glanced across the ballroom. Mae stood slim and tall in the corner, a bright candle amidst a crowd of sober-clad gentlemen. Let her shine her light on them— as long as she didn't start aiming it at him again.

He glanced about. 'But never tell me you've come alone? After the difficult time your mother has expe-rienced, I would have thought she'd enjoy a spot of society.'

Matthew frowned. 'You would think so, but she hasn't thrown off her mourning yet.'

'Not yet? But surely it's been…yes, well over a year since your father passed on.'

'True.' Matthew sighed. He slapped his thigh where the extra length of his breeches was neatly pinned over the peg that replaced the rest of his leg. 'But I vow, she's mourning this leg of mine as deeply as she does my father.' He sat silent a moment. 'She's convinced my life is over as well.'

Stephen's jaw tightened against a surge of resentment. He'd felt this before, on behalf of his friend. Matthew's mother's sentiments reminded him painfully—and infuriatingly—of his own mother's maudlin excuses. Weak, defeatist drivel. It put his back up and made his gorge rise.

But Matthew's face had hardened. He looked up at Stephen with a glower. 'I'm here to prove her wrong.'

Stephen relaxed. 'She couldn't possibly be more wrong.' He grinned to lighten the mood. 'Does she know how frightful a dancer you always were?' He gestured to his friend's elaborately carved peg. 'Surely you can do as well with that contraption as you ever did on your own two feet.'

Matthew gave a startled chuckle. After a moment it turned into a genuinely rueful laugh. 'No, this is the perfect excuse to give up dancing.' He eyed Stephen's blond hair, cut far shorter now than when he'd been living a fashionable life in London. 'But I still have my wits about me and a damned good head of hair above them. Surely there's a young lady or two who won't mind sitting out a set.' He sighed. 'Or there's always the card room.'

'You forget where we are. It's Newmarket, man! And you're as good a judge of horseflesh as any man I've ever met. You could talk of nothing else for the entire week and still be thought a sparkling conversationalist.' He clapped him on the shoulder. 'Now, let's introduce you around.'

* * *

For the next hour Stephen stayed at Matthew's side, presenting him to all and sundry. It was no easy task. Never in all of his life had he had to work so hard to maintain an air of complacent good humour. For while a few grasped his friend's scarred hand in easy welcome, it was clear that many others were uncomfortable with, even scornful of, his deformities.

Stephen wanted to berate every fool who allowed his revulsion to show on his face and he wanted to shake the idiot woman who flatly refused to offer her hand, but fortunately Matthew was in a jovial temper—and he wasn't above a self-deprecating joke or two. Together with Stephen's hearty laughter and calm acceptance, they managed to quickly soothe most of the discomfort they encountered.

But Stephen was beginning to feel stretched too thin. He felt like a juggler with too many balls in the air. He was happy to work to secure Matthew's acceptance, of course, but at the same time he was watching for an opportunity to re-engage Ryeton. The earl had been about to include him in his party tomorrow. He wanted to give the man the chance to finish the invitation and he wanted to accept it with alacrity.

And he wanted to forget Mae Halford's presence. She certainly appeared to have forgotten his. It was almost unnerving, in fact. He could scarcely recall a time when he'd been in the same room as Mae and had *not* been the centre of her formidable attention. He told himself firmly that he was glad of it.

Yet suddenly she was looking up, as if the weight of

his regard had been a tap on her shoulder. Their gazes met. The ghost of a smile crossed her face.

Stephen pivoted away. Matthew was engaged in conversation with a wide-eyed young miss. To hide his confusion he looked about for Ryeton.

There. The earl and Toswick stood talking just a few feet away. Ryeton met his eye, but quickly averted his gaze, as Stephen had just done to Mae.

Something scuttled down Stephen's spine. A warning, perhaps. But he was determined and a little desperate. 'Come,' he interrupted Matthew. He smiled an apology at the girl. 'I must introduce you to the man who is set to fleece us all. I believe the lucky devil's got a favourite in every damned race. We'll all end up indebted to him by the end of the week.' He took a step towards the two men.

And then it happened—one of those moments that can occur naturally in any crowd. The orchestra wound to a finish. Conversations paused as guests lightly applauded, and the Earl of Ryeton's words rang out unusually loud over the quiet moment.

'What is he thinking? This is a ball, for God's sake. It's the height of poor taste for that man to expose the rest of us to his disgusting abnormalities. And has Manning run mad? To squire the cripple about in good company?'

Toswick whispered urgently, trying to shush the earl, but Ryeton paid him no mind and suddenly that donkey's laugh hung in the air. 'The man's lucky he wasn't born a horse. Were he one of my nags I'd have him shot.'

Time stopped. All around them men stilled and

ladies gasped. Stephen halted in midstep, caught up in a torrent of icy-cold shock and heated fury. For the fraction of a second, he reached for his usual control, scoured his brain for a jaunty bit of humour that might salvage this horrifying moment. But then he saw the flush of anger and embarrassment spread across Matthew's face. He thought of the incredible courage it had taken for his friend to show up and act as if his life and his body had not been shattered—and he saw the moment Ryeton realised what had happened, right before his nose tilted up and his expression settled into a belligerent scowl.

This was it, then, one of those moments by which a man defined himself and shaped the course of his life. Stephen allowed himself the briefest sliver of a moment in which to mourn his lost opportunities, to prepare himself for an added burn of guilt, before he embraced the wrath surging through his veins and entered the fray.

'I dare say you would, Ryeton,' he ground out. 'But what if the case were reversed? Surely it would be better to be shot for a heroic warhorse than a dim-witted, braying ass.'

'Excuse me?' Ryeton turned his reddened face to their host. 'What did he say to me?'

Toswick only sputtered helplessly.

'You heard me, my lord. Feeling better about yourself, are you, for having judged a man by the bits he is missing?' Stephen's fury raged through him, opening wounds he'd thought long buried. Suddenly every mocking slur cast against his unorthodox family, every whispered taunt about his sad and lonely mother stung him again, releasing their venom into his veins. 'It's obvious, though, that he's not the only one here missing a few vital pieces. And were I forced to choose between your affliction and his, I'd gladly give up my leg and the use of my hand if it meant I could keep my honour and integrity.'

Another round of gasps went up from the crowd. Ryeton, nearly purple with fury, thrust his glass at Toswick. 'I shall find a great deal of pleasure in making you regret those words.' Ryeton's voice took an unexpected turn to a higher octave at the end of his threat.

Stephen might have laughed if he hadn't understood just how many ways it could come true. He took a menacing step towards the man. 'You are welcome to consider whom you would like as your second. I believe we were in the process of arranging to meet in any case, it would be just as well to make it a dawn appointment.'

'No.' Matthew's voice rang out this time, the authority inherent in his tone a direct contrast to Ryeton's bleating. 'It's my infirmities he mocks, and did I think him worth it, it would be me meeting him at dawn.' He gave Ryeton a hard stare. 'And though I may have only one good hand left, my lord, I've killed more than a few Frenchmen with it. I doubt I'd have any trouble dispatching you.'

He paused and swept a steely look across the gawking guests. 'But I don't find him worth the trouble. He's entitled to his opinion. Whatever he thinks of my "abnormalities", I know I obtained them on a field of honour, defending my fellows and my country, and my king.'

Matthew might have said more, but he was interrupted by a softly uttered, 'Oh, bravo!' from the chit he'd been talking with. He coloured once more and looked to Stephen.

'Let's go,' Stephen said shortly. He gave Ryeton a last glare before gesturing to the crowd knotted around them. A path opened up, and he waited for his friend to set out before him.

But the evening held one last shock. Stephen stared as several footmen burst into the ballroom. Two pulled up just inside the door, but one had his head down and a dogged expression on his face. Guests shrieked, scattering before him. Drawing closer, Stephen saw the reason behind it all. Fleet as a frisky colt, a boy dodged and darted just ahead of the man—a grime-spattered boy who, cap in hand, caught sight of the cleared aisle and pelted down the centre of it. He skidded to a stop at the sight of the earl.

'Lord Ryeton,' he wheezed. He bent over to catch his breath. 'There's trouble in the stables. 'Tis Pratchett, my lord!'

The crowd began to murmur. All the buzzing, gossiping people who had begun to turn away surged forwards again, eager to catch a glimpse of the new commotion.

Stephen noted that the high colour had drained from Ryeton's face. 'Well?' he barked at the child. 'Spit it out, boy! Pratchett, you say? What's amiss with my best horse?'

'He's been stolen, my lord!' He sucked in a breath. 'Pratchett's gone!'

Chapter Four

Back and forth Stephen paced, from sagging stall to weathered doorway. Lord Toswick's stables were a hive of activity, nearly as busy as the house. This ancient hay barn, tucked at the edge of the stable block, looked as if he might knock it over with a good push, but it was redolent of sweet-smelling hay, just the right size for a good, agitated pace and wonderfully, blessedly quiet.

It might be the only peaceful place in Newmarket this morning, for the entire town was still abuzz with gossip from last night's ball. Already London's newspapermen and inveterate rumourmongers were descending on the town, eager to hear the latest details. Oh, and wasn't there a good deal to hash over? A good bit of it centring around him. He sighed. It was familiar ground, performing as the meaty chunk in the centre of the scandalbroth.

Except he didn't want to be there any longer. Leaning up against the corner stall, he deliberately breathed in straw-dusted air. He'd worked hard to leave the shrill boy he'd been, so hungry to be noticed, behind. Side by side he'd laboured with Fincote's people, desperate to pay back some part of the debt he owed them, but just as intent on proving himself, too.

The old plough horse in the stall approached. Curious, she nudged him. 'I don't suppose you'd be available to race for me, would you?' He rubbed her cheek and stroked down her fine, strong neck, taking comfort in her simple affection.

Simple. This foray into Newmarket was supposed to be simple. Two notable horses to match up and draw racing's elite to Fincote Park. Once there, they'd recognise the superiority of his challenging, well-maintained course. They'd experience the hospitality and eager gratitude of the local business owners and merchants and soon enough they'd all be on their way to becoming a well-known, much-frequented part of the racing circuit.

And he would, at long last, put the ghost of his mother's neglect to rest.

But those plans lay in tatters now. And because it was natural to do so when his mind was full of chaos or destruction, he conjured up the image of Mae Halford as she'd been last night, challenging him from across the ballroom with that grin on her pretty face—the one that was both familiar and intriguingly new at the same time. She'd moved through the crowd with confidence and grace, as if fidgets and restless energy had never been her natural state.

Stephen had watched the candlelight ferret reddish highlights out of her golden curls and experienced a deep foreboding. She'd been a force of nature when he'd known her before. The thought of what she might be today—with full knowledge and possession of her power—defied description.

He experienced a profound sense of mortification, too, knowing that she'd witnessed the débâcle with Ryeton. Perhaps because it had been so spectacularly melodramatic. He rolled his eyes and left the horse to her clover-scented hay. The evening had possessed a taste of the theatrical, but Stephen wouldn't take back a word. Ryeton was an arrogant, small-minded imbecile—but he had been perfect for his needs. The man sat on top of the racing world right now. His horses were well blooded, well trained and practically unbeatable.

And now, unobtainable. Stephen paused at the entry to the tack room and traced the horseshoe hung above the door for luck. He needed a new plan. A new patron. But Ryeton was influential. He had the ear of the Jockey Club stewards and most of racing's important figures—and Stephen had mortally insulted him. There was damned little chance he could get back in the man's good graces. Indeed, the earl could kill all of his dreams with just a word.

He set off again, thinking and pacing his way around and around the small open space—until the very path he walked sparked a sudden idea.

A hell of an idea. A thought so simple, so complicated and so brilliant all at once that it set his heart to pounding and his feet to travelling even faster. What if he could get *around* Ryeton? He could well imagine the state the man was in today. By all reports he was frantically following up every lead, trying to get Pratchett back in time to race the Guineas. But what if

Stephen was the one to find the horse? He could return the thoroughbred to Ryeton with all due pomp and circumstance. It would create a sensation—one that he could use to benefit Fincote Park.

He'd thought himself past the need for the spotlight—but this time he could use it to accomplish all of his goals in one fell swoop. The racing crowd would go wild—and claim him as their hero. It would create the perfect opportunity to convince Ryeton to run Pratchett at Fincote. The earl would look like a fool were he to continue to hold a grudge in such circumstances. He would have to agree—and the racing world, so eager for a spectacle, would stumble over itself to witness it.

Stephen could barely contain his excitement. It was perfect. It would work—if only he could locate the missing racehorse first.

The thought stopped him dead in his tracks. That was the complicated bit, wasn't it? Though Ryeton had put on a convincing show of shock and bewilderment, he had to have an idea of what motivated such a bizarre incident. And knowledge would give him an advantage that would make him hard to beat.

Stephen started moving again. Society being what it was, someone else might have a hint at what lay behind it, too. Surely someone, a trainer, groom, the earl's friends—or enemies—knew something. It would be a race to ferret out information and connect the pieces before Ryeton did.

He nodded. It could be done. He could search out the truth. But the job was too big for one man. He would stand a better chance if he had help.

Silently, he considered his prospects.

Toswick, perhaps? Quickly, he discarded the notion. His host was an upstanding gentleman, too honourable to chose between his acquaintances in such a manner. Landry, then? With a stab of disappointment, Stephen recalled the viscount's tirade against Ryeton. Landry was unlikely to help with any scheme that helped the earl get Pratchett back, even if it aided Stephen at the same time.

No, he needed someone uninvolved. Someone with a quick mind and a sense of discretion. His mind raced. Owner, trainer, black leg and groom—every man-jack involved in racing was knee deep in speculation right now. Yet gossip was likely thickening the air in Newmarket's social circles as well as in her barns and training courses. Ryeton's name would be whispered over every teacup, the man's history and his every social gaffe dug up, dissected and served up alongside the cucumber sandwiches. The information he needed could come from anywhere.

Stephen needed a partner—someone who could help him cover ground, explore every avenue and then come together to sort, sift and piece answers together. Surely he knew someone not averse to a bit of adventure and ready to embrace a good scheme…

He stopped short once more. The answer was at once obvious and frightening. It floated, a red-gold beacon in his mind.

What he needed was Mae Halford.

No! He exploded into motion again, moving faster than ever and setting the old mare to prancing nervously as well. It was an absurd notion—too foolish to be contemplated. And yet he could think of no one better suited for the job. Mae had been an ally once. Hell, they'd cut their milk teeth on more outrageous schemes. But that was before he'd turned her into an opponent—and she made a formidable foe, indeed. He'd far rather confront Ryeton than her.

Last night she'd insisted that she no longer carried a torch for him. It was not difficult to believe—he doubted her tender feelings could have survived their last encounter. But Mae was nothing if not tenacious. If she did still harbour yearnings for him, he'd be granting her a prime opportunity to catch him in a leg-shackle. If not—well, he'd already hurt her once. That knowledge was one of his heaviest burdens—could he risk adding to it?

And what of her father? She'd indicated that Barty Halford did not wish her to continue their association. The man was nearly as influential in the racing community as Ryeton. If crossed, he could crush Stephen's plans just as easily as the earl.

No.

Stephen closed his eyes and experienced again the burning need to make Fincote a success. The goal loomed ever larger in his mind—a holy grail that he could not stop chasing. He would never rest easy until it was done.

He groaned and leaned back against the tack-room door, gazing up at the horseshoe above him. He was going to need all the luck he could get. Could he truly be considering this? And the question remained—even if he convinced himself, how on earth was he to convince Mae?

* * *

'Mademoiselle!'

Mae blinked. Her maid's tone was sharp, the hairpin she'd just jabbed at her skull sharper yet. Still, it took a heroic effort to focus on Josette's exasperated face in the mirror.

'Almost I can see the very busy turnings of the wheels in your mind, but three times I have asked if you prefer the plain comb or the pearls.' Josette wagged a finger at her reflection.

'I'm sorry, Josette.'

'Do not be sorry. Only pay attention, just for a moment. You can go back to your scheming once we have you ready for the day.'

Mae stared at her image. Good heavens, but her shoulders were drawn tight up around her ears. Deliberately, she relaxed and reminded herself that she *liked* what she saw in the mirror.

Yet thoughts of Stephen and his friend from last evening continued to trouble her. Mr Grange, who likely did not enjoy his reflection any more—but with whom she felt a kinship, none the less. He was an outsider, just like her. They were each undeniably different from the people about them—only Mr Grange wore his differences on the outside.

She sat straighter in her chair. 'Josette, are we doing the right thing?'

'What?' the startled maid asked. 'The pearls?'

'No, no. The pearls are fine.' Turning around in her seat, Mae let the words rush out. 'The campaign. I know we've laid our plans and devised our strategies, but I'm beginning to wonder if it is a mistake to hide my...foibles.' She paused. 'From the gentlemen I am meeting, I mean.'

Josette clucked and turned her around to face the mirror again. 'Do you know what you are, *mademoiselle?* You are like a banquet prepared by the greatest chefs of my country, rich with ingredients and fascinating layers. But these Englishmen! Bah!' She tucked in a curl and waved a dismissive hand. 'Too long have they lived on bland, tasteless fare. They do not know enough to know what is best. You must give them a small taste at a time. Slowly they will become accustomed to the many delicious flavours that make you who you are. Only then will they discover it is too late to go back to their plain English misses.'

Mae laughed. 'Bad enough my father puts me in the same category as his fillies, now you make me feel like a cassoulet.'

'Either way,' Josette said with a smack of her fingers to her lips, 'you are *magnifique.*'

Mae studied her reflection once more and chose to believe her. She knew she was not the same as most girls—had known it since she'd discovered that none of the others improved the efficiency of the kitchens by reorganising the cook's battery of pots in order of frequency of use. At school she'd been the only one to keep her clothes hung in the wardrobe according to colour and age of the garment. But she'd always chosen to embrace her differences, to believe that they made her interesting and unique. She was different, not less—but it had been a battle to convince the world to believe it along with her.

Josette set down her brush and began to smooth and

arrange curls with her fingers. 'The servants are buzzing like bees—there is so much gossip in the air, it is
like pollen from the flowers.'

Mae looked up sharply. Josette's tone was entirely
too casual.

'Many interesting things I have heard—including
the name of one of the gentlemen.' She met Mae's gaze
in the mirror now. 'He is here, isn't he?' she asked
quietly. 'The one who so troubled you in the past?'

A heated flush started low in her chest. Mae ignored
it and nodded.

The maid pulled away. 'Aha! I knew it. This is why
you begin to doubt yourself—and your purpose.' Whirl-
ing away in disgust, Josette began to murmur in low,
rapid French. Mae flinched when she swung back and
poked a finger at her.

'Mademoiselle,' her maid began heatedly. She
paused and took a breath and the exasperation in her
face faded to concern. 'You said you were strong, that
you would not let his indifference inflame you.'

'There is no need to worry. I acted exactly as I must.
We've promised to keep our distance. Our meeting was
bound to be traumatic, but except for the slight damage
to my ankle, I am fine.'

'So it is true, then—it was he who caused your fall.'
Josette began to grumble again. 'I must catch a glimpse
of this man who causes so many difficulties. Surely
he must be handsome.' She eyed Mae slyly. 'I know
his brains must not be the attraction, since he did not
have the sense to fall in love with you when he had the
chance.'

Mae laughed. 'Well, you must be careful when

you seek him out, dear. His mind might not be up to your standards…' she let out a teasing sigh '…but the rest of him…' She paused and closed her own eyes. 'His eyes—dark blue on the outside, but I'd forgotten how they change toward the centre, fade to the lightest shade, so clear you think you could see right down to his soul, if only he would let you.' After a moment she marshalled herself and tossed a wicked grin over her shoulder. 'And his shoulders! I know how you feel about a nice set of shoulders.'

'Eh! Blue eyes, broad shoulders. *Et voilà!* So easily she falls.' Josette shook her head in dismay.

Mae straightened. 'No one is in danger of falling,' she said flatly. She'd made that mistake once already— at her first encounter with Stephen Manning, years ago. The fateful afternoon had been branded on her heart. Her friend Charlotte had only laughed when the two of them had been caught spying on Charlotte's brother and his friends—the older boys had been sparring with fencing foils in the wooded groves of Welbourne Manor. Mae, at first, had cringed. She'd waited, head down, for the teasing to begin. But then she'd raised her chin in defiance. She'd been mocked before, for odd starts and hoydenish behaviour. She'd resolved to endure it again, with her head held high.

Incredibly, there had been no mocking. No snide names or even the common disdain older boys felt for younger girls. Stephen had laughed and diffused the situation entirely. And then he had reached down a hand, and offered to teach her to fence.

Thunk. Fallen was exactly what she'd done.

'Oh, but your papa,' Josette reminded her, morose. 'He is not going to be happy.'

'He has not the slightest cause for worry,' Mae insisted. She'd already wasted years on Stephen Manning—and what had it got her?

After a lifetime of battling the many voices who insisted she must change, adjust, squeeze herself into an ill-fitting mould, after years of fighting to bolster the pedestal of her own confidence, he'd knocked her off almost without effort. Stephen Manning had been the only one who had ever made her doubt herself.

All the old anguish and heartbreak threatened to resurface at the thought. Mae refused to allow it. It had taken a long time to accept that all the glorious potential she'd seen between her and Stephen had been nothing more than friendship tinged rosier by her own juvenile dreams. It had taken longer for her to accept that romantic love was not to be a part of her life. For she had never felt a connection with any other man the way she had with Stephen.

Accept it she had, though, at last. And when the time came that marriage could not be put off any longer, her Marriage Campaign had been born. She'd come back home with her goal in mind and her plans fixed firmly in place. She would find someone who could appreciate her—for her. And then the long battle would be over.

She met Josette's approving gaze in the mirror and pushed all of her doubts aside. She wasn't going to allow Stephen Manning—or anyone else—sway her from her purpose. The campaign for her happiness had begun.

Chapter Five

'Lord Stephen,' his hostess exclaimed. 'You are back early!' The pleasure faded from her expression. 'You are the only one, I am afraid. The other gentlemen have all abandoned us for the Heath, the Jockey Club and the other pleasures of town.' She didn't look pleased. 'We don't expect them back until dinner, at the earliest.'

Stephen grinned at her. 'Thank you, Lady Toswick, but I find I'm more interested in the whereabouts of the ladies at present.'

She returned his grin. 'How very obliging of you.'

The matrons in the room smiled at each other over their embroidery and correspondence. 'All of the young ladies have gone strolling about the grounds,' a silver-haired lady offered.

'Yes, they've taken the forest walk,' the countess added, 'except for dear Miss Halford. Her ankle is not up to the exercise just yet, so she's gone to feed the birds in the meadow.' Lady Toswick waved an encouraging hand. 'But the rest of the girls have only just left.

If you hurry, you should be able to catch them before they've gone far.'

'Thank you, my lady.' Stephen cast a conspiratorial wink across the room and pretended not to notice the bent heads or the tide of rising whispers following him from the room. He paused in the entry hall and tossed a waiting footman a coin. 'The meadow?' he asked, his voice pitched low.

'Not far.' The coin disappeared and the footman leaned closer. 'Just past the terraced gardens at the back of the house. The path begins next to a large chestnut tree.'

Stephen nodded his thanks and hurried on his way, hoping his feet would get him there before his head convinced him to turn back. It was the height of irony, finding himself chasing after Mae Halford. No—it was the measure of his desperation. How many times had he told himself that he would do anything to bring about Fincote's success? Well, now he knew it was true. He would do anything—even ask for help from the one person from whom he least deserved it.

The crunch of gravel underfoot faded as he left the formal gardens behind and found the tree marking the tiny path. A thick canopy of elms and chestnuts spread overhead, filtering light and muting sound. Stephen quickened his pace, unwilling to be alone with his doubts and his conscience for longer than necessary. It was only a few moments, though, before he reached the clearing and paused on the edge to drink in the beauty of the scene.

It must be man-made, this perfectly symmetrical open spot in the midst of the wood. The ground was covered in a vibrant carpet of wildflowers, the edges punctuated with rustic, curved seating. Mae sat quietly, off to the right, her fingers drumming on the thick-crusted loaf in her lap. She was clearly not part of the scene—dressed immaculately as she was, from kid boots to her charming, if ineffectual hat, in rich shades of brown and contrasting cream—yet it was as if her very separateness enhanced the image. Bird-song echoed in the glade, but she hadn't yet broken her bread. She looked lost in thought—and he suffered the sudden urge to ruffle her feathers, yank a lock of that shining hair, flop down next to her and tease her until she confessed what troubled her.

He shook it off. Breathing deep, Stephen stepped forward. He called out to her before he could change his mind. 'Mae? Good morning.'

She turned and he nearly stopped in his tracks. The wary distrust on her face was such a shocking contrast to the enthusiasm with which she had greeted him all of their lives. He pushed on, but that look gave him pause in a way that all of his reservations had not. He summoned the image of Fincote's empty courses, her hopeful people, and he spoke again. 'Would you mind if I joined you? I was hoping for a chance to speak with you today.'

She sighed. 'I thought we had agreed to keep away from each other, Stephen?'

'We did. But I believe I owe you an apology for the harshness of my words last night. I… You caught me by surprise.' He'd reached the curved bench. He gestured, silently asking permission to sit.

With bad grace she moved aside. She fixed a stern

eye on him and shuffled a little farther away as he took his seat. 'It *was* unexpected, but I should have been prepared.' She turned her gaze away from him, looking up at the treetops. 'I think our first instincts were correct. It seems we both have work to do here. Why don't we just leave each other to it?'

Stephen bit back a bitter laugh. It was almost reassuring, really, to see that nothing had changed. This was Mae—and she wasn't going to make this easy on him. 'I can only wish you better luck with your mission than I am having with mine,' he said with all seriousness.

She didn't answer right away, just tore a piece from her crusty loaf. As if it had been a signal, the air grew abruptly heavy with excited chirping and the flurry of wings. In an instant a veritable swarm of sparrows, finches and swallows swooped down from the trees.

Not even Stephen could hold on to his sobriety at the sight of them, preening and pecking, squabbling like fishwives over food that hadn't even been thrown yet. He chuckled. She held her silence and he did too, sure her innate curiosity would take the conversation where he needed it to go.

'I heard talk of your racecourse last night,' she said eventually. 'I'm sorry to hear that you've already hit a snag.'

He sighed. 'A wall is a more apt description, after that contretemps with Ryeton.'

She glanced in his direction, then quickly looked away. 'I hope you are not regretting your actions last night? You gave that horrid man just the set-down he deserved.'

Her approbation warmed him—and gave birth to a

tiny thread of hope. 'I will never regret defending Matthew. I'd do it again, a thousand times over. But I do regret the necessity of it,' he admitted. 'Ryeton's good will was essential to my plans.'

She said nothing, just cocked an inquisitive brow at him. But something in the set of her shoulders told him that she didn't expect him to explain.

Stephen drew a measured breath. This was where he had to step carefully. Mae was bright, inquisitive—and relentless. Worse, she saw far more than most others ever did. It was what made her so dangerous, and him so wary. It was what had ultimately led to their last, disastrous confrontation.

Yet Stephen knew he owed her more than glib words and skilful evasion. The answer he would have given anyone else, that is. She deserved the truth—both the facts and the gut-felt emotion that went with it.

He looked away. 'If you don't throw some of that bread, we're going to be besieged.' And then he forced himself to meet her gaze square on. 'Perhaps I should start at the beginning?'

Her eyes widened in surprise and she nodded.

He drew a deep breath—and found himself unable to do it. Not even with Mae, perhaps *especially* not with Mae, could he lay bare the devastation he had discovered at Fincote, and the equal damage it had wrought upon him. So he deliberately skipped those details and concentrated instead on the birth of his plans.

She watched him, all the while he spoke, with those incredible, alarming eyes, and, because it was Mae, he allowed his intensity and passion to show. The words came slowly at first. But she listened without comment and he tried to relate at least some of the blood, sweat and tears that he had poured into the project, and a great deal of the respect and obligation he felt for the people who had worked alongside him.

He told her of his idea to use Pratchett's notoriety to add to Fincote's. Above all, he wanted her to see all of the hope and excitement that he'd brought with him to Newmarket.

She idly tossed bits of bread to the waiting birds, but her gaze remained on him. Silently she studied him. He had the peculiar sense that she was trying to reconcile what she knew with what she saw. He could understand her confusion. It felt at once old hat to be sharing intimacies with her again, and yet it felt somehow…new, as well.

'Do you find it all difficult to believe?' he asked with a self-deprecating laugh. 'The last time we saw each other, I was still pulling pranks and chasing skirts about town.' He chuckled again. 'Life is certainly different now.'

'I think we've both had a chance to grow up,' she said simply.

'Sometimes I wake up and I forget. For a moment I'm still that same attention-starved boy—willing to do anything to get a rise or a laugh out of my brothers and sisters. Or my parents.' He grinned, reminded of their old camaraderie. Except that never before had he been tempted to reach out and test the softness of the curls at her nape, or ease the tension in her frame with a quick caress. 'Or you.' His smile died away. 'And sometimes the feeling lingers and I know it's the truth. I am still the same.'

She frowned. The chunks of bread she tossed were too big now. They scattered the birds at their feet like grenades. 'Of course you are not.'

'It's all of a piece, I think sometimes.' He focused on the squabbling birds for a long moment. 'Brenner helped me to see, both myself and others, more clearly.' He spoke of Viscount Brenner, who had married his half-sister, Justine. 'He is so different from my father. Father was formidable, of course. But Brenner is so solid. Not at all like the fast crowd that used to hang about Welbourne.' He cast another grin in her direction. 'He gave me a view down a different path.'

'I think perhaps I know what you mean. He's well known and well liked and absolutely respected.'

'Exactly. I got a taste of that, building Fincote. Heady stuff. I don't wish to lose their respect.' He sighed. 'That's what worries me.'

She nodded. 'It was a good plan. The best you could have come up with, I think, given all the circumstances.' She cocked her head at him. 'But what will you do now? Now that Pratchett is gone?'

Stephen's breath caught. His muscles tensed. Every instinct cried out for him to stop, to turn away before he could make the mistake of leaving himself open and vulnerable.

'I want to find Pratchett,' he said, throwing himself on the mercy he hoped to find in those blue eyes. 'I want to be the one to return that thoroughbred to Ryeton, to create a spectacle that will capture the hearts and minds of the racing community and that will leave the earl obligated to race his horse at my course.' He swallowed, then took her hand in his. 'And I want you to help me.'

* * *

Mae was so occupied keeping rein on her traitorous body that it took several minutes for the impact of that last statement to sink in.

Stephen sat close, too close, and, despite their past, her resolve and her head's desperate pleas for caution, she had to fight to keep the rest of her from quivering at his nearness. Outwardly, her fingers beat out the only sign of her agitation, drumming on the remains of the thick loaf in her hands as if the rhythm would soothe the butterflies cavorting in her belly.

But inwardly it was another matter entirely.

Handsome, virile male, shouted her pounding pulse. *Mine,* whispered the thousands of nerve endings in her fingertips, all straining to touch him. But her weak and foolish heart was the worst offender. It was caught up in his easy manner and open expression. *Look,* it insisted. *He's talking, sharing…*

Listen! Her beleaguered brain's last desperate shout jerked her straight in her seat.

'…if you would consider it,' he was continuing. 'Wouldn't it be almost like old times?'

'What?' Aghast, she blinked, breaking the spell of his clear blue gaze. 'What was that? I can't have heard you correctly.'

For the briefest moment he stiffened. Mae's heart sank at the familiar posturing—but her anger blazed. Now it would come—another argument. Another metaphorical shove. Just another way to keep her at bay—and from getting too close.

It was an old dance, one that they'd performed

together too often already. She cut her gaze away and turned to go.

'Mae?' Her name was a plea. She glanced back and saw that he'd dropped his battle stance and watched her quietly. 'I know I should not have asked, but I really need your help. I can think of no one better suited for the job.'

Mae hesitated while once again her inner landscape went to war. This wasn't part of her plan! She had her future to arrange. Hadn't she already proved that she couldn't afford a distraction like Stephen Manning? Heaven knew this was not the time to risk the sort of doubt and pain that he was capable of inflicting on her.

'No,' she said flatly. She lobbed the last of the bread. It hit the ground with a *thunk*. Birds fluttered out of the way, then descended on the thing *en masse*. Mae stepped around them, swept around the bench and headed for the safety of the house.

'You know me, Mae,' he called after her. 'I wouldn't ask if my need were not dire.' He followed in her wake and she tried to harden her heart.

But this was *Stephen*. Part of her had to look past the drama and the pain of their last encounters and to the years of friendship and camaraderie that had come before. Part of her positively longed to help him—to fix things so he was smiling and lighthearted again.

Except—she knew that the carefree Stephen was only a mask. The glimpse she'd seen today, of Stephen enthusiastic, determined, worried—that was the most genuine that she had perhaps ever seen him. Her step faltered. Could she turn her back on something she'd waited her whole life to see?

Yes. For her own sake, she could. She strode ahead again.

At the first turn in the path, she paused. The very air felt heavy, momentous. She'd reached a crossroads. Suddenly she knew that this moment might for ever define and divide the segments of her life.

She glanced back. Stephen had given up his pursuit. He turned away, every line signalling his dejection. Her heart sank.

And her head snapped abruptly up. Her own words echoed in her head. *For her own sake...*

Hadn't she just this morning vowed to do anything to forward her campaign, to achieve her goals? Surely it wasn't a good idea to alienate a potential ally? Perhaps instead of pushing Stephen away, she should *recruit* him.

'Stephen, wait!' she called. Her pulse pounded loud in her ears and she prayed she wasn't making a huge tactical error. But she couldn't deny that it *felt* right.

He'd glanced over his shoulder at her. He stood, one hand gripping the curved seat, hope alight in his eyes.

'I might consider your request, but I propose an exchange,' she said, coming closer again. 'My help for yours.'

'My help?' he asked. Relief visibly flowed over him. 'Of course. Anything.' He reached out, grasped her hands. 'Thank you,' he whispered. He tugged her back towards the bench. 'There's so much to discuss. We must get started right away.' He frowned. 'But wait, I don't know what your goal was… What was it that you need help with, that you mean to accomplish?'

She smiled. 'Marriage.' She said it loud and clear and without hesitation.

And took a great deal of satisfaction in witnessing the shock on his face.

Chapter Six

Stephen's blood surged. His senses sharpened in an
instant, keen as a knife's blade. *Idiot. You blind, bloody
fool.* He knew Mae was capable of playing deep. And
he'd played right into her hands.

Careful. He swallowed a surge of anger. He had no
call to be angry in any case. He was the one who had
started this—and he had known what he was getting
into. Plenty of women could identify what they wanted,
but *no* one else threw themselves into achieving it with
even a fraction of her passion and abandon. He admired
that about her. He only found it disconcerting to be at
the centre of it.

'Mae.' He hesitated. 'You know how fondly I think
of you. I don't believe I've ever admired a woman's
tenacity and intelligence as I do yours, but all of my
energy is focused on Fincote Park right now. It's no
time for me to be thinking of anything—'

Mae's laughter pealed out across the glade. 'Oh, to
have a mirror right now, so that you could see your

face,' she said. She'd flushed red, but her eyes twinkled with mischief. 'Stop, please, before you embarrass us both. I don't mean marriage to *you,* Stephen. I did mean what I said last night. I'd prefer to leave the past where it lies and look to the future.' She rolled her eyes. 'Papa would never countenance such a thing, in any case.'

For the second time in as many minutes, relief swept through him. He couldn't help grumbling a bit, though. 'Well, glad as I am to hear it, I can't help but wonder why your father holds me in such disregard. He never objected all those years we ran wild all over Welbourne Manor.'

Mae's smile grew reminiscent. 'Did you know that he wasn't aware of it, at first? He was always away in London on business, leaving Mama and me alone in Richmond. She wrote that I had befriended a duke's daughter and he was content.'

He had to suppress a laugh. 'No, I didn't know. Until he discovered *which* duke, I would guess?'

'Precisely, and by then it was too late. He might have judged them to be fast, but he also knew better than to risk offending your parents.' She shook her head. 'I know he only wants what he thinks is best for me. I suppose one cannot fault him for entertaining higher aspirations for his only daughter.' Her mouth turned down in a wry curve. 'Unless you are the only daughter.'

'Higher aspirations, is it?' He ran an evaluating eye over her, but she waved her hand, dismissing the subject.

'Let's settle down to the business at hand.' She eyed him, considering. 'I have to say, I admire your thinking on this. Based on the gossip at breakfast, the people of

Newmarket—and all of England, soon enough—can talk of nothing else but Pratchett's kidnapping. Lord Toswick said that the London journalists are already swooping through the town.' She sat back, a mischievous smile on her face. 'Especially after your disagreement with Ryeton—can you imagine the fevered reaction of the crowd here at Newmarket should you be the one to return England's most famous Thoroughbred? They'll go mad with the delicious irony of it. You'll be a hero, practically a legend, in a moment's time. They'll talk of it all over England.'

Insidious, the notion wound its way inside of him again, caressing all of his weak spots. The idea of being lauded as a hero held an undeniable appeal—as Mae of all people would at least dimly understand. But the chance that such notoriety would give Fincote Park was what truly mattered.

'You are right,' she continued. 'Ryeton will look like an ill-tempered fool should he continue to hold a grudge. And meanwhile, racing enthusiasts will be strewing a path of rose petals leading you straight to the Jockey Club.'

Lord, she did know how to get a man stirred up.

She frowned. 'But finding Pratchett? That's going to be the difficult part.' Her brow furrowed, she heaved a great sigh.

He wished she wouldn't. He couldn't recall that she had ever possessed such an inclination for deep breathing and gusty sighing. Surely he would have noticed, before now. He eyed her bosom with a considering stare. Or perhaps she just had not yet possessed the equipment to make the habit worthwhile.

He shook his head to clear it. 'It's not going to be easy. There are plenty of experienced racing men who are already convinced that Pratchett will never be recovered—that he's likely dead already.'

'No, no!' She waved an impatient hand. 'Surely you know better than to listen to such idiocy.' In the past, Stephen might have been irritated at her manner, but just now he found he did not mind seeing Mae worked into a state of agitation. It did lovely things to her colour and the brightness of her eyes. He glanced down once more. And the rate of her breathing. It also tipped the scales of justice slightly in his direction. Fate and all the heavens knew she'd agitated him often enough in the past.

'You don't go to all the trouble of kidnapping a horse if you want him dead. No, someone took that horse for a reason,' she said. 'Discover the reason and you'll discover the horse.'

'I agree.'

'Surely it will have been someone involved in racing. But who? And why? A rival owner—someone tired of Pratchett stealing the limelight? Someone with a grudge?'

'Or perhaps Ryeton owed someone money and they thought to get their return back,' Stephen said thoughtfully. 'Anyone could make a fortune siring foals by him, even off the Stud Book records. He could be on his way to a stud farm in Ireland as we speak.'

'No.' She frowned. 'Too easy to be caught. That horse is still somewhere quite nearby. I'd bet on it. If the kidnapper does mean to keep him rather than return him, he'll leave once the racing's done, along with the hundreds of other horses that will be moving on the roads out of here.'

She continued in that vein, musing or perhaps thinking aloud. And Stephen listened, following in the wake of her incredibly thorough mind. This was exactly why she was the person he needed at his side. When Mae Halford told you exactly how to get what you wanted, anyone acquainted with her knew to listen. But only half of his brain was truly engaged.

The other half was being troublesome.

Very busily, the other half was looking her over, measuring her up. There were new and deeper layers to her. Her enthusiasm and energy felt familiar, but they'd been enhanced with knowledge and a nascent sensuality. And somehow it all combined to form an ever-changing, irresistible whole.

'We'll need to move quickly. Have you any ideas on how you wish to proceed?'

Her question jerked him back to the present. 'Yes. I think that together we can cover a lot of ground, each of us investigating in our respective spheres to collect information.'

She raised a brow, encouraging him to continue.

'I can tell you what is happening in every stable in town, right now,' he assured her. 'Owners, black legs and jockeys, they are all pontificating right now, telling everyone who will listen what they know, what they think they know and why such a thing would never have happened to them. Somebody knows something— it'll be my job to separate the wheat from the chaff.'

She nodded, thinking it through. 'And me?'

He chuckled. 'Well, you are just newly arrived back

in England. Clearly you will need to be brought up to the minute on all the gossip. And the ladies, no doubt, will be thrilled to indulge you. Right now, all over Newmarket, women are delicately whispering of every social *faux pas* that Ryeton's ever committed. If there are any jilted fiancés, family feuds, former lovers, any skeletons of any sort in Ryeton's closet, they'll be laid bare in the parlours and sitting rooms all over town.'

Her mouth twisted into a grin. 'I can hardly wait.'

'As we're both guests here, finding a way to come together to compare notes and put pieces together shouldn't be too difficult.'

She nodded again, but her gaze had grown unfocused and he could tell those indefatigable wheels were turning in her head. He held his breath and watched hers for a sign of what she was thinking. Or so he told himself.

'I think we should add a third prong to your investigation,' she said at last. 'If you don't mind my making a suggestion—I think we should use Josette.'

'Josette?'

'My maid.' A wry twinkle showed in her expression. 'Not even your thoroughbreds travel faster than servants' gossip. And they are often privy to details to which ladies are not. Josette is a treasure—and a genius at sorting through to the heart of the matter.'

'Then by all means, have her set her ear to catch what news she may.'

'She's also a very pretty girl. She might come in handy if you need to get information from your stable hands or grooms.' Mae's chuckle told him all he needed to know about the two of them and the sort of mischief they had likely got up to together.

'I'll keep that in mind.' He stood, eager to get started. 'We can begin at once—'

'Stephen.' Mae stood too. She watched him, hesitation in her manner and perhaps something…defensive, too?

'There's something else.'

He waited.

She turned away. 'I'm not sure…' Abruptly she spun around, her arms folded before her and a challenge in her eye. 'I have some information, something that might be of even further use for you, but perhaps we had better just define my role in this right here and now.' She lifted her chin. 'If I have ideas, thoughts, then I want to know now that I can bring them up without recrimination or resentment—'

'Have you forgotten whom it is you are talking to?' he interrupted her, irritated. '*I* asked for *your* help! Do you think I'm going to suddenly act the snippy little girl if you give it?'

They glared at each other a moment. It was as if a span of years had suddenly fallen away. Yet at the same time Stephen was aware of a newfound tension crackling in the air between them. He felt hot and edgy, entirely uncomfortable and incalculably curious.

'Very well, then,' she relented at last. 'First, let me ask you a question. Have you heard about the filly my father brought over from France?'

He nodded. 'Yes, she's said to have deep hindquarters and a quick gait. But an unknown filly is not what I—'

Her raised hand stopped him cold. 'Do you know her name?'

'I'm sure I've heard it, but I can't quite recall it now.'

'Barty's Shill.'

'Unusual.'

'*Apt* is the word for it. My father's little joke.' She shook her head. 'Really, we've only been abroad for two years, and already these racing men have forgotten who my father is. They are all agog over that pretty little filly, and they are ignoring the string of other horses he's stabled here in Newmarket.'

Stephen straightened. 'And I gather that they should be paying attention?'

She smiled. 'Indeed they should. For mixed in with that group is Ornithopter, a high-necked bay that looks like he was put together from pieces from the knacker's yard.'

Mae leaned in and he tried to look more interested in her words than the view.

'He can fly, Stephen. I've seen racehorses from Dublin to Deauville, but I've never seen anything like him. Papa meant for him to give Pratchett his first taste of track dust. *That's* going to be the horse everyone's talking about after the Guineas are run. You would do well to talk to Papa before then.'

He felt some of his interest leached away. 'Ah, but if your father doesn't care to have me near his daughter, I doubt he'll feel any differently about his prized horseflesh.'

She gave a huff of exasperation. 'Such a flattering correlation—and one Papa is likely to make as well. We'll have to be careful. But as I said last night,

Stephen, Papa taking us abroad had less to do with you than it had to do with me. He wasn't angry with either of us, but he thought we would both be better for a bit of distance between us. As long as he believes my interests to lie elsewhere—and that I'm not making a nuisance of myself or harassing you—then he'll be impressed that you have the superior understanding to see the potential in Ornithopter.'

Stephen was relieved, but his mind was travelling further along the new path she had pointed out. 'I see what you are saying. Even if we do return Pratchett quickly, it may be that the Jockey Club stewards will not allow him to race the Guineas. Without a true challenge from Pratchett, Ornithopter will win—'

'He'll make it look like child's play,' she said eagerly. 'And afterwards, every racing man in the kingdom will be clamouring to see them matched against each other. It will be the most natural thing in the world! *You* must be the one to give it to them.' She tilted her head, her smile a fascinating marriage of triumph and allure. 'And when you do, Fincote Park's future will be secured.'

He stared at her. Such a familiar feeling, always being one step behind Mae Halford. Curious how it didn't send him flying into fits of annoyance like it used to. Instead he had to curb the impulse to sweep her up, twirl her about the meadow and kiss her soundly. 'This could work,' he whispered instead. 'This could be the making of Fincote, Mae!' Jubilation and real hope surged in his veins. He scrubbed a hand through his hair, already thinking out a timetable in his head. 'We can start now,' he said with excitement. 'I'll head into town right away—'

He stopped. Her arms were crossed again, and if he wasn't mistaken then that pretty little kid boot was tapping in his direction.

'Not so fast, Stephen.' Yes, he definitely recalled that crotchety tone. 'This is to be an exchange. Or had you forgotten already?'

He deflated a little. 'Oh, yes. No, of course I did not forget.'

'I've agreed to help you. I've risked much, revealing my father's secrets, against his express wishes. I think I more than deserve your help in return.'

He nodded. 'Yes, my help. Regarding your marriage.'

There it came again; another damned distracting deep breath. 'Marriage is indeed in my future. Papa has decided it is time. But you know how he is.' She glanced about the empty glade and lowered her voice. 'He's going to consider his balance sheets with at least as much attention as he will my inclinations. Or worse, he'll choose somebody he thinks can shape me into the right sort of woman.'

Stephen clamped firmly down on an inarticulate note of protest.

Mae didn't appear to notice. She was wrapped up in her own miserable view of such a future. 'I can't live like that, Stephen. I've fought this battle my entire life—tooth and nail I have resisted as people have tried to squeeze me into a mould that does not fit. I have no desire to spend the rest of my life fighting my husband's efforts to do the same.' She glanced away. 'Perhaps I am not delicate and quiet and well trained, like a daughter or a wife should be. But I do possess a few good qualities. I should like to be appreciated for them.'

'As you should.' His voice had gone hoarse.

'And so I *need* your help. I've been away, and even before we were never very active in the highest society. I need information. Your opinions, as well, if you would share them. Somewhere there is a gentleman, perhaps more than one, who's strong enough, secure enough with his own quirks, so that mine won't seem such an obstacle.' She shrugged. 'I just hope to find someone to accept me as I am. Will you help me?'

Surely it was relief travelling in waves through his veins right now. Relief, pure and simple, unadulterated with anything as hypocritical as pique or resentment. That would be childish in the extreme and entirely too *dog in the manger* to contemplate.

'What would you have me do?' he asked.

'Nothing onerous, and nothing that will distract us from the job we have to do. Introduce me to the right people. Share what you know. Help me evaluate likely men based on the criteria I've come up with.'

Criteria? He shuddered. But truly, this was the least he could do for her. 'Of course. I will do whatever I can. There are always a few social entertainments to go along with the racing. We should make an inroad on quite a number of gentlemen.'

'Thank you.' Against all his expectations, her expression radiated gratitude and hope.

Who are you? He prayed that this turn of events was genuine, that Mae had indeed moved past her girl-ish infatuation. But part of him could not forget that she was devilishly skilled at manoeuvring people and events to her satisfaction.

'We've a bargain, then,' he said.

'Yes. And a great deal of work to do.'

And then, just because he had to know, he did what he had *never* done with Mae Halford before. He summoned up his most devastating smile. With heat in his eyes and seduction in the low rasp of his voice, he rose and extended his hand. 'Then shall we seal it?'

Her mouth set primly, she stood as well and shook his hand. But she snatched her hand back as if his had burned.

He took a step closer. 'So formal? And we such old friends.' He shook his head slowly, his gaze locked to hers. 'Surely we can mark our agreement in a more memorable fashion. With a kiss, perhaps?'

Perhaps it was cruel to test her this way. But he must know, in order to proceed with confidence. The Mae of old would leap at this chance. Hell, she'd likely leap into his arms, sure her tactics had been a success.

Breath suspended, he waited.

She stilled. He could see the pulse leaping in her throat, the rapid rise and fall of her breast.

A little spike—mixed triumph and dismay—sent his pulse ratcheting.

Her gaze broke free from his. Stepping back, she dusted off her hands. 'Four days! That's all we'll have until the running of the Guineas.' Her voice wasn't even shaky. 'Let's get started, shall we? Lady Toswick is hosting a tea today for her guests and some of the ladies also in Newmarket. I will discover all that I can. Tonight she plans an evening of cards for her guests and a few others, but if you cannot return by then, we should be able to catch up at her party tomorrow here in the gardens.'

He should be finding it reassuring, that air of indifference. Yes, of course he did.

'Very well.' And because whatever other feelings Mae might inspire, without a doubt she deserved his gratitude, he bent over her hand. 'Thank you, Mae.' Lightly, he brushed his lips over her knuckles.

The scent of her skin caught him, holding him bowed before her for several seconds too long. Between them the very air flared and crackled into life. He dropped her hand. Only long years of training and practised smoothness kept him from rearing back.

'Until tomorrow, then.' She turned on her heel and spun away.

He watched her leisurely retreat. So Mae Halford had indeed grown out of her schoolgirl crush. This was a cause for joy, not annoyance, he told himself firmly. She needed his help, just as he needed hers. He'd left the house this morning in a cloud of despair. She'd helped give him back purpose and hope.

Stephen moved to go. He caught himself up quickly, though, before he could step through the shining strands of a spider's web. The spider was busily at work, constructing her masterpiece. Good luck, that—to find a spider spinning in the morning. And so appropriate, as he and Mae began to spin out another scheme of their own.

Stepping carefully around the web, Stephen headed back. Perhaps he and Mae would move on to new equality in their relationship. Truly, she did have a remarkable mind—and a definite talent for scheming. She deserved happiness. She was warm and giving, intelligent and loyal to a fault. And annoying. The memory of her detachment pricked him again.

Definitely annoying.

...

Chapter Seven

Mae and her mother paused outside the parlour door. Lady Toswick's butler stepped forwards to grant them admittance, but at the tug on her arm, Mae signalled him to wait.

'Perhaps I'll just take a tray in my room, after all.'

Mae patted her mother's hand. Lady Toswick had done a marvellous job of easing her anxiety, for which Mae could only be grateful. Her mother had appeared to be comfortable enough when the mature ladies of the house party gathered at their sewing or to write letters, but she still found the larger entertainments to be nerve-racking.

'It's only tea,' Mae said with an encouraging smile. 'And only the ladies are to be present, I heard.'

'Oh?' The news did seem to brighten her mother's spirits. She nodded. 'Perhaps just for a little while, then.'

Mae was nervous herself, if for entirely different reasons. She'd informed Josette of their new mission.

The maid hadn't been happy, but she'd promised to find out what she could. She'd also interrogated her mistress ruthlessly. Mae had confessed everything, right down to her pride in her own acting abilities. She could easily have become the toast of Drury Lane, had there been a theatre director in that meadow this morning. At the very least she deserved a standing ovation for the way she'd disguised the intensity of her response to Stephen's blandishments.

He'd been testing her. She supposed she could not blame him, considering their past. Josette assured her she'd passed with flying colours. *And weak knees,* Mae had mentally added. *And a leaping pulse and the nearly irresistible urge to throw herself into his arms.*

She clenched her fists and prayed she hadn't made a mistake, agreeing to work with him. But the more she considered the matter, the more certain she grew that he was the right person to help her. True, she was a little worried about the intensity of her reaction to him; he'd but sat next to her on the bench and her insides had unfurled like petals in the sun. But surely she'd already made it over the biggest hurdle—she'd withstood the full force of his considerable charm. It would only get easier from here, and she had to believe that the benefits outweighed the risks.

He certainly knew and understood her capabilities. Far from being threatened, he'd sought out her help! He would know exactly the sort of temperament she required in a husband. After everything, he still trusted her; she would trust him to steer her on the right course.

She need only keep a cool head. And all of her petals tightly furled.

The door swung open and Lady Toswick's butler bowed them in. The parlour itself felt inviting. Warm with shades of green and cream and touched with gilt highlights, the room reflected the welcoming smiles of their hostess. 'Here you are, Mrs Halford!' the countess sang out, coming to greet them. 'And Miss Halford!' She gestured toward a sunny corner where ladies sat grouped about several tables. 'We'll be serving tea shortly. Won't you join us?'

Some of the tension left her mother's arm. Mae cast a grateful smile upon Lady Toswick. 'Mother, Lady Corbet is beckoning. Shall we join her?'

The door opened again. 'Ah, here are the tea carts.' The countess grinned. 'Now, we shall enjoy cook's wonders, and then I shall share with you some exciting news!' She radiated a sense of good-natured mischief that piqued Mae's curiosity.

Mae's mother was pulled into an empty chair near their hostess, but Addy called Mae over to her. 'Here you are at last!' Reaching out, she pulled her into a swift embrace. 'Watch the one in the ice-blue,' she whispered. 'She's as spiteful as a cat.'

Mae nodded her understanding. A round of introductions was made and then the servants began to unload the carts.

The tea was of a fine quality and the accompanying savouries were delicious. The conversation, however, was general, light and innocuous. Fashion was the topic of interest at their small table—the hazard of sitting with so many of the younger members of the party.

'You certainly look delicious today, Mae.' Addy picked up her tea and looked her over with a critical eye. 'Those browns are rich indeed—you look like my cup of morning chocolate.' Her eyes twinkled over the rim of her cup. 'I predict the gentlemen will fall over themselves for the chance to drink you up.'

Mae flushed. Being singled out would not help her win any of these ladies over. What she needed was a way to introduce the subject of Pratchett and Lord Ryeton.

Miss Metheny, the cat, took up the thread of conversation. 'Your fabrics are indeed lovely,' she agreed. 'But your waistline is so low.' Smooth and guileless her face remained, but spite shone clear in the hooded gleam of her eye. 'It's too bad.' She sighed. 'No one in London is wearing their waistlines low.'

'It is unfortunate, isn't it?' Mae agreed, all good cheer. 'London does always seem to be a step behind Paris. No doubt the English ladies will catch up by next Season.'

She never had been one to back down when confronted by a bully, social or otherwise.

'Ooh, Paris!' Exclamations and questions arose from the circle of ladies.

'How lucky you are.' The cat's younger sister, Miss Lucy Metheny, sighed. 'We never get to go anywhere.'

'I certainly had no wish to be dragged to Newmarket.' Her sister's unfortunately broad face had gone sour. 'But Father will force us along, every year.'

'There is a bright side this year,' Addy told her. 'The scandal of the Season happened right here and you were a first-hand witness.'

'Pah. Horses,' Miss Metheny scoffed. 'Who cares for a scandal involving *horses?*'

'Corbet says that all of London is already talking about it. People are already beginning to arrive, hoping to catch the rest as it unfolds.'

Mae mentally blessed her friend. 'Lord Ryeton certainly makes a tragic figure,' she offered helpfully. And hopefully. Anything to ferret out gossip about the earl.

'My mama says he makes himself ridiculous,' one of the other girls piped up. 'With all of those outrageous wagers.'

'Wagers?'

'He does bet on anything, and at the drop of a hat.' Addy's waving hand dismissed the importance of such a habit. 'So childish! But he's hardly alone. There are gentlemen aplenty at White's who will bet on the next person to walk in the door. Or the colour of the hat worn by the next lady to pass by.'

'How funny you should say so.' Miss Lucy laughed. 'Lord Ryeton made just such a wager with my papa. They bet a shocking sum on whether Papa's favourite mare would foal a colt or a filly.'

'Lucy!' Her sister's tone held a warning.

'What?' The girl continued, unheeding. 'I was so happy Papa won, because I had been longing for ages for a particular tall bonnet, with the most cunningly curled ostrich feathers. Papa said it was beyond our budget, however. But with the winnings, he was able to buy it at last!'

An uncomfortable silence ensued. Miss Metheny's face flamed. Mae felt a stab of sympathy for her.

They all turned eagerly when Lady Toswick cleared her throat and called for attention.

'My dears. I would like to thank you all for coming today. I'm having a marvellous time and I do hope that you are too.' She gave a sad smile. 'Many of us are here frequently throughout the racing season and repeatedly through the years. Of course, we do try to add a little gentility to our time spent here. We schedule our teas and explore the shops and the local sights. But it is a shame that so many of our social engagements are separate from the gentlemen.'

There were heartfelt sighs of agreement from several of the younger ladies.

'It is a bit tiring, to be left out of the constant talk of weight and handicap at my breakfast table. In London it is one thing for my husband and son to spend their days drinking and smoking at their clubs. I am occupied there. But here? They are off to their stables, their prize fights and their Jockey Club rooms and I struggle to fill my days. I find myself becoming resentful as my interests are placed such a far-away second.'

Murmurs of accord rippled around the tables.

'I have corresponded at length with my dear friend Lady Ryeton about this dilemma. To date her solution has been to refuse to come to Newmarket at all. But we have hatched a more delicious answer. We fail to distract our men from their preoccupation with trial runs and touts, so we shall join them in it.'

Excited talk erupted throughout the room. Miss Metheny groaned.

Lady Toswick waved them down. 'We shall do just as they do. *En masse,* we will observe the practice trials, tour the training stables, make our bets and watch the races. Together we will become educated and passionate about this sport of theirs and we will regain their attention as we do so. Lady Ryeton is travelling to Newmarket and she has promised that we shall have a tour of her husband's stables, reputed to be the best in all of England!'

She grinned. 'It shall be great fun, giving them a taste of their own medicine as we become busy and preoccupied with our new interest, but it shall be great fun also to come together in the end.' Her lips pursed in an expression of pure delight. Pausing, she allowed her gaze to drift about the room. 'What say you? Are you with us?'

A great babbling broke out. The ladies abandoned the tea tables to gather in groups. The room came alive with the ear-piercing prattle of women a-twitter, ready to seize the bit in their teeth. Mae smiled at the commotion. There might be benefits to this development. Her own scheming might not look so…odd, against the background of a townful of society ladies angling after the attention of their men.

Addy gripped Mae's arm and drew her towards a secluded corner. 'Ryeton's countess hasn't been to Newmarket in years,' she whispered in confiding tones. 'Pratchett was just the beginning of the earl's troubles. He must be the most wretched man in Suffolk, with his horse gone missing and his estranged wife on her way here. If I didn't know better, I'd say Lady Ryeton cooked up this idea about getting us all involved in racing as an excuse to punish him.'

Mae perked to attention. 'They are estranged? Is her

husband's devotion to racing the reason for it?' Perhaps Lady Ryeton had conspired even further back to punish her husband. Could she have arranged for Pratchett's disappearance from afar?

'Her husband's devotion to his mistress, rather.'

'His mistress?' Miss Lucy, eyes bright with interest, interrupted their tête-à-tête. She sidled up beside Mae, glanced across the room and lowered her voice. 'I heard something of her just this morning! Lord Ryeton's lady-bird—Charlotte Hague, the woman he's kept so cosily here in Newmarket for the past two years—has cast him out!'

'Lucy Metheny!' Her sister was next to join their group, and distaste outweighed the shock in Miss Metheny's tone. 'That is hardly a fit subject for a young girl. Where on earth would you have heard such a thing?'

'I heard the cook telling one of the kitchen maids,' answered the girl as if it was the most obvious thing in the world. 'They were gossiping this morning when I went to fetch Mama's posset. They said Miss Hague has ejected him from her house, boxed up all of his things and left them on the street!'

'Is that what those boxes were?' Another of their tablemates had joined them. 'I passed the stack of them myself on the way here.'

A chorus of whispers began all about them. Mae was delighted. An angry wife? A disenchanted mistress? Either one of them might have taken Pratchett—if only to make the earl miserable.

'Lord Ryeton certainly is having a difficult time of it,' she said. 'Perhaps Miss Hague *is* interested in racing. That may be what has inspired his wife to come up with this particular plan.'

'The kitchen maids said that she's giving up the lease on her house. Perhaps she means to relocate to London. Likely she's on the lookout for a new protector.'

'Lucy, that is the outside of enough! If you keep on, I'm going to tell Mama.'

Nobody paid the least bit of attention to Miss Metheny.

'Perhaps not,' the other girl said, keeping her voice low. 'My sisters put their heads together when we passed those boxes and said that Miss Hague has been seen driving out of Newmarket every afternoon.' She raised her brows. 'Perhaps she has found Lord Ryeton's replacement already.'

'I insist that we leave this subject behind.' Miss Metheny was becoming sincerely disturbed. Mae felt a twinge for the fate of their household's kitchen maids. 'Let's talk of something else.' Pointedly she turned to Mae. 'Have you been long acquainted with Lady Toswick, Miss Halford?'

Mae blinked. 'No, indeed. I never met her before this house party.'

'How kind of her to invite you and your family, then.'

'Very kind. I credit Lord Toswick. He and my father are racing cronies.'

'I credit the fact that the countess's nephew is not yet married,' Addy said with a smirk. 'I rather think she wanted to get a look at you, Mae, before you made your début in London.'

'Well, Delia won't like that!' Miss Lucy said, with

a look of alarm. 'My sister is the toast of the Season.'
She leaned close. 'And she's not fond of rivals.'

'If you cannot open your mouth without making a
quiz of yourself, then I wish you would keep it closed!'
Miss Metheny had gone off crimson again.

Mae could not suppress another pang of sympathy
for the difficult Miss Metheny. Miss Lucy had proven
quite helpful today, but she possessed a definite gift for
discomposing her sister.

'Surely you jest, Miss Lucy. Your sister appears to
have every social advantage over me. She has knowledge and experience of London society, while I have
been gallivanting abroad.' Mae cast a smile of camaraderie towards the beleaguered girl. 'She can have no
need to feel threatened by me.'

But Miss Metheny was in no mood to form
alliances. Or perhaps she had been pushed past her
endurance. Raising her chin, she speared Mae with an
unmistakable challenge. 'The word is that you possess
a dowry of fifty thousand pounds. That's enough to
make you a threat to every unmarried girl in London.'

Mae flushed. Or perhaps Miss Metheny was just a
shrewish vixen. Whatever the case, she would not allow
the girl to vent her spleen all over her.

'But I saw you speaking to Lord Stephen Manning
last night.' Miss Lucy broke in, her eyes alive with
interest. 'Perhaps your interests lie in that direction?'

Mae struggled to control both her colour and her
temper. 'Lord Stephen and I are old friends. We practically grew up together. Are you well acquainted
with him?'

Miss Lucy's face lit up. 'No, but I should certainly like to be.'

'I can easily arrange an introduction.'

'To one of the Fitzmanning Miscellany?' Miss Metheny broke in. 'Don't be absurd. That family has made its home in the scandal sheets for the last twenty years. It wouldn't be seemly.'

Every trace of empathy for the girl died a quick and fiery death. Mae straightened, her fists clenched.

But Addy leaped to Stephen's defence even before Mae could. 'Lord Stephen Manning—'

'Is a second son of a disreputable duke,' the nasty bit of baggage interrupted. 'And likely in need of an heiress. He would do very well for *her*.' Not finished yet, she looked down her nose in Mae's direction. 'You might also consider Viscount Landry, Miss Halford. He's been sniffing about the house party. He's pockets to let and growing quite desperate. I shouldn't think he'd object to a merchant's daughter.' She let loose a bitter laugh. 'In fact, he has fifty thousand reasons not to object, does he not?'

Her chest tight, Mae took a step closer to the odious Miss Metheny. 'Has the viscount perhaps shown an interest in you?'

Miss Metheny, her lips pressed tight, did not answer.

Her sister did. 'Indeed, no! But then Delia does not have—'

'A pleasant manner? A gracious temperament?' Straightening her spine, Mae stared at the girl who seemed so determined to be nasty. 'Well then, the viscount will have at least fifty thousand and two reasons to prefer me over you.'

She stepped back and looped her arm in Addy's. 'Come, Addy. I understand there is to be a card party tonight. Let's go and prepare ourselves, shall we?'

'Let's,' Addy said firmly. They stepped away. 'I never did care for toast.'

Stephen had been right about one thing. Every man-jack in Newmarket was still talking about Pratchett's disappearance—and they all had a theory on what had happened to the horse, and why.

The grooms he spoke to all suspected a rival owner had done the deed—and they were all fearful for their own four-legged charges. The black legs he encountered shared the grooms' suspicions and went about muttering about pots and kettles and shades of black. Just to make things interesting, the owners and enthusiasts he talked with were all convinced the job was the work of a crooked leg or, even worse, a consortium of them.

'It makes sense.' Lord Toswick was morose, mourning Pratchett's loss as a stud. Stephen had encountered the earl and his cronies along Moulton Road, mounted and heading to a cockfight at the edge of town in an effort to restore his spirits. 'Ryeton has been very vocal about putting a stop to the cheating legs and their skullduggery. He wanted them to answer to the Jockey Club.'

'If it was them, then perhaps they meant it as a warning.' Matthew Grange, driving a smart cabriolet, accompanied the earl's group.

'I doubt it,' Stephen said with a frown. 'It's not their usual mode of operation. Normally the legs allow a clear favourite to build. Once the betting is high, they *then* arrange something, a laming or a poisoning right in the last hours before the race. When the horse shows poorly or doesn't run, they rake in a fortune. There's no profit to be made if the horse disappears before the bets are made.'

Toswick shrugged. 'Perhaps Ryeton's wife had a hand in it. She's been giving him the devil of a time.'

'I think I like her already,' Matthew said with a grin.

'That's because you haven't met her,' Toswick answered with a shudder. 'She's a sly thing, just the sort of woman to come up with such a bizarre way to punish a man.'

'Bizarre, but effective,' retorted Matthew.

Toswick's horse began a restless dance. 'Let's be off, then. Care to come with us, Manning?'

'Thank you, Toswick, but I'm still searching for a decent match up for Fincote Park.'

'Very well, then.' Impatient, the earl's horse pranced again, setting off several other mounts. But Toswick paused. 'You might consider fillies. My Butterfly runs a very decent trial and I hear that Halford has brought over an exceptional animal from France. You should go and have a look at her. I wouldn't be averse to a match between them.'

It was a very generous offer. Stephen was grateful for it, even if he did have something bigger and better in mind, thanks to Mae. Had there ever been another like her? Gad, he'd barely presented her with his dilemma, yet she'd sized up the situation and seized upon a brilliant, all-encompassing plan. 'Thank you, Toswick. I'll do that now.'

The group departed and Stephen made the rounds of several stables, including Mae's father's. Barty Halford had spared no expense, renting space on Mill Hill, near to some of the greatest trainers of the day. Well built and modern were these stables too, with spacious loose boxes and more than adequate ventilation. Stephen spent some time observing Halford's famous filly, but he unobtrusively sought out Ornithopter as well.

Mae was right. The horse was no beauty, but Stephen dallied, gossiping with the stable hands until a groom took the horse out for exercise. He saw for himself how the animal carried a gorgeous stride, long and smooth.

The sight of it renewed his determination. Pratchett and Ornithopter. What a contest it would be—between two such magnificent animals! Their names—and Fincote Park's along with them—would be spoken for years. But he had to find Pratchett first, for any of it to be feasible. He moved on, praying for a hint of the information he needed.

Everywhere the talk was of Ryeton's predicament and Pratchett's fate. Everyone had an opinion, some claimed more knowledge than they ultimately possessed, but none cursed Ryeton with more animosity than Viscount Landry, whom Stephen found loitering about the training stables.

'I told you, didn't I? Not an ounce of generosity in the dastard,' the viscount said, leaning heavily on a paddock rail. 'The man is black of heart and soul.' He glanced askance at Stephen and squinted in the sun. 'You cannot say I didn't warn you.'

'I wasn't sure if you were still there, when it

happened.' Stephen kept his tone casual at first. Wind blew sweet and strong from the Heath. He lifted his face, let it wash over him before he spoke again, with just a shade of bitterness to colour his words. 'The rotter can say all he likes about me and my enterprise, but I'll not hear him disparage a good man who gave his all for king and country.'

'Rotter,' Landry agreed glumly. 'That's the nicest thing you could say about the man.'

Stephen studied his old associate. Something was going on between him and Ryeton. And Landry still wasn't talking about it. In Stephen's mind, that only highlighted the significance of the thing. He pushed away from the fence. 'This breeze is drying me out. Care to stop in a pub?'

Landry's expression brightened, yet he hesitated.

Ah. The wind blew in that direction too, did it? 'Come, I'll buy you a drink, man. Enemy of my enemy and all that.'

'All right, then. I suppose you're right—those of us who can see Ryeton for what he is should stick together, eh?'

Stephen merely clapped the man on the back and hoped he was still a talkative drunk.

He was—and a melancholy one as well—but he took a damned long time to get there. The hour grew late and Stephen's pockets grew lighter, and though Landry eventually bemoaned fate and bad fortune at the gaming tables, hard-hearted wenches and tight-fisted fathers, he steadfastly declined to say more about Ryeton.

His refusal piqued Stephen's interest even further. He

wanted to curse in frustration when Landry slammed down his pint and declared he must go.

'Toswick's giving a card party, you know.' Morose, he looked down at the disarray of his clothing. 'Going to try to weasel my way in. Should go and change, but there's no use. Even my valet has abandoned me.' He turned to stare into his empty tankard, his lower lip quivering in drunken abandon. 'I don't even have a clean neckcloth to my name.'

Staring at the viscount, Stephen executed several slow and solemn blinks. He hadn't drunk nearly as much as Landry, but the viscount didn't need to know that. When a man dived so deeply into his cups, he rarely liked to go alone.

'Come as my guest,' Stephen said at last. 'I've linen. I'll loan you some.' His gaze traced a wobbly path up and over the man. 'A clean shirt, too.'

'Will you, by God?' Landry slammed his pewter mug down again. 'Tapster! I'll have another. There's still a bit of generosity left in this world and I would drink to it!' He downed the last mug in one long swallow. 'Manning…' he staggered to his feet '…you're as good a friend as I've ever had. Must get into that party, you see. The play won't be deep, but the company…'

'I'm happy to help.'

'Halford will be there. Man's got more gold than Midas, or so they say. Looks like a troll, though.'

Stephen's stomach twisted. He'd forgotten Landry's determination to meet the 'new heiress'. 'Shall we go? We've no wish to be late, I'm sure.'

'He's got a daughter, did you know?' Landry's gaze had gone suddenly intense.

'I did know.' Firmly he ignored the sudden vision of how Mae had looked at Toswick's last-evening entertainment, glowing from the inside and casting all those about her into the shade. Or this morning, when she had shone brighter than the sun.

'Still haven't managed to meet her. Mean to, though.' He sighed. 'Tonight.'

'Come along, then, and get dressed. I'll introduce you.' And then he'd make sure that Landry stayed far away from Mae. Surely there was another woman of means in Newmarket he could be turned towards.

Stephen finally coaxed the man away and got him safely to Titchley. To be safe, he sneaked him up the back steps and rang for a hot pot of coffee. He'd thought the viscount would sober up a little as they dressed, but Landry appeared to be feeling the delayed effects of his afternoon of drinking.

At last the viscount was poured back into his superfine. They stood a moment, facing their reflections in the room's small mirror. Stephen had heard the ladies liken Landry to a Greek god. He was indeed handsome, with strong, even features and dark hair just a touch too long. Cut specially to tempt the ladies' fingers, likely. He bent down to ruffle his own short curls. A sour twang thrummed in his gut at the thought of the viscount making his bow to Mae.

Higher aspirations.

He shook his head. Landry was his friend, but surely not even Halford would crave a title so badly that he'd sell his daughter to the man.

Without warning, Landry broke down. Stephen stepped back in alarm. The viscount's hand braced on the mirror's frame, his body shook with the force of his sobs. 'It's a damned cruel world, that's what it is,' he wailed. 'I vow—a title's a damned heavy thing.' He met Stephen's gaze in the mirror. 'Almost, I could wish myself a second son. Free. Like you.'

With visible effort, he pulled himself together. Sniffing audibly, he reached into a pocket for Stephen's handkerchief. 'But I'm not. I've had my time in the sun and I'll pay the piper like a gentleman should.'

He tried to clap Stephen on the shoulder, but ended up leaning heavily against him. 'I wish better for you, Manning. I do. I pray you never know the depths to which a man is forced to sink, the things he must do, if only to survive.'

Ears pricked, ignoring the tingling travelling down his spine, Stephen steadied him. 'Sounds like a heavy load you're carrying.'

'You can't know,' Landry sighed in answer.

'You might want to share it—bound to lighten your burdens.'

'No.' The viscount heaved a dramatic sigh. 'I will soldier on, as so many of noble blood have done before me.' He pushed away. 'Come. It won't do to be late.'

After his outburst, Landry appeared to sink into a daze. He kept silent as they made their way along the long, dark corridor. He stalked down the stairs, almost as if he'd forgotten he had a companion. Stephen hustled along beside him, his mind racing far faster than their feet. He had to find a way to get the viscount to talk.

They'd reached the marbled hall. Again the parlours to the right had been opened up to form one great room.

Warmth and laughter drifted from beyond the doors. Stephen made one last desperate attempt as the butler prepared to admit them. 'You don't suppose Ryeton will be here this evening, do you?' he drawled low to Landry. 'I'd heard he was chasing word of Pratchett all about the countryside.'

'Ryeton?' The word appeared to clear the mists in Landry's head. He sprang to life, spinning about and glaring at Stephen as if he'd never seen him before. 'That black-hearted cretin? He'd better not be within, or I'll draw his cork for him!' He stepped close and grasped a handful of Stephen's coat. 'Do you know what the dastard has done to me? Pratchett was mine! Ryeton stole him out from under my nose!'

Chapter Eight

~~~~~~~~~~~~~~~~~

Stephen was not in attendance at Lady Toswick's card party. Despite her disappointment—she couldn't wait to inform him of Ryeton's troubles with his wife and mistress—Mae was having a fine time.

The countess's long, converted parlour was nicely filled with card tables and lit with brightly glowing sconces. Mae's father was in a good mood, her mother was relaxed and the room was filled near to bursting with the cream of Newmarket society. Even better, Mae was making definite progress towards her own goals.

Lord Corbet's friends, to Mae's intense satisfaction, were all in attendance. Addy, with significantly raised brows and widened eyes, introduced her to a handsome young nobleman. Lord Banks partnered her in whist, and when they weren't trouncing Addy and her husband, they talked of Paris and of horses and of where in Europe the best riding might be pursued.

Eventually the game ended and they continued their conversation alone. The baron was a perfect gentleman;

his gaze never once lingered on her, despite the elaborate embroidery gracing the high collar and low bodice of her gown—and the jewellery she'd selected just to invite attention to it. She sighed and, remembering Mr Fatch, listened to him discuss the renovations he planned for his own stables and his hope to start up a stud. Mae, who had visited the Continent's finest breeders with her father, only listened, asked leading questions, and pretended to be impressed, even when it became clear she knew more about the subject than he.

'I hate to give her up,' Lord Banks assured Addy when she came to fetch her, but Mae felt no desire to linger in his company. It was a tedious business, this acclimating a gentleman's palate. Conversation was far more interesting when a man had already had a full taste—she blushed at the *double entendre*—as Stephen Manning had.

In perfect unison with this thought, a prickle blossomed on the back of her neck. She spun towards the door just as the butler announced his name.

Pleasure bubbled up inside her, erupting into a slow grin. She had hoped to see Stephen tonight. But certainly neither she nor anyone else had expected to see him framed in the doorway with his neckcloth tangled in another man's fist. The unknown gentleman spoke low and urgent, very close to Stephen's face. He didn't appear to be daunted by it. In fact, he appeared to be listening intently. She was too far away to hear any of their conversation, but like a ball on a bowling green, the word *Pratchett* rolled across the room, bouncing and ricocheting from table to table.

Her grin fractured into a chuckle of delight. She'd thought she be forced to put Stephen's mission on hold this evening, but perhaps they could find a way to work on both goals at once.

The two men separated at their host's approach. Mae whispered to Addy and left her to head towards the group. She knew the instant Stephen's gaze fell on her, for the weight of it warmed her from the inside out. She smiled, but he lowered his brows at her. With a frown and darting eyes, he warned her off.

Confused—and annoyed—she stumbled to a halt. Trying to look natural, she took the first empty seat she encountered, next to Mr Matthew Grange.

Mr Grange, bless him, expressed his delight. *He* wasted no time admiring her jewellery.

'Your sapphires are stunning, Miss Halford, but I can't help feeling sorry for them.'

'*Sorry* for them, Mr Grange?' She glanced down where the heavy sapphire pendant nestled tantalisingly at the top of her cleavage.

'Indeed, for they are completely outshone by the brightness of your eyes.'

She laughed up at him. 'Very nicely done, Mr Grange.'

'Thank you.' He followed the direction of her glance, towards the doors. 'My social skills have grown rusty. I'm happy for the chance to air them out.'

Mae glanced about at the empty chairs at his table. 'I see you've been left without a partner. Shall we search out another game?'

'Truthfully, I'd rather not. I had enough card play to last several lifetimes when I was confined to my sickbed. I was hoping instead to find a lovely lady willing to accompany me on a gambol about the room. I'm in need of practice there, too, you see.' With his scarred and reddened hand he slapped the wooden leg strapped to his thigh. 'What do you think of her?'

'Her?' asked Mae with a smile. The piece was intricately carved and highly burnished.

'Aye. She's my prop. Always there when I need to lean on her, helping me to achieve all that I want. Just as a good woman does for her man.' A grin only barely concealed his tension as he waited for her answer.

'I think she's an object of beauty, practicality and great worth, just as any woman should be in her gentleman's eyes. How could you, or anyone, not love her?'

His smile widened as his shoulders relaxed. 'Shall we stroll, then?'

They did, with their heads together and with much laughter punctuating their conversation. Mae's gaze returned repeatedly to Stephen, but he showed no awareness of her at all. He and his companion had been absorbed into a group that included Lord Toswick and her father, although it appeared that Stephen was trying to lure the other man away.

'You mentioned social skills earlier, Mr Grange. Tell me, do you believe that a woman seeking to impress a man must learn to downplay her own accomplishments?'

'In general, I'm not a fan of hiding anything, Miss Halford.' He gestured towards his missing limb, but frowned thoughtfully. 'Although, I believe I have met more than one person whose character seemed suited to extreme modesty. Hiding their light under a bushel, as my old nurse used to call it.'

'Ah, then you believe it to be a function of character, rather than gender?'

He gave her a gentle smile. 'I confess, the war made me a student of character.'

She met his gaze squarely. 'And what did you learn in your studies, sir?'

'Oh, several things.' He glanced in Stephen's direction. 'I learned that many people are not familiar with who they are beneath the surface.' His expression grew rueful. 'I learned that nothing strips a man and exposes the truth of his character like hardship and deprivation. And I learned that nothing brings more misery— or a quick and certain death, in the army's case—than finding oneself in a position that one's character is not suited for.'

She blinked at him. 'I think your studies have made you a very wise man, Mr Grange.'

'And a tired one, I'm afraid.' He gestured toward a nearby sofa. 'Now, I am going to sit down a moment.' He thrust his chin towards Stephen's group. 'You go on—and rid yourself of the bushel.'

Mae squeezed his hand. 'I'll consider your advice, sir.'

She stepped away. Stephen, she'd noticed, had finally succeeded in separating his friend from the others. She started in their direction, stopping to collect Addy on the way. 'Play along with me, please,' she whispered in her friend's ear. Stephen had dragged the man to a secluded corner. She tugged Addy towards them.

'Of course. But what are we doing?'

'Reconnaissance.'

Addy's countenance lit up.

'Who is that man who arrived with Lord Stephen?' she asked, low.

Alarm replaced the mischief in Addy's expression. 'Mae—that's Viscount Landry, the very one that spiteful Miss Metheny told you about.'

'Ahh. That will only make this that much more enjoyable.'

'You'll have to be careful.' Addy's gaze lingered on the man in question for a long moment. 'He may be lovely to look at, but he hasn't a feather to fly with. Corbet says he's in dire straits indeed.'

'I'll take care to admire his beautiful feathers without allowing him to pluck my own.'

Mae pasted on a smile as they reached the two gentlemen. 'Stephen, the earl was not sure you would be here this evening. How happy I am that you've come.' She eyed the viscount in appreciation. 'And you've brought a friend.'

Stephen merely nodded.

'Yes,' the other man answered for him, blinking rapidly. He appeared to be having difficulty focusing. 'Manning is a brick.' He frowned. 'He brought me along.'

'And we haven't had a moment to talk since.' Stephen's annoyance rang clear.

Landry's wandering gaze hit upon the sapphire pendant at her breast—and sharpened immediately. An overly long beat of time passed. Still he didn't look up.

'Landry.' Stephen's frustrations appeared endless tonight. Served him right.

Looking closer, Mae noticed the viscount's flushed cheeks and glassy eyes. The man was foxed. A happy little flutter beat in her chest. So much the better. 'Will you make the introductions, Stephen?'

Thunder collected across his brow. Short and curt, he performed the niceties. 'And now, if you ladies will excuse us,' he said even as he finished. 'Lord Landry and I were interrupted in the midst of a crucial conversation.'

But something had hung the viscount up. 'Wait,' he ordered again. 'Halford? Halford's daughter?' He squinted at her. 'But you're a pretty thing!' He turned it into an accusation.

Mae laughed. 'I'd apologise if I hadn't worked so hard at it.'

Now his accusation was for Stephen. 'Holding out on me, Manning?' His face drooped. 'And after all of our years of drinking together? I'd expected better of you.'

Mae nudged Addy.

'Oomph!'

Mae glared.

'Yes!' Addy said, too loud. 'Lord Stephen, it sounds as if the viscount has monopolised you long enough. You must come with me. We promised one of the ladies that we would introduce you.'

'Perhaps later.' Glares were *de rigueur* in this corner of the room and the one Stephen directed at Mae was a winner. 'I have important matters to discuss with Landry.'

'You have not the slightest cause for worry, then.' Mae wrapped her arm about the viscount's—the better to support him should he stumble. 'When matters are important, they are best left to a woman.'

'Mae.' Dire warning lived in that one word.

She stiffened. 'You run along with Addy. And I shall take the viscount along to greet our hostess.' She tugged on Landry's arm. 'Come along, my lord.'

'Just a second—'

Addy led a protesting Stephen away. Mae smiled at Lord Landry.

'You're a pretty thing,' he said once more.

'Thank you. Are you enjoying Newmarket, Lord Landry?'

'Wasn't. Was having a devil of a time. Things picked up, though.' He leered at her sapphire again. 'And now I'm having a wonderful time.'

'You flatter me.' Tilting her head just a bit, she looked up at him through her lashes, just as Josette had schooled her.

He straightened, tried to rally. 'You've been away from England, have you not? Travelling?' He swayed alarmingly on his feet, but appeared not to notice. She doubted she had much time before he passed out on his feet.

'Yes, indeed. I love to travel, but I admit, after so long, I'm glad to be home. I'm looking forward to seeing London again soon.'

'London?' Horror creased his face—and it appeared to be too heavy an emotion to handle. He tilted towards her. She braced herself, but at the last second he got his feet back under him.

'Yes.' She ran a considering eye over him and shifted her strategy. She'd better get this done quickly. 'Perhaps it is not very English of me, but while I was in Paris I developed a taste for strong, black coffee. Would you care to join me in a cup?'

'Happy to.' He came along compliantly as she started off, not willing to relinquish his hold on her arm. Or her steadying influence.

'Oh, dear, it appears that Lady Toswick is busy arranging the buffet supper.' Shyly, she glanced askance at him. 'Would you mind if we took our coffee in a more...private setting? I confess I could use a moment of quiet.'

'A brilliant suggestion,' he said fervently. 'Where shall we go?' He'd discovered her matching sapphire earrings. His gaze was now fixed firmly on her left ear. 'Does the family have a sitting room upstairs, perhaps?'

'I think the yellow salon across the hall will do nicely.' She called over a servant and gave several quiet instructions. 'Come, Lord Landry, let's find you a comfortable seat.' On the way across the room, she also stopped to whisper a word in her mother's ear.

The salon was only steps away, but the viscount sighed in relief as he eased onto the jonquil sofa. 'Don't do it, Miss Halford. Don't go to London. Town is crowded and dull.' He laid his hand over hers. 'You should stay here in Newmarket.' He did his best to summon a charming smile, but it came out lopsided. 'With me.'

'Do you reside full time in Newmarket, my lord?' This surprised her.

'For now.' The crafty crinkle about his eyes disappeared as they closed in a yawn.

Servants bustled in with the coffee. Mae perched on the edge of the sofa to pour. She handed the viscount a cup, but judged it had come too late. He was having difficulty keeping his eyes open.

'I heard you discussing the Earl of Ryeton with Lord Stephen. Is the earl a friend of yours?' she asked innocently.

'Good Lord, no.' He blinked rapidly at her. Trying to keep awake. 'The man's a rotter.'

She rescued his cup as he lost the battle and laid his head on the back of the sofa. After a long moment's silence he let out a giggle. 'Rotter,' he repeated with delight.

Mae judged her moment to have arrived. She leaned in and asked her question low in his ear. 'Did you steal Pratchett, Lord Landry?'

That woke him up. He pulled his head back up in a hurry. 'Damn and blast—did that devil Ryeton tell you that? Hell, no. *He* stole that horse from *me!*'

'He stole Pratchett from you?' She made her eyes wide.

'Next thing to it.' His eyes pleaded for her understanding. 'A while back, I owed him some money. A pittance, really, but he wouldn't wait for me to come up with the blunt. He wished to take Pratchett as payment instead.'

She sat back. 'Well, that showed significant foresight, didn't it?'

'Horse was young then. Promising, but no significant races to his credit.' His head nodded again. 'Funny.

Horses don't have credit, do they?' He sighed. 'Neither do I.'

'And then Pratchett began to win.' Mae was all sympathy. 'You must have wanted him back.'

'That horse has made Ryeton rich several times over. All I wanted was the money I could have got for him if I'd sold him instead of turning him over outright.' His drunken indignation was fading.

'It seems only fair.'

'Ryeton wouldn't even hear me out.' His eyes closed and he laid his head back again. 'It'll be Marshalsea for me, before long.'

His eagerness to get her alone became clear. 'Unless you marry?' she asked sourly.

'Marry,' he agreed with a yawn. 'Halford's daughter.' He smiled with his eyes still closed. 'Who knew she was such a pretty thing?'

Mae had outmaneuvered him.

She'd charmed Matthew Grange. The man was half-besotted, singing her praises in Stephen's ear until he wished to plant his friend a facer.

'Just wait until you know her better,' Stephen had told Matthew.

She'd flirted shamelessly with his friend; he'd witnessed it himself. She'd snatched Landry away, too, preventing Stephen from discovering information vital to their mission, and then she'd disappeared with the man.

She'd better not be *breathing* at him.

She was off alone with the most flagrant fortune hunter in the *ton* and he was stuck here, caught in a choppy confluence of emotion. Some of it held a definite flavour of familiarity; he'd swum through waters of irritation and exasperation often enough when dealing with Mae. His old weaknesses were flaring tonight, too. He was not used to being ignored, could scarcely abide it, but never had his shameful need to be noticed blazed so painfully as tonight, when Mae had so blatantly disregarded him and his wishes.

But what was this burning madness that had seized him as he watched her slink off, alone with Landry? He refused to believe it was jealousy. It was concern, naturally. Although even that was an overreaction. What was Landry going to do? Ravish the girl? Of course not. He was more likely to grab that dare-you-not-to-look sapphire between her breasts and hie off to the nearest fence.

The image kicked him hard in the gut. Landry's hands. Mae's breasts.

Without a word he abandoned Matthew and went in search of them.

The parlour door, standing half-closed, flew the rest of the way open with a bang.

'Shh,' Mae admonished Stephen. 'You'll wake him.'

He blew into the room, a thundering storm looming over the questionable shelter of the sofa. Mae kept her gaze fixed steadily with his. This was no time to back down.

'What do you think you are doing?' he demanded.

'Practising my wiles,' she answered, leaning away from the viscount and rising up to meet Stephen. She had the feeling she'd want to be steady on her feet for this.

'Practising…' His words fell away. Clearly this was not the response he'd been expecting.

'Yes—and putting them to good use, too.' She gazed down at Landry with regret. 'Unfortunately our mystery is not going to be solved so easily. The viscount did not steal Pratchett away.'

That dissipated some of his blustering. 'No?'

She shook her head.

'Damnation. He accused Ryeton of stealing the horse from him, so I'd hoped…' He stared at the sleeping man in disappointment.

'No.' Mae explained what the viscount had said. 'So,' she concluded, 'Ryeton took Pratchett to cover a trifling debt and made a fortune off him. Landry's been trying to weasel a share of it.'

Stephen heaved a sigh. 'I suppose it would have been too easy, had it turned out to be him.'

'Easy would have made for a nice change.' Mae sighed right along with him. 'But there is good news. We're not left completely without leads.' She outlined all that she'd learned at tea this afternoon.

He'd lost his words again, but his glare was back. 'You think Ryeton's wife—or perhaps his mistress—might have orchestrated this? Out of spite?'

She shrugged a shoulder. 'He is miserable, by all accounts. And it would appear that they both have reason to make him so.'

'But they wouldn't…' He sounded aghast.

'Why not? Because they are women? Do you judge

them incapable of such a thing because of their sex?' She raised a brow at him.

'Point taken.' His shoulders slumped. 'But I don't relish the idea of investigating the man's wife. Or his...' He paused. 'Oh, Lord, I shouldn't even be speaking of these matters with you.'

'Don't be missish, Stephen.' She rolled her eyes at him. 'By the way, Josette's ruled out Pratchett's groom being involved.'

'What? How?'

'I sent her into town this afternoon. She asked around, found his favourite tavern and spent several hours with him. She said he's distraught with worry over the horse. And the cat.'

'Cat?'

'Yes, apparently Pratchett has a cat as a constant companion in his stall. Like the Goldolphin Arabian and his faithful Grimalkin.'

'Damn the cat.' Stephen exhaled mightily and began to pace. 'Damn it, Mae! I'm proud of you—look at all that you've accomplished in such a short time. But I can't condone your methods!'

'What have I done that is so terrible?'

'I brought Landry along, but you shut me out!'

She straightened in indignation. 'You shut me out first!'

He speared her with his glower. 'You should never have come in here alone with him.'

She crossed her arms. 'Why not?'

'Why not?' He spun away, pacing again. 'Why not, she asks! What goes on in those European salons, I have to wonder?' He turned back to her. 'You shouldn't have done it because it's not seemly!'

His attitude was a flame setting her anger to simmer. 'You asked for my help. You don't get to dictate the manner in which I give it.'

He rolled his eyes. 'You're after a husband. I understand.'

'Yes! We have a bargain in that regard,' she snapped. 'I hope you have not forgotten!'

'I have not.' He'd descended into condescension now. 'But you asked not just for my help, but for my opinion. You should have given me a chance to express it before you went traipsing off alone with a jug-bitten fortune hunter like Landry! The man is at his limits and he's growing desperate. Who knows what he's capable of? He could have kidnapped you. Or compromised you beyond saving.'

She laughed. 'This situation is too much for you. You've gone histrionic.'

He gaped at her. 'I am not histrionic!'

'And I'm not a fool.'

'I didn't say you were!'

Mae knew she'd taken on her most mulish, unattractive expression, but there was no avoiding it. 'You implied it—and the alternative is worse. If I'm not foolish, then you must think me a wanton! Is *that* what you meant to imply?'

His mouth dropped open. She didn't give him time to come up with a reply.

'I left word with my mother before I left the long parlour. She's aware of both my location and the viscount's condition. The servants have been in and out with coffee and a footman has been parading up and down the hall at regular intervals. I had only a few minutes alone with him, but I managed to discover what I needed to know *before* he passed out from all the drink you've poured down him.'

She set her hands on her hips. He stood near now; close enough to catch the scent of his spicy cologne and freshly starched linen. Close enough to feel the warmth rising off his broad chest and notice that it was rising faster than it had been just a second before.

'He was in more danger from me than I was from him.' She pitched her voice low, kept her expression cool and taunting.

In contrast, his face darkened. 'That's the God's honest truth.'

'Perhaps you should consider your own welfare, then.' She exhaled. 'Perhaps you'd better run.'

He made a strangled sound of protest. He took a step closer instead, closing the small space between them. He looked like he wished to strangle her.

'Or perhaps you might begin to fulfil your part of the bargain.' She gestured towards the unconscious viscount. 'Twelve hours it's been since we made our pact and between Josette and myself we've eliminated two suspects and one potential husband.' She showed him no mercy. 'It would appear you're falling behind, Stephen.'

His only answer was a growl, laden with frustration. She froze as he took the last, infinitesimal step. If she moved but an inch, she would find herself pressed up against him.

He didn't speak.

She wouldn't back down.

Stalemate. It lasted moments. Or centuries. She waited. He held himself aloof. Immobile. His breath sounded like a bellows, and his expression might have been carved from stone.

'Good Lord,' he moaned. 'Perhaps this is not going to work.'

'Perhaps not.' She sighed.

He stepped back, scrubbed a hand in his hair. Even now, mad as a fury, she longed to follow suit.

'Did you agree to this, Mae, just so that you could get even with me?' He sounded exhausted. 'Were you only after a little revenge?'

Flabbergasted, she stared at him. 'Revenge for what?'

'For the last time we were together.'

It hurt, that he would bring the subject up again. But she tossed her head to hide the pain, and gave a deprecating snort. 'I begin to think that you ascribe more importance to that night than even I do.'

He turned away, his head hanging low. 'I was in a lot of pain that night, Mae.'

'I know.' And that had been the problem all along. She'd known things, seen things that he didn't want seen. She'd chased him, yes. Manipulated him into kissing her once. But the real problem had been that she had asked for more than he was willing to give. She wouldn't make the same mistake again.

'I'd only just returned from my first visit to Fincote, since my mother's death. I...' His voice trailed away.

Mae did not make the mistake of urging him to continue.

Finally he turned back to face her. 'It wasn't you I was angry with.'

'It's fine, Stephen. I'm fine. You did what you had to that night—you told the truth. You made me see that there was nothing more than friendship between us.'

'I shouldn't have lashed out so harshly.'

'It was better that you did.'

'I never thought your father would pack you off to the Continent.'

'He did the right thing, too. I was hurt, and young and headstrong. He'd been aware of my...pursuit...of you. I think a good deal of his sympathy was for you, actually. He saw me that night, after we argued. He knew I was upset and suspected that something had occurred between us. He knew enough of my tenacity to take me away before I did something foolish.' She sighed. 'It *was* the right thing. It gave me time to deal with my disappointment and plenty of other things on which to focus my energies.'

He was going to say more. She could see that he wanted to. She waited, but he held silent, stood immobile. His breathing grew harsh and laboured once more.

Her own breath caught the rhythm and followed along. Behind them the viscount slept on. Between them the air crackled with intensity, sizzled with spiralling heat. And inevitability.

She saw his intention in his eyes a moment before they closed, before he gave a groan of frustration, reached out and pulled her hard against him.

She froze at first, rigid with disbelief. Feebly,

she reached up, put her hands on his chest to push him away.

Instead, she melted. Gone. All the rigidity of her bones and the strength in her muscles—gone to mush under the angry heat of his kiss.

This was nothing like their first kiss. Her first kiss. That had been all tentative exploration and giddy excitement. This was heat and anger and denial and want all wrapped up in the taste of his lips and the insistent stroke of his tongue.

This was no boy's kiss, nor green girl's response. Stephen loomed above and all about her. He felt bigger, darker and more demanding—and she thrilled to it. She opened wider to take him in, revelled in the abandon with which he ravished her mouth.

From behind them came a loud, rasping snore.

It shattered the spell. They stilled. Stephen pulled back, staring at her with bewilderment and accusation in his eyes.

She raised her chin. 'If I didn't like you so well, Stephen, I would slap you a cracking good blow for that.'

'Perhaps now you will understand why you should not go off alone with strange men.' He lacked the conviction with which he'd been arguing before.

She forced a laugh. 'You may have been the first strange man to have kissed me, but you're not the only one. And I doubt you'll be the last.'

His fists clenched at his sides. 'Made a habit of it, have you?'

She raised a shoulder. 'A girl does what she must. But I'd hoped that your help would mean *less* of this sort of…research.'

He gaped at her.

'I don't mean to disparage your skills, of course. You are a lovely kisser. But I already knew that, didn't I? Now, we have a horse to find. And a husband. Let's get on with it, shall we?'

With a swish of her skirts, Mae turned and left the parlour.

Chapter Nine

'The world's gone upside down.' Lord Toswick stared down into his mug of coffee like he was looking for the way to set things right again.

'You have no idea,' Stephen agreed with him. He still couldn't wrap his mind around the fact that he'd kissed Mae Halford. Not a friendly kiss, either. He'd practically devoured her. He'd tossed and turned all night long and rose from bed still hungry for her. All of that was bad. But the worse part, the most disturbing and painful truth, was that it hadn't been at her instigation. This time it had been his doing.

He pushed the thought away. Almost as bad was the memory of her indifference to his kiss. A blow to his pride, to be sure, but a good thing. He repeated that to himself once more. That kiss had been a mistake. One he couldn't allow to happen again. He was going to apologise—profusely—and move on. He was damned lucky Mae *didn't* want him—had she been another sort of woman she might have had his head in a noose and tugged him to the altar already. But she had her goals and they in no way coincided with his.

And it was time he began to concentrate harder on his. What if her father had found them? He would have been ruined. The people at Fincote would have had nothing again. Nothing but hunger and despair. Again. Such a thing would kill him. He didn't think he could handle another burden of guilt like the last one.

He looked about him, at the men settled comfortably in this thoroughly masculine environ. They all sat at peace with their papers or grouped together, debating tomorrow's racing with muted excitement. He was here, in the Jockey Club Coffee Rooms. He should be savouring this moment.

'This morning at the breakfast table, my wife asked me what I looked for in a jockey.' Toswick frowned at Stephen. 'When I answered, she took out paper and pencil and began to take notes.'

'That is odd.' No wonder Toswick had been in a strange mood. The earl had met him on the stairs this morning and invited Stephen to the Coffee Rooms as his guest. He had eagerly accepted, but now he began to wish he hadn't. The rooms were a shrine to horses, dogs and manly pursuits, but he felt like a fraud. He wanted to be here on his own terms, recognised for his own merit.

'And that's not all. I think Ryeton's run a little mad, what with Pratchett gone and his wife just arrived.' By Toswick's tone, Stephen was given to understand that the two events carried the same disastrous weight. 'He even questioned me—as if he thought I might have known something about Pratchett's disappearance!'

'His search doesn't go well, I presume?' Stephen had to disguise his surge of pleasure and relief.

'Not at all.' Toswick cast a careful glance about. 'But after listening to all and sundry—my money's on Cray. As the culprit, I mean.'

Stephen took the statement literally—he knew there was voluminous betting taking place, on just who the horse-napper would turn out to be. 'Cray?' he asked. 'Chester Cray, the leg?'

'Aye—that's the one.' He lowered his voice. 'There's bad blood already between him and Ryeton, you know. Ryeton suspected he might have been the one to poison the feed at his home stables.'

'Is Cray even in Newmarket?'

'Reputed to be, though he must be laying low. I haven't caught a glimpse of him myself.' Toswick looked about once more. 'I'd appreciate you keeping this to yourself. Cray's not a character I'd want to cross.'

'Of course.' Stephen's spirits lifted a little, while his heart began to beat a more hopeful rhythm. It didn't make good business sense for a leg to steal a favourite horse, but if Ryeton had a contentious history with the man, the matter might have become personal.

'I say…' Toswick's amused tone woke him from his reverie '…what have you done to Halford?'

'Halford?' Stephen straightened in his chair.

'Yes. He just passed us by on his way out—and the look he cast your way was distinctly…odd.'

'Perhaps it was only that he didn't expect to see me here.' Surely it had nothing to do with the fact that he'd lost control with his daughter last night. That he'd let her daunting confidence and the challenge in her eye goad him into silencing her with his kiss. A kiss so devastating that his nether regions felt the echo of it even now.

'Have you spoken to him about his filly?'

'I did.' He'd mentioned Toswick's idea to Mae's father last night while she'd been flaunting her jewel-adorned cleavage at the bleary-eyed Landry. 'He appeared amenable to the idea.' Stephen had also taken the opportunity to mention the promise he saw in Ornithopter.

'Splendid,' said Toswick with satisfaction. 'The fillies go off tomorrow. If both animals perform well, there will be that much more interest in seeing them matched against each other.' He set down his coffee and checked his pocket watch. 'Halford is likely returning for the garden party.' He groaned. 'I don't suppose my wife would look favourably upon either of us if we missed it.'

'I don't suppose she would.' Mae would be there. Lord, he'd be better off taking her advice and running the other way.

He stood. 'Shall we go?'

Toswick sighed. 'I'll have to show my face, at least. But then I'm off to watch Butterfly's time trial.' The earl stood as well. 'I wonder if my wife will be inviting a jockey as her guest?'

Lady Toswick had invited a jockey to the garden party, as her guest. All of the ladies had been made privy to the scheme. Her orders, given at the end of her tea and spread across town yesterday, had been for everyone to ask questions of their men and come ready to share what they'd learned.

Now women were milling about the lawn in terrible chaos, ignoring the lovely setting, the refreshments and the men. Some clustered about, questioning the jockey, a Mr Kincaid, late of Dublin. Others stood about or flitted from one group to another. Bonnets nodded and parasols pointed as the ladies of Newmarket discussed sires and dams, and furiously argued favourites and odds.

At first the pandemonium barely registered with Mae—likely because it so perfectly echoed her own inner turmoil. She, usually so clear-headed and focused, found herself floundering. It was uncomfortable, intolerable—and all Stephen Manning's fault.

He'd kissed her! She didn't understand it. She'd done just as she'd ought. She'd followed each carefully planned step, adhered to every painfully plotted stratagem, even down to squelching the heat, the thousands of tiny explosions of desire that had beset her as they argued.

And yet the results had been mixed at best. Yes, she'd made a favourable impression on Lord Banks, and she'd eliminated Lord Landry both as a potential husband and as the person responsible for Pratchett's disappearance, but she'd also somehow goaded Stephen into kissing her.

Worse, she'd succumbed completely. Forgotten every design and objective and allowed herself to be overpowered by the glorious heat, strength and taste of him, and by her own heady desire for more.

There would be no more, she told herself sternly.

One kiss had left her lost; her straight and narrow path degenerated into a swampy marsh of too many choices, too many voices.

They clamoured in her head as she looked about at the confused picture the ladies made. All they wanted was an occupation, a bit of attention. Well, they had it. The men stood about, looking amused. Or annoyed. Mr Fatch in particular was looking sour, standing aside in deep consultation with Miss Metheny.

Mae resisted the almost violent urge to take the ladies in hand. It was what she had intended to do when she arrived in England: behave prettily, as her father wished, blend in and present her best face to rigid English society. But Stephen Manning was watching, his head close to Lord Toswick's, as they and all the gentlemen tried to work out what had gotten into the women. And suddenly it was Matthew Grange's voice echoing in her head, and it spoke of the misery that came with hiding one's true character.

She decided to listen. Breathing deeply, she stepped into the midst of the hubbub and clapped her hands until the chattering ceased. It was but a matter of minutes before she had the ladies gathered into a cohesive group. She saw that everyone had refreshments and invited Mr Kincaid to speak on the qualities he looked for in a successful racehorse. A word whispered into the ear of their hostess and a chair was brought from the house. Another whisper—and a little flirtation— and Mr Matthew Grange took the chair once Mr Kincaid was through. He talked for a while about how the legs went about taking bets and 'making their books'.

The women listened, asked intelligent questions

and began to be as excited about the actual sport as they had been about the idea of gaining the attention of their men. Even Mae's mother looked to be caught up in the fun. The male guests were still flummoxed at their behaviour, but at least the ladies were presenting a more impressive image.

As Mr Grange finished, the group began to break up. Their hostess called them together for a last moment. 'The gentlemen are puzzled, ladies. Some are intrigued and a few are a little put out. I'd say we've had a successful start to our strategy, but for now let us go forth and mingle as if all of this was perfectly ordinary.'

She shooed them off. Mae glanced towards Stephen. He was decidedly not looking at her. She scanned the crowd until she located Lord Banks. With a toss of her head, she made a beeline for the baron, joined his group and took his arm.

'I'm afraid I missed the chance to explore the forest walk with the ladies yesterday,' she told him. 'Would you care to join me as I make up for the lack today?'

He readily agreed and it was with a grim smile of satisfaction that she felt the stealthy weight of Stephen's gaze, as he pointedly did *not* watch her set off.

The path they took was longer than the one she and Stephen had taken to the little meadow, and enhanced in spots with cleverly planted groves of elm and sycamore. At one point it became clear that the trail had been designed to showcase a pretty little stream lined with willows.

They had not been walking very long before Lord Banks cleared his throat. 'That was a masterful display back there, Miss Halford.'

She raised her chin. 'Thank you. The ladies were only in want of a little management.'

He nodded. 'I could use someone with an orderly mind like yours, as I plan my stable renovations. It will be a large undertaking, especially when combined with the start of my stud.'

A little hitch of pleasure had her catching her breath. Perhaps Mr Grange had been right! Still, Josette's warnings rang in her ears. Eyeing the baron carefully, Mae decided to give him a taste of the real Mae Halford.

She crossed over to the bank of the little stream, where several individual stone seats had been placed. They both remained standing, though. 'I would be happy to help in any way I could. I have a good deal of experience in helping to manage renovation projects. My father and I have also visited many of the finest breeders on our travels.'

Lord Banks's pleasant expression grew more shuttered. 'How kind you are.'

Watching him closely, she continued. 'Your enthusiasm is quite catching. I confess, though, a question did occur to me, listening to your plans yesterday.'

'Oh? What question was that?' He sounded only curious, which Mae took as a good sign.

'You mentioned that the estate is small. Most breeding enterprises do require a good deal of acreage.'

'Ah, yes, you are right about that. Actually, I'm hoping to acquire a nice bit of land marching our eastern side.'

Mae didn't try to hide her surprise. 'How lovely that a small estate provides enough of a profit to do so.'

Now the baron began to look a little uncomfortable. 'The estate does well enough to support itself.'

'But not well enough to support your dreams.' She nodded her understanding. 'Then I hope you have a plan to raise the money. It's unlikely that you would get enough in stud fees, for several years at least, to cover such an investment.'

He looked her over with an odd smile. 'I do indeed have another plan.'

She waited, but he didn't continue, only watched her with amusement in his eyes. And finally, realisation dawned. 'Oh!'

She supposed she should be flattered, but instead the laughter and quiet confidence in his expression set her back up. At least he was honest. She could do no less, really, than return the favour. What had Josette called her? A feast of strong flavors? She smiled, and hoped he was hungry.

'Quite sensible of you,' she said with a nod. 'I do have a substantial dowry—though clearly not enough to purchase land, update your stables *and* fund the beginning of a business.' She cocked her head at him. 'I feel I should warn you, though, that my father and I have already agreed that the bulk of my money will remain under my own control after my marriage.'

He did look startled. 'Why would your father agree to such a thing?'

'Because he knows me,' she answered simply. 'I was raised at his knee, you know. Interest and investment and insurance were the regular topics of dinner conversation in our household.'

He blinked. 'How unusual.'

'How fortunate,' she corrected. 'I assure you, I am perfectly familiar with and capable of performing all the duties of a lady—it's just that I am capable of much more, as well.'

Clearly he did not know what to say.

She smiled. 'Many girls get a new gown for their sixteenth birthday. My father gave me two weeks to sort out the dreadfully mismanaged books of a bankrupt warehouse that he had just purchased.' She grinned. 'I had the best time of my life.'

'I see.' The words came out faintly.

'So perhaps I would invest in your stud, if your bloodlines and your projected profits warranted it.'

Lord Banks heaved a deep sigh. With a rueful smile he turned to her and took her hand. He bent over to kiss it. With detachment, Mae realised that there was none of the pulse-pounding excitement in the air that had been present when Stephen had done the same thing, just yesterday afternoon.

'I regret that I shall have to change my plans, Miss Halford.' He gently released her hand. 'You are lovely, and clearly a woman of many talents. It's just that I am not prepared to take on such a…challenge in a wife.'

Mae wondered that she did not feel sadness, or at least a bit of regret. Instead she was left only with a sense of relief.

'I am sorry,' he said.

'Don't be,' she assured him. 'I need a man who is up to a challenge.' She smiled to ease the sting of her words. 'Why don't you head back to the party? I will follow along in a moment.' She turned towards the stream. 'Good day, Lord Banks.'

'Goodbye, Miss Halford. And good luck.'

Chapter Ten

The world had indeed turned upside down. Toswick had no idea how true he'd spoken this morning. And it was all thanks to Mae Halford. Mae Halford who had tossed them all arse over teakettle.

It was hard to tell just what the ladies of Newmarket society were up to this morning, but easy to see that Mae was in the thick of it. Stephen had been amazed at how she'd tamed the crowd of cackling women. In a matter of minutes, right in the middle of a social event, she'd organised an impromptu but thorough lesson on the subject of racing.

All about him, men had watched in awe. Some had looked disapproving, some amused. A few had been so thoroughly absorbed that Stephen was sure they were learning something. But they'd all been impressed with the swift transformation Mae had effected.

And just look at what she'd done to him. He'd been getting ready to take his leave, but he'd seen her go off—alone—with Banks and his gut had started to

churn. Soon after he'd seen Banks come back—alone—
and his feet had started to move.

Upside down. He'd spent a lifetime running from
Mae Halford; now, for the second time in twelve hours,
he found himself chasing after her.

He found her sitting on a seat next to a tiny stream.
She glanced back at him over her shoulder, then turned
back to contemplating the water with a sigh.

'Have you come to upset me, too?'

She was all covered up today, in a soft green walking dress under a darker green spencer. Part of him
appreciated the effort. The other part knew that the
tightly fitted garment was a wasted effort. The feel
of her yielding curves lived still in the palms of his
hands.

But as he drew closer, he slowed. She looked lost,
sitting there. Smaller, somehow. Not like Mae at all.

'Yes, indeed I have. But I'm annoyed to hear that
someone has beaten me to it.' Light words, but the emotion underneath was true enough. 'Who's been upset-
ting you?'

'No one. Everyone. Or perhaps just me.'

He sat beside her on the bench and stretched his legs
out. His feet came within inches of the dancing water.

They sat in silence. The babbling stream did the
talking for them. All about them birds twittered and
rustled while the faint buzz of party chatter drifted
towards them along the path. Stephen felt tension flow
out of him. Maybe it would float downstream to burden
some other poor sot.

His eyes fell closed. He always had been able to
sit like this with Mae, in companionable silence, but

never before had there been this slurry of excitement and anticipation thrumming low inside of him. The memory of their kiss hung bold and vivid in his mind right now, but so did the peace of the scene in front of him. He sat still, enjoying the pleasurable contrast.

Mae broke the silence at last with a heavy sigh. 'I've always known just where I'm going, what I want. Now, there are too many ideas, too many voices telling me how to get there. I don't know who to listen to.' A heartbeat of silence passed before she said tentatively, 'Today I listened to your friend, Matthew Grange. I think I'm glad I did.' She paused again. 'He seems a lovely man.'

Stephen pretended not to notice the question hidden inside that innocuous statement. Was she asking for his opinion? Because she was considering Matthew as a potential suitor? Matthew was the best man he knew— but he couldn't force words to that effect past the lump of anger lodged in his throat. How could she kiss him so fervently last night and talk of other men today? Besides which, Matthew was *not* the man for Mae.

She spoke again and saved him from finishing that thought. He'd been successful so far at avoiding the question of just who might be the right man for her.

'It's not going to be easy, is it?'

He snorted. 'Which part of all of this did you expect to come easily?'

'I did have hope, if not expectations.'

He waited. She wore a bonnet to protect her face from the sun, but several curling locks had escaped. He could have sat there all day and watched the stray sunbeams search out the red-gold in her hair.

'That was the smallest part of myself that I allowed to show back there. All I did was organise a flighty group of women, for heaven's sake! Every time I allow a bit of the real me out and into the light, I face nothing but instant censure.'

He shrugged. 'So?'

'So, in case you hadn't noticed, I'm not fond of censure.' She sighed again. 'Perhaps I should go back to Europe.'

He straightened. 'What's this? Hiding in the woods? Talking of running away? Giving up? I don't think you should go back at all, if this is what you learned over there. The Mae I knew was a fighter.'

Her gaze softened. The rest of her followed suit. Right before his eyes her posture changed, opened, yielded. She looked him over thoroughly. 'Perhaps I only learned to choose the battles that are worth fighting for.'

'And give over the rest?' Stephen laughed. 'I don't think so. You've never yielded so much as an inch in all the years that I've known you.' He paused for a breath. 'I've always admired that about you.'

She tightened again. '*Admired* me?' A small frown of disbelief creased her brow.

'Yes. Admired.' He scoffed until he saw that her surprise was genuine. 'Why this talk of voices? You've only ever listened to one voice, and that's your own. Why would you change that now?'

She turned away. 'Because I'm afraid.'

He shrugged again. 'Everyone's afraid. Not everyone has the mettle to do something about it.' He stared. 'Mae, can it be that you don't know how courageous we

all know you to be?' He took her soft hand. 'Mannings
and Fitzmannings alike, we know you to be incredibly
brave. We took you in, welcomed you into the circle of
our outlandish family and knew ourselves lucky to have
you.'

Her eyes filled with tears. The sight of such a thing
startled him—and touched something inside him,
something elemental and entirely masculine.

'Mae Halford,' he said gently, 'you are the single
most courageous soul I've ever known. The rest of us
live in hiding. We put up fronts, build walls, all the
while hiding our true selves safely in the shadows.
But not you. Every day you stand in the sun, flaunting
everything that you are and daring the world to reject
it.' His grip tightened. 'None of us can hold a candle to
you.'

Her eyes still shone bright with unshed tears.
Stephen held his breath, unsure just what he would do
if she actually cried. It seemed an unnatural possibility—the sun might as well rise in the west. He feared
the sight of her tears might push him into an equally
unthinkable act—something incredibly unwise.

Last night's kiss reared up to haunt him again, bath-
ing him in a wave of heat. His nether regions, already
poised in interest, began to stir. He waited.

She didn't cry.

She took his hand. She blinked back her tears and
met him eye to eye. 'I see the real you, Stephen,' she
whispered. 'I always have.'

God, but she had the heart of a lion. He knew that
at least part of her wanted him to pull her close, to use
his body to comfort her. But she didn't take the easy

way out. Instead, she spoke the truth—and said the one thing most likely to send him speeding away.

He swallowed. If she could show such courage, then surely he could match it. It took every ounce of will he possessed to stay calm and stay seated, but he did. 'I know.'

And he had known—it was the reason he'd resisted her so hard, for so long. For that was the ridiculous conundrum that lay at the heart of him. He longed for everyone to look and no one to see. He wanted to be seen and heard, but he could never, ever let anyone truly close.

He pushed back the mental image of his forlorn mother and pulled his hand away.

'Why were you so upset?' she asked in a whisper. 'That night—our last night?'

He swallowed. He wasn't upside down now; he was twisted into a knot. Tangled parts of him wished to snatch her close, run his hands over her and kiss her until she forgot everything she thought she knew. The twisted other part of him only wanted to ignore her question, to walk away, to leave even if it hurt her. Better now than later, better to hurt than to be hurt.

Except that he couldn't even contemplate doing such a thing. Either thing.

'Was it because of Charlotte's marriage?'

It did exist—buried deep, a piece of him that wanted to answer, that had always wanted to talk to Mae, let her in, let her *see*. It had always been smothered by fear, crushed by the need to protect, to shield. But he owed Mae. God knew why she wanted to examine this ugly piece of his past, but he'd be damned if he wasn't going to give her *something* for her help, her support.

'No, of course not. Charlotte and Drew were happy, and so was I.' What he'd been was a mass of conflicted feelings.

Silent, she waited.

'I'd just come from Fincote. From my first visit there since my mother's death.' He closed his eyes. 'It was… disturbing. The estate, the few people that were left—they were in terrible shape. Destitute.'

And he had been devastated.

'I felt horrible. I knew I had to help them. I didn't want to ruin Charlotte's wedding, though. I tried to laugh, to take joy in the day.'

He'd needed to hide his failure from his family.

'I could see that you were upset. That's why I followed you.'

And he had been conflicted all over again. Torn between relief at being seen, and a great, terrible fear that she would see too much. It had all been too much to contain. 'I'm sorry—I should never have been so harsh with you.'

He rose to his feet and walked a few feet away to squat at the side of the stream.

She let him go. Didn't press the issue. He appreciated her restraint.

'What did you do to Miss Metheny?' he asked eventually. Just normal conversation. Nothing momentous happening here. 'She was glaring daggers at you earlier.'

She drew a deep breath. 'Not a thing. There was

no need. Showing up in Newmarket with my dowry dragging behind me was enough to turn her sour.'

'I'm afraid to ask what's happening with the ladies back there. Most of them only tolerate racing, now they appear to be diving head first into it.'

'A social experiment, I should call it. Nothing that will interfere with our plans. In fact, I'm finding it quite useful. Lady Ryeton is planning a tour of their stables on Thursday, with a picnic to follow. Who knows what I might discover?'

He got to his feet and turned to face her. 'Lord, I hope we're not still looking on Thursday.' A little spike of panic went through him. 'We've got to wrap this up soon.'

'Speaking of which, I know Ryeton has his own stables here in Newmarket, but he does use a local trainer, does he not?'

'Yes. Felton.' Still he kept his distance.

'Have you an acquaintance with him?'

'No. Why?'

'Josette has been doing her best to gain an introduction. He would seem to be a good source of information.'

'Felton's more than a step above a groom. It may be difficult for her to arrange.'

A fond smile spread across her face. 'Josette will find a way.' As he watched, her expression changed. Fascinated, he watched the transformation. She'd just gone distant. Away. This was her thinking face. 'As will I,' she said quietly.

'I am terrified on Lady Ryeton's behalf.'

'There's no need to be.' With a flick of her finger

she dismissed one of the leading hostesses of the *ton*. 'It will be easy enough to speak to her during the tour or even perhaps at the racing.' Briefly distracted, she smiled. 'Although I am looking forward to meeting her. She sounds like a schemer. There aren't that many of us around, you know.'

'Who then?' Had she come up with information he didn't know about?

'The mistress—Miss Hague. She will present a challenge. How shall I get to her without compromising myself?' By her tone, she was thinking again. 'But I am working on an idea.'

Stephen's heart stuttered. He sent up an urgent prayer that he'd heard her wrong—although he knew he had not.

'What?' She had noticed his silence. Up on her feet she hopped, challenge emerging back into her eyes.

'Get it out of your head right now, Mae.' It was an order, sure to get her back up. But this was worth a fight. 'You will go nowhere near that woman. I will not let you ruin yourself on my behalf.'

'On your behalf? I thought we were in this together? Are we not meant to help each other?' She folded her arms. 'Not that you've been much help, I might add.'

'I'll do better,' he vowed grimly. 'I'll parade a line of eligible young bucks past your bedroom window, if you wish. But you will not go near Ryeton's mistress.'

'Ah, Stephen.' Dangerously gentle, her voice. 'You really are a clodpole. I thought you'd learned years ago that the best way to get me to do something is to forbid it.'

'I've heard things of this woman. She's no Miss

Metheny, to be easily outwitted and outmanoeuvred. She's got claws—and ripping your reputation to shreds would be but a moment's amusement to a woman like that.'

Mae only looked intrigued.

'No, Mae! You'll get skewered. And if anyone hears even a hint of it—it will all be over. And there will go your dreams of marriage.'

She rolled her eyes. 'Have you no faith in me, Stephen? I'm disappointed.'

'What you'll be is tainted. Untouchable.'

She looked disgusted. 'What I will be is married to some ore magnate or a stuffy nobleman who only wants an ornament for his arm. Dreams are fine, but they require work to turn them into reality.' She huffed at him. 'You are taking risks. Do you expect less of me?'

Stephen groaned. 'I will not allow you to do something so foolish!'

'Foolish?' That wasn't the part that he'd thought she would seize on. 'Again, I am foolish?' Scorn was writ large across her face. 'We've covered this ground already, Stephen. I begin to grow bored.'

Bored? It was a childish taunt, but remarkably effective. He wanted to stomp his feet. Or grab her up and show her a better use for that mocking mouth.

She had turned away from him, her dainty nose in the air.

Look at me. He wanted to scream it. He said nothing instead.

With one last disdainful glance over her shoulder, she moved to leave.

He let her go. She picked up her pace. He held himself frozen until she reached the line of alders, then he set out after her. Chasing her again.

Damn her.

He caught her before she'd made it more than a few steps into the wood. Grabbing her by the wrist, he scooped her up. Ignoring her protests, he dragged her deeper into the shelter of the trees and pressed her up against a sturdy elm.

She let out a gasp. 'Stephen! Let me go!' It was an order, but her wriggling attempts to free herself acted as a spur to his fury and lust.

'No, damn you. The first time, you manipulated me into kissing you. Last night you tempted me beyond reason.'

'I did no such thing.'

'You did. But this time we are going to kiss…' He leaned into her, pressing himself slowly against her, starting at his thighs and continuing on until they were chest to chest. 'This time we kiss at my behest.'

'Your behest? Ha!' She was practically spitting in anger. 'If you—'

He stopped her with the press of his mouth on hers.

A hard shiver ran through her. And just like that, all of her rage died away. Fluid, she dissolved against him.

In response he gentled his kiss. Easing his hands from her shoulders, he ran them lightly along the length of her arms. Eager, trying not to hurry, he burrowed under her spencer to span her waist.

Through straining against his chest, her hands spread flat. Quick and nimble as the rest of her, her fingers climbed up across his collarbone and along the length of his neck. Only a moment's hesitation, and they took the plunge into his hair.

A shiver skipped down his spine. The feel of her fingertips on his scalp triggered a hidden spring. Just like that, the knot inside of him unravelled. There could be no room for conflict when he was filled with the achingly sweet taste of her. Fear and doubt retreated, helpless against the press of her soft bosom.

Unbidden, she opened beneath him. He deepened the kiss, only to be struck by an agonising thought. Other men. He'd been the first to kiss her, but some other man had taught her this—how to drive him mad with the heat of her mouth and the sweep of her tongue.

He redoubled his efforts. He would kiss her senseless and erase any memory of another man's touch.

She moaned her approval. He took the sound as permission to cover the more-than-satisfying mounds of her breasts with his hands. Her breath caught in the back of her throat. He paused, unsure, but she thrust herself into his hands.

He broke the kiss, but only long enough to look down and address all the buttons of her spencer. Pushing it wide, he cupped her again, thrilled to discover the sharp little peaks of her nipples through the muslin of her gown. Deftly, his fingers explored.

Her gaze fastened helplessly on his. 'I don't think...'

This was an affront. His brain function had ceased minutes ago. Unfair that she retained sense enough for thought. 'Don't think.'

Did she never stop? Her mind was a formidable

opponent, but no match for his skills. He kissed her again. Down and down, through levels and layers of logic-stripping, emotion-entangling embraces.

Her décolletage loomed gratifyingly low. With one swift tug he hooked a finger in and drew it down, taking the soft linen of her chemise along with it. Dappled sunlight filtered through the canopy of leaves overhead and across the beauty of her breasts, limned the dusky pink of her nipples.

He growled. Like an animal, low in his throat.

With no further warning he bent his head and licked. Her gasp echoed in the secluded glade. Hot ribbons of pleasure unfolded, tugging his erection higher as he circled her nipple with soft, biting kisses before drawing it in his mouth.

Lust swamped him. Good God—who knew that they would be so good together? He didn't want to stop. He wanted to part her thighs right here against this tree and bury himself in her heat.

But beyond the soft rustlings of the wood, happy voices echoed closer. A giggle sounded dangerously close. This had to stop.

Her nipple slid from his mouth with a slick pop. He leaned his forehead against hers and tried to gather his control.

His breath came fast and heavy. 'I'm discovering new things about you every day, Mae Halford.' He pulled back and gazed helplessly at her half-naked, eminently beautiful form. 'But it's the things that I'm discovering about myself that are most disturbing.'

She opened her mouth to reply, but someone called

out from just beyond their haven. Starting in alarm, she silently began to set her clothing aright.

The group of revellers passed. Stephen, his blood still boiling, fought for control.

Finally Mae was put back together. Finger to his lips, he pulled her onto the path and they headed back towards the lawns.

'The racing starts in the morning. I'll find you at the course.' They had reached the mouth of the pathway. Stephen bent low over her hand and fixed her with a hard stare. 'You will stay far away from Miss Hague.'

A tingle pricked at the back of his neck. He looked up to find Barty Halford watching them with a frown.

'Don't fight me on this, Mae.'

Her father still watched, but it was a rash of other, more accusatory gazes that weighed down Stephen's soul. Many faces that could see all the way from Sussex only in his imagination, but stabbed him with sad and critical stares none the less.

He turned on his heel and strode away.

Chapter Eleven

'These tears? I do not understand them.' Josette sounded as baffled as she looked. 'You didn't *want* that English lord. No?'

'No.' Mae, perched on the edge of her bed, dabbed at her eyes. 'They aren't tears. I'm not crying. I'm just… leaking a little.'

It was no wonder Josette was confused. This morning, Mae had felt lost. Now, after yet another physical encounter with Stephen—there were no words for her bewildered state.

Why did she allow him to affect her this way? Every time she found herself adrift in a mass of confusion and doubt, she could lay the blame squarely at Stephen Manning's feet.

Or could she?

At least in the past they had both been consistent— she in her pursuit and he in his retreat. But now, cracks were forming in his reflective surface. He was allowing her a peek inside, if just a little. And physically—

No. She couldn't lie to herself. The pattern was clear. This was just a new approach to pushing her away. He'd let her in, the tiniest bit, and then he'd pick a fight, use his kisses as a punishment for getting too close.

She flushed, and it came back to her then—the sight of Stephen nuzzling her breast, his lips and tongue stirring to life a frenzy of want and need...

'It is a good thing that you did not let this Lord Banks kiss you,' Josette said suddenly, her eyes fixed on the hem she was repairing.

Mae fought to concentrate on her maid. 'Why?'

'The kissing,' she said with a dire shake of her head, 'it makes them stupid. They become domineering, think they can order you about. And then it is much work convincing them otherwise.'

Mae considered this. Stephen had changed, become more critical, less accepting of her ideas. After telling her to listen to her own voice, he'd started issuing orders.

She shook her head. It was just another example of him sending one message, then instantly following up with its opposite. What could she conclude except that he was as confused as she was?

Mae started to roll her neck, but suddenly stopped. As angry and perplexed as Stephen made her, at least he hadn't bound her shoulders into knots.

She glanced across the room, at the mirror, and she knew that she must take his advice—his first advice. She was going to follow her own instinct, both to find that damned horse and to find herself a husband. And right now, her inner voice was telling her to talk to Ryeton's mistress.

Mae swivelled about in her chair. 'Josette?'

'Yes, *mademoiselle*?'

'Fetch my riding habit, please.'

If Chester Cray was in Newmarket, he was playing least in sight. This was not sound business practice for a leg. Perversely, this gave Stephen hope that Cray might have a reason to hide—the theft of England's favourite racehorse, perhaps?

Guilt had spurred him away from the party and on to an afternoon spent trawling among the pubs, inns and taverns of Newmarket. Unfortunately, he had turned up no sign of the well-known leg, and damned little word of him, either. The search had served admirably, however, as a means of avoiding any thought of what had happened between him and Mae earlier.

Until now, damn it.

She'd given him another chance to repay his debt to the people of Fincote. He owed her thanks, but he owed them his full effort and concentration. Mae was stealing it away. Somehow Stephen was going to have to find his balance in this topsy-turvy world, this planet on which suddenly he had more interest in Mae Halford than she had in him. Lord, it was like learning to walk again to even contemplate such a thing.

Fortunately, the rest of the town appeared to be immune to this shocking upheaval. Talk of Pratchett's disappearance, old hat to the diehard racing men who had been in Newmarket these last few days, was being kept alive by the influx of new arrivals. Men gossiped endlessly over who might take the Guineas, with Pratchett out of the way. They speculated nearly as much on

the Earl of Ryeton's behaviour. Some whispered that
he'd locked himself away in his office. Others insisted
that he was chasing over the countryside, searching out
every lead to his missing thoroughbred. Either way, the
lack of his presence was as noticeable as Cray's. Both
gave Stephen much to worry about. Time was growing
short. The tangled muddle of conflicting emotions that
was his response to Mae Halford was going to have to
wait.

Or perhaps not. By late afternoon, feeling dusty and
defeated, Stephen returned to Titchley for a change of
clothes. The garden party had wound to a close; only
the servants were about outside, clearing up. Inside,
the house echoed with silence. Lady Toswick's guests
must be recovering in their rooms or gone on to further
entertainment in town. Stephen retreated to his room—
only to find a request to call upon Barty Halford. At his
earliest possible convenience.

Politely worded and printed on thick vellum, the
thing still felt like a summons to the gallows.

That odd look Mae's father had directed at him earlier haunted him. Had someone seen him with Mae?
Had her father somehow quizzed out the truth of what
they'd been up to?

He groaned. He was in trouble no matter what Barty
Halford knew. He changed quickly, not willing to wait
to find out how much.

He found the man in the library at the back of the
house. Mr Halford smiled as he rose to greet him.
There was no sign of Mae.

'Lord Stephen—' Halford extended his hand '—thank you for coming. Won't you have a seat?'

There was a single chair across from the substantial desk. Two more sat comfortably close to a cheery fire. Halford stood next to one plush chair by the fire and indicated the other.

Mystified, but feeling somewhat hopeful, Stephen took it.

'It's good to have you and your family back in England, sir.'

'My thanks to you, young man. I admit it is good to be back.' Though the room wasn't cold, he rubbed his hands together before the fire. 'I'm particularly looking forward to the start of the racing tomorrow.'

'As are we all.' Stephen grinned. 'I admit I put down a wager on your filly for tomorrow's run. She's a beauty.' He leaned forwards. 'I appreciate your willingness to race her at Fincote Park, sir. More than I can say.'

'I'm happy to do it.' The older man's genial expression changed. Stephen met his shrewd gaze and caught a glimpse of the man who had single-handedly amassed one of England's largest fortunes. 'By all accounts, you've done a stupendous job with your enterprise. I hear you've a solid, challenging course and adequate stables. Support of the community, too, which will make all the difference.'

Stephen blinked. 'You've checked up on Fincote Park?' He didn't know whether to be insulted or impressed.

'Of course. Information is power, young man.

Surely you've learned a bit of that by now. A man in my position can't be too careful.'

Which position? Stephen's mind spun a little wildly. A man with a significant horse to race? Or a man with a marriageable daughter?

Halford sat back. 'I have to say, I'm impressed with you, Lord Stephen.' He raked a hard, measuring look over him. 'I didn't used to be. You were a young hellion when last I saw you.' He held up a hand when Stephen might have responded. 'Though I know that even then, you handled my Mae with tact and finesse.' He chuckled. 'Not an easy thing to do. I appreciated it.'

Stephen shifted. 'Mae was merely young, sir.'

'Young, yes. But being Mae—' He shook his head. 'She was formidable even then.' He turned toward the fire, perhaps to hide the trace of a fond smile on his face. Kitchen noises drifted in from the hall. The door, not fully shut, had drifted open. Halford didn't appear to notice. 'Ah, but just have a look at her now. She's a young lady to be reckoned with, to be sure.'

A footman passed in the hall outside. Stephen didn't respond. Agree or disagree, he was sure to dig himself deeper into trouble.

'You've spent some time together, these last couple of days.' Halford's gaze was measuring now, laced with perhaps a hint of a warning.

Stephen nodded.

'You might have shunned her for the way she acted a couple of years back. Or shamed her. But my wife told me how you looked out for her when Lord Landry sniffed a little too close.'

Heat swept over him. 'It was what any gentleman

would have done, sir.' His face must be flaming. 'Mae mentioned that she is…ah, gathering information. About potential husbands. I agreed to help her out, share my opinions.'

Halford's mouth fell open. 'She asked for your help?' He snorted, suddenly clearly delighted. 'Ah, my Mae. She will stir things up wherever she goes—but she's been making a real effort since we returned.'

Halford suddenly slapped the arm of his chair. 'Well. I admit, I was fearful that she'd fall back into her old habits, make a nuisance of herself, but if that's the way of it, then…I like all that I've heard of you, young man. I think your father would be proud.' Halford bit out the words in his blunt way, but somehow that made the compliment all the more meaningful. 'I'll be happy to race my filly at your track—especially up against Toswick's Butterfly.'

'You won't regret it, sir. I promise a demanding race, run clean.' He sat straighter, hoping to open the subject of Ornithopter, but Halford wasn't finished.

'I'd also like to sponsor you for membership into the Jockey Club Coffee Rooms.' He tilted his head. 'It's not a full membership, but it's a start.'

Pleasure wrestled guilt into submission. This was compliment and opportunity both. 'Thank you,' Stephen said with real gratitude. He stood and extended his hand. 'Your sponsorship would be an honour and a privilege.'

Halford clasped his hand, then crossed before the open door to a small table on the same wall. 'There will be a vote, but it will be a formality, really. Can't think that anyone would object to you—not now that

Ryeton's busy, eh?' The older man laughed as he raised the lid on an elegant humidor. 'Shall we smoke to celebrate?' He raised a thick cigar.

Stephen nodded. 'Thank you. But I did wonder if you might also consider racing Ornithopter at Fincote Park?'

Halford clipped his cigar. He didn't look up. 'Ornithopter, eh?'

He didn't expect an answer. This was fortunate, as Stephen suddenly found himself unable to provide one. Someone else was passing in the hallway. A curvy someone in a navy riding habit who just happened to be creeping along with her boots in her hand. She froze when she glimpsed him through the doorway.

Stephen glared.

His back to the door, her father approached. 'And who would you have in mind as a match for Ornithopter, lad?'

Stephen took the offered cigar. Halford bent slightly to light it and Stephen shot his daughter an evil look over his shoulder.

Mae gave a silent laugh. Deviltry lit up her whole face. With a wave of her hand, she disappeared down the hall, towards the back of the house.

'I'm working on that, sir,' Stephen said, his tone grim.

Mae's heart pounded as she flew through the kitchen, startling the help and flipping the cook an apologetic wave. Her mother was napping and she hadn't expected her father to be in the house at all, let alone to have Stephen Manning with him.

The kitchen step radiated cold even through the thick layers of her habit as she sat down to pull on her boots. She couldn't suppress an amused snort. Oh—the look on Stephen's face! He'd known exactly what she was up to—she could tell by the order implicit in his gaze. Even without words, she'd made sure that he could tell that she felt no compunction to follow his orders, implicit or otherwise.

Her fingers flew as she buttoned up the last boot, and then she was up and nearly running to the stables. It had looked as though her father had Stephen well and truly trapped, but she would take no chances. Stephen would never give her away—but he would come after her. She wanted to be well away before he escaped her father's clutches.

The groom had her mount saddled and waiting. She thanked him with a big smile and a larger coin, but he was wise to her ways. 'Just give me a moment to saddle up, miss. Ye know yer father does not want ye riding out alone.'

'Not to worry, Henry,' she assured him. 'Lady Corbet is already waiting for me at the end of the drive. She's in dire need of new ribbons for her bonnet, before the start of the racing tomorrow.' She grinned and cocked her head at the groom. 'You wouldn't happen to be in dire need of any ribbon, would you?'

'Cor! No, miss, not me.' He eyed her doubtfully. 'If yer sure the lady is waiting?'

'I'm sure!' she called, wheeling her mount about. 'In fact, I'm running late.' Hiding a grin, she was off, hooves clattering over the cobbles, hopefully before Stephen had puffed his cigar to a full burn.

Newmarket was not far, and Mae kept to a slow pace as she made her way along High Street. Her heart beat a good deal faster, though, as she hoped she would encounter the person she sought before Stephen caught up to her. She had been ambling along for nearly ten minutes when her target breezed past.

Miss Charlotte Hague. It could be no other. She drove the pretty little cabriolet, painted a bright red, that the girls at the tea had described. She looked beautiful in her scarlet driving suit, her matching ribbons trailing merrily from her bonnet. She was heading east, out of town, just as she'd been reputed to do every day since she'd turned Ryeton out.

Mae fell in behind her, keeping her in sight, but making sure that plenty of traffic separated them. This grew more difficult as they left Newmarket proper and began the climb south and east out of the town. Mae kept her distance, but in a matter of minutes they were the only two on the road.

Miss Hague must have known she was being followed, but still she continued on, through the grassland and occasional tree belts until she reached a pretty little farm, nestled like a jewel in a valley of green chalk land.

Watching, Mae pulled her mount to a stop. The woman turned on to the track leading towards a small farmhouse and beyond. She continued directly past, heading for a clapboard barn at the edge of the valley. Pausing at the mouth of the rutted drive, Mae watched Miss Hague pull her carriage to a stop. She tied her single horse to a post and entered the barn without a backward glance.

Mae hesitated. Stephen's warnings rang in her head. What could the chances be—that Pratchett might be hidden in that barn? Slim at best. The opportunities for danger suddenly felt more likely. She bit her lip. In the past she'd done a great many foolish things in pursuit of Stephen Manning. This one had the potential to put all the rest to shame.

She thought of all the voices, urging her to act or to not act, or to act in a certain way: Josette, her father, Lord Banks and even the lovely Mr Grange. She thought of Stephen, simultaneously inviting her in and shutting her out. Three days ago her life had been simpler, her goals clear.

She heard it then. Echoing from across the valley, emanating from the barn, the high call of a horse. A greeting.

Her hands gripped tight on the reins. Perhaps things would look simpler again, once Pratchett was found and all the distractions removed.

Urging her mount forwards, she headed for the barn.

Chapter Twelve

Stephen left Barty Halford as soon as he was decently able—which turned out to be about fifteen minutes too late. Fifteen minutes. The damned chit could be anywhere.

Nevertheless, he stormed along High Street in high dudgeon—because he knew where she'd gone to, didn't he? Right where he'd forbidden her to go.

Naturally.

He held his anger and fear for her in check while he made enquiries. Tamped it firmly down while he searched out Charlotte Hague's house and used a combination of bullying and bribery to intimidate her discreet servants.

But now he had a destination. And a mount under him. And plenty of time to indulge in visions of punishment as he made his way out of Newmarket and into the surrounding countryside.

And indulge, he did. He could not stop himself. The girl needed tying up. Or a padded cell. Mae had gone too far this time. He knew that once she made a commitment, it was heart and soul. He knew that she was likely to get caught up in the excitement and beauty of seeing her plans unfold. But it was one thing to blithely spout nonsense about ruination being preferable to an unwanted marriage. It was another thing altogether to court such a disaster with unruly, childish behaviour.

Mae didn't understand what a misery a life shut out from all good society could be. Stephen did.

He knew all about the horrible loneliness. How, when the world forgot you, you began to lose yourself. He'd seen his mother fade away in isolation and exile, through no fault of her own. He'd be damned if he'd see the same thing happen to Mae.

Swallowing a curse, he urged his mount to a faster gait.

What had Mae expected to find as she followed Charlotte Hague? A clandestine meeting? A lover's tryst, perhaps. Standing in the doorway, she blinked her eyes, fighting both disappointment and the gloom of the interior. This was no love nest disguised as a barn. Miss Hague stood within, alone at a stall's opened half-door, stroking the neck of a dappled grey.

Miss Hague chuckled as the horse imperiously butted her shoulder. But when she spoke, her words weren't directed at the grey. 'Well—come in, then. I give you full marks for audacity. Now that you've come all this way, you might as well have your say.'

Mae took a tentative step inside. 'Miss Hague?'

The woman turned and Mae paused. Charlotte Hague was an utterly incongruous sight in such a homey, everyday scene. The woman was lovely, beautiful in a striking, dramatic way. Her dark beauty belonged in another time and place, in a Venetian gondola perhaps, or reclining on a Roman couch. Her lips were red, her skin an exotic olive—but her eyes—Mae's breath caught when their gazes met. Charlotte Hague's eyes were dark and heavy, full of too much knowledge and more than enough experience and, roaming over Mae, her expression took on an inordinately weary cast.

'Well, aren't you a fresh young thing?' She didn't wait for an answer. 'I don't know what nonsense Ryeton has told you, but if it's the house you're after, or anything in it, then you can turn right back around. It's all in the contracts—and it's all mine.' Her beautiful bow of a mouth twisted a little. 'But his lordship? You're welcome to him.'

Mae shook her head. 'No, you've mistaken me. I'd like to ask you a few questions, if you wouldn't mind.'

'I won't promise answers—or answers you want to hear, in any case. And if you've come for a fight, then you are in for a disappointment. I don't fight over men, darling. There are more than enough to go around.' She waved a negligent hand. 'And if you've questions regarding Ryeton, then I've only one answer—pick another mark.'

Mae started again to correct her, but stopped. 'Why?' she asked simply.

'Ryeton spends his money on his horses, not his women. It was not so bad at first, but lately?' She shook her head. 'Ah, perhaps he is too old to maintain more than one obsession. Or it might be that we are just too familiar—we have been together for a good spell.' She raised a shoulder and pursed her lips. 'Either way, I've no talent for playing second fiddle.'

She spared Mae another glance. 'Nor should you start out that way.'

'I don't intend to,' Mae answered truthfully.

Miss Hague turned back to her horse. 'In any case, Lady Ryeton is in Newmarket—which would scratch any chance of you hooking him now.'

Mae took a few steps farther into the barn. 'Is that why you are leaving?'

The other woman laughed. 'Word is out already, is it?' Her sigh was almost swallowed in all the soft, rustling sounds of the barn. 'It's partly the reason. Why not? She's invaded my territory, so I shall breach hers. I'm in need of a new protector—and all the nobs here will be gone in a matter of days.' She shot a glance over her shoulder. 'I'd advise anyone starting out to hie to London and do the same.'

Approaching the stall, Mae got close enough to see that the grey mare had gone heavy with age and indulgence. There was nothing wrong with her nose, however. She had only just reached the pair of them when the mare swung away from Miss Hague and took a step in her direction. She pushed her nose past Mae's outstretched hand and straight to her pocket.

Miss Hague chuckled. 'You must have something good in there.'

'Sugar,' Mae answered with a smile. 'Would you mind?'

'Of course not.' The other woman's voice took on a note of almost parental lenience. She reached out and ran a fond hand down the arch of the mare's neck.

'This is Minna. She's my oldest and dearest friend. I can't even begin to tell you all the adventures we've had together.' She sighed. 'I sold her once, when things had got so bad…' The words trailed away.

Silence hung in the air a moment, along with all the strong and oddly comforting smells of a working barn. Miss Hague gave herself a little shake and continued on as if nothing had happened. 'I bought her back as soon as I was able—at twice the price. And I've never parted from her since. It's a nice set-up we have here in Newmarket. She has plenty of room to roam, a nice man to spoil her, and I can drive out and visit her any time I like.'

Mae shivered at the tickle of the mare's velvety nose against the palm of her hand. She heard Miss Hague's unspoken words—and saw the sorrow they lent to her caressing hand. 'It sounds like you'll miss her while you are gone.'

The other woman shot her an amused glance. 'Indeed I will. I've been fitting in extra visits as I prepare to leave. She's not young any more and I fear…' Unable to finish the thought, she gestured towards the back of the stall. 'But Minna won't be completely bereft. She'll have Argus to keep her company.'

'Argus?' Mae stepped to the side until she caught a glimpse of black towards the back of the stall. A small goat lay curled in a bed of straw, regarding her with unblinking eyes.

'Argus is Minna's special friend,' said Miss Hague with a smile. 'He was already living here on the farm when I first boarded Minna here. They took one look at each other and have barely been more than a few feet apart since.' She chuckled. 'At this point, I think it would be far more difficult for my darling to be separated from Argus than from me.'

Immediately, Mae thought of Pratchett and his cat companion. 'That is an odd coincidence. I'd only just heard about how some animals strike up such relationships.'

'Yes, they are all talking about Pratchett, are they not? And he does have a friend—a solid black cat.' She shivered. 'They do say as black cats are odd, and that one is no exception. I've seen that thoroughbred in a right towering temper tantrum, and that cat will just walk up, cool as you please, and rub up against his leg—and just like that, the horse goes flat and easy as a becalmed ocean.' She gave a rueful laugh and her grey responded with a nod. 'Now Minna would be the opposite. She's as easy going as the day is long, until Argus is out of her sight, and then she starts to get agitated.'

Mae took a step over to the next stall, where a bay with four white stockings stood with his hindquarters towards them. 'But where does that leave this lovely boy? If those two are so close, I wonder if he feels left out?' She turned to Miss Hague with a smile. 'He looks to be in wonderful shape. Is he yours as well?'

'No. He's one of Lord Ryeton's. I don't think he's been here long enough to feel left out.'

Mae's heart began to pound. Ryeton's? The earl kept a horse tucked away out here?

But Miss Hague had continued, and even through her excitement, Mae caught the bitter note in her voice. 'If money is such an issue, it makes no sense to me that Ryeton would spare the expense to board this one all the way out here instead of keeping him in his own stables. Heaven knows that his horses are more pampered than his women.'

Intense and hopeful excitement made Mae incautious. 'Miss Hague, could this be Pratchett?'

'Pratchett?' The other woman's surprise was genuine, as was the slightly mocking trill of laughter that followed it. 'Good heavens, no. My dear, you must learn more about horses and racing if you are hunting for a protector among the racing set. Pratchett is a full bay, for one thing, and he *looks* like a champion, with a proud and regal bearing. He's as temperamental as any stage prima donna as well, with a fiery heart and a tendency to nip out at anyone who would dare come this close to his stall.'

She waved a dismissive hand. 'This one is fine enough, but he doesn't have the spirit of a true champion—he cannot even be bothered enough to be curious about us!' She cocked her head at Mae in curiosity. 'And why in heaven's name would Ryeton kidnap his own horse? It doesn't make sense.'

Mae flushed, but more from disappointment than embarrassment. Oh, would it not have been the grandest thing to have found Pratchett so unexpectedly? How she would have loved to march back into Newmarket and toss that little nugget of information—along with his imperious orders—right in Stephen's lap!

Still, she would find out what she could. 'As you say, none of it makes sense to me. Do you have an idea why anyone would kidnap that horse? What gain could be got from it?'

Miss Hague shrugged. 'A rival, perhaps? Pratchett

wins everything he enters. I wish I did know who had done the thing, for I would like to extend my personal thanks. I don't think I've ever seen Ryeton so unhappy.'

Mae arched a brow at her. 'If making Lord Ryeton unhappy would count as a motive towards this crime, then you would seem a likely suspect.'

The woman appeared to be more irritated by the observation than alarmed. 'And you would seem a little fool to have confronted me about it, here where we are all alone. Were I that desperate, what would keep me from doing you a harm as well?'

Suddenly weariness descended over Charlotte Hague once again. 'Good gracious, I'd forgotten what it's like, to be so young and earnest. You exhaust me.' She rubbed her hand across her forehead. Mae could see the conscious effort she made to smooth her expression. 'It's only bitterness that makes me wish to see Ryeton as miserable as he's made me over the last few months. But I've neither time nor energy to waste on such pettiness. I have my own future to worry over.' Her tone grew sardonic. 'And fewer resources with which to approach it.'

She looked away from Mae. 'Some day you'll understand. The time will come when you are not so firm as you've always been, when you begin to need the tricks of light and the magic in your dressmaker's fingers. If you are anything at all like me, then that will be the first time you actually fear what the future might bring.'

Mae had never had to worry about where her next meal was coming from, had always known she would have a place to lay her head, but still, she did know something about the uncertainty and anxiety that went with fearing for your place in the world. 'I know a little of what you mean,' she said softly.

Both women startled at the crunch of gravel outside. Minna lifted her head and nickered a welcome and the other woman eyed Mae in knowing amusement. 'Well, this is unexpected.'

Mae flushed and turned towards the open door. Could Stephen have found her already?

Charlotte Hague dropped a kiss on her mare's nose. 'I thought that today was going to be all about endings and goodbyes. I find that it makes things easier to think that it might also be about a beginning.' She trailed one last caress across the grey's nose. 'Goodbye, my darling.' The smile she cast at Mae was crooked and bittersweet. 'And good luck to you.'

She strolled towards the barn door, but the light dimmed as a male figure suddenly blocked it. Mae's heart began to pound. It *was* Stephen.

Anger shimmered off him in waves. He glared at Mae with a heavy-lidded gaze that stirred her insides to life. He ignored Miss Hague completely, instead raking Mae with a burning, head-to-toe glance. She straightened her spine and braced herself for battle.

Miss Hague gave him a solemn nod, as if they'd met along the streets of London instead of in the wilds of Suffolk. Without looking directly at her, he returned the gesture. She slid past him into the lengthening shadows.

Stephen stood in the wide barn door and smouldered. The gold sunset of Mae's hair glowed against the dark night of her navy habit. The sight fanned the flames inside him even higher. He feared that if he set foot inside, he'd set the place alight. 'You just cannot do it, can you?'

Unrepentant, she cocked an eyebrow at him. 'I'm sure I don't know what you mean, Stephen. I can do a great many things. And I do most of them extremely well.'

'Perhaps I should have said "won't" instead. Because from my perspective, the list of things that you should do, but won't, is longer than my arm.' He took the risk and entered the shadows of the barn. 'Certainly you refuse to listen to perfectly rational suggestions—even when they are meant to safeguard your welfare.'

'Suggestions? Your suggestions sound unfortunately like orders. I have told you repeatedly how I feel about that. I have no wish to be ordered about and treated like my brain caved in when my bosom popped out!'

Her flippancy made him insane. He'd worked himself into a frenzy riding all the way out here. 'Can't, won't. Suggestions, orders. Stop arguing about semantics, Mae! The end result of your folly will be the same, should anyone find out about this little jaunt.' He stalked towards her, but she held her ground. Like always. Just once he wished he could frighten her enough to *listen*. He grabbed her arms. 'I won't see you ruined!'

'I cannot see where it is any of your concern.' She scowled up at him. 'Kissing me twice in twenty-four hours does not give you any say in my future.'

'If you have a future,' he said scathingly. He let go of one arm and tugged on the other. 'Come, we need to get you back to Titchley.'

She resisted. 'Don't you even wish to know what I've found out?'

'Nothing you could have discovered would be worth the risk you've taken.' He paused. 'I harbour serious doubts regarding your theory that Charlotte Hague stole Ryeton's horse as a parting shot in their relationship.' He crossed his arms. 'Did she?'

'No.' The admittance came out sulky, like a child's. 'But Ryeton does have a bay boarded here.'

He dropped her other arm and stared at her in disbelief. She gestured to the farthest stall. His heart rate ratcheting, he crossed to look.

'That's not Pratchett,' he said, his gut heavy with disappointment.

'No, but it is odd that he would keep a horse out here, isn't it?'

'Four white feet, do without him,' Stephen mused.

'Excuse me?'

'Nothing, it's just an old superstition. It goes something like this:

One white foot, buy him
Two white feet, try him
Three white feet, look well about him
Four white feet, do without him.'

'Well, fortunately we're not looking to buy him,' Mae said with sarcasm. 'Although maybe that is why he's here? Could Ryeton be selling off his stables? From some things that Miss Hague said, I'm beginning to suspect Ryeton might be having financial difficulties.'

He sighed, suddenly more weary than angry. 'Did she *say* he was having financial difficulties?'

'Not outright, but several things she mentioned suggested the possibility. She did say that his—'

Stephen threw up a hand. 'Stop. I don't care what she said. I only care about getting you safely—and quickly—back home. Who knows what Charlotte Hague is going to say when she gets back to Newmarket?'

'She won't say anything. She thinks I am a fledgling lightskirt.'

He shuddered. 'Is that supposed to make me feel better? Oh, Lord. Fine, then, let's get you out of here before the farmer who owns this place shows up and finds us here.'

'So what if he does? Will you shout my name at him?'

'I won't have to! Think, Mae. You are not exactly a fade-into-the-background sort of girl. Everyone in Newmarket and its vicinity will have heard of the beautiful and rambunctious heiress with the gold hair. How long do you think it will take that woman—or this hypothetical farmer—to work out who you are? Our best defence is to have you safe and sound at home, with no one else the wiser about this idiotic adventure of yours.'

Her expression had softened. 'Beautiful?' she asked softly. But then she frowned. 'Idiotic?'

'Yes—to both of those words. There are a host of others I could throw in. Irritating. Exasperating.' *Mine.* He brushed that thought away and took her arms again, this time with a gentle touch. 'I am not trying to stifle you. Don't you see, Mae? You say that you are resolved not to live a life where no one knows or respects the real you. But how much worse would it be if everyone refused to know or accept you at all? *I'm* resolved that you should never know the pain of seeing your friends and family abandon you.'

He slid his hands along her arms to take hers. 'You are indeed rambunctious and irritating, but you are also happy and fun and full of life and energy. I don't ever want to see you left alone to grow lonely and listless.'

Comprehension chased the obstinate expression from her pretty face. Some of the tension melted from her frame. 'Like your mother.'

His every muscle tensed. How could he speak of it? He never had—not even with his brother Nicholas. It had been the secret they kept for and with their mother—even after her death.

And look what disaster that secret had wrought! It—and his irresponsibility—had destroyed Fincote. Speaking of it now would be painful, dangerous even, but he would lay bare at least part of the awful truth if it kept Mae from ruining her life.

He sighed. 'Yes, like my mother. I know her scandal occurred on a grand scale, but it only takes a small scandal to ruin a young woman.'

'But…I know it must have been horrible for her— when your father left, I mean. But none of it was her fault—surely once the talk died down—'

Bitterly, he interrupted her. 'You are right about that—not a bit of it was her fault. She wasn't a shrew or spendthrift or a wanton. She was merely a wife whose husband loved another. So much so that he couldn't live without her.'

'But your father recovered eventually, socially, I mean. Even Lady Catherine was accepted after they stayed together for so many years. And your brothers and your sisters have done well.'

'Yes, Father and Lady Catherine recovered.' The bitterness had drained away, leaving only resignation. 'And they wouldn't have cared if they hadn't, for they had each other, and their crowd of loyal, if fast, friends and all of us children. But my mother was left alone to bear the brunt of society's cruelty. She wasn't living openly with a lover, but still she was mocked, shunned and ridiculed. And, ultimately, forgotten.'

He rubbed a hand across his brow. 'Her pain and shame were burdens too heavy for her to overcome. She hid away, with sorrow and disgrace as her only companions.'

'I never knew,' Mae said. 'All the time I spent at Welbourne Manor and I never thought…' Her words died away and she moved closer.

'No one ever thought of her. She lived alone, nursing her grief. It ate at her until she died.'

Her eyes filled with the tears that he had never let fall. 'Oh, Stephen, I remember that you and Nicholas would sometimes go to visit her.' She stopped abruptly. Her hands slipped from his and circled around his waist. 'I'm so sorry.'

'Don't be sorry.' His tone had gone harsh with emotion. 'Just don't let it happen to you.' Her arms tightened and he knew he should step back. Away. But the barn had grown dimmer and the light inside Mae was shining through, glowing from every inch of exposed skin and pricking him with tiny rays of her warmth.

'I'm not my father, Mae. I couldn't bear to be responsible for your disgrace, the reason for your suffering.'

When had she ended up in his embrace? She cradled his jaw in her hand. 'No. I think you've enough burdens,' she whispered. 'I'll do my best not to add to them.'

All of Stephen's anger and fear had gone. There was nothing now except the feel of her yielding curves and soft heat. There was no mischief between them now. No bickering. Only the tenderness in her eyes and the racing of his heart.

Her hands came up. His brain gave a last feeble try, shouting out a distant warning, but it was no match for the much closer press of her bosom to his chest or the rush of desire clogging his veins. He closed his eyes, went under and pulled her close for his kiss.

Chapter Thirteen

Her heart overflowing, Mae leaned into Stephen's kiss. He'd done it. It had been horribly difficult for him, that much had been obvious, but he'd opened a piece of his heart to her in a way that he never had before.

And this time it hadn't been due to her prodding and probing. At last he'd taken the step himself, grabbed both edges of a tiny crack and pulled it wider, shared a dark part of his past that he clearly didn't care to—and he'd done it to protect her.

She well remembered the times when Stephen and Nicholas had gone away to visit their mother at Fincote Park, how Nicholas had nearly always been subdued when they returned, but Stephen had come back full of energy, almost frantic in his desire to play a bigger prank, tell a better joke, or make everyone laugh until their sides hurt.

His desire for attention as a boy made perfect sense now. How horribly it must have hurt those brothers to see their mother fading away, retreating from life. How frightened Stephen must have been that the same thing might happen to him.

She mourned for his sad mother, and for all the years that he had carried such a burden all alone. But she also revelled in this new openness, and in the incredible difference in this kiss. Their other embraces had been full of heat and excitement, thick with desire—and with more than a hint of combat. This…felt more like a plea. She could almost feel his inner turmoil begin to quiet.

She feared the opposite was happening to her. Her body was vibrating as his hands moved over her. He made her feel alive in a hundred places, in a thousand ways.

He broke their kiss and buried his face in the angle of her neck. She gasped. His tongue brushed her earlobe at the same time as his hands closed over her breasts and a line of fire jumped to life between all three points. A moan tore its way out of her. She was burning, from the inside out.

She didn't care. She wanted more.

There was no undoing the many tiny buttons marching up the back of her habit. Stephen didn't even try. He just pinched her nipple through the heavy fabric of her habit with one hand and started pulling up her skirts with the other.

And she was helping him. He pressed her up against a rough wall and she lifted her leg up high, along with her climbing skirts. She wrapped it around him, dug her fingers into his hair and held on. Stephen was above her and around her, solid and reassuring. Her position should have felt precarious, but she'd never felt safer. Or more filled with hope.

His fingers slid along the length of her leg, following the sweep of her garter on to the soft flesh of her inner thigh. *Yes.*

'No.' Stephen pulled his mouth from hers, but his fingers were still creeping higher. 'We should not be doing this.'

She suppressed a groan and agreed with him instead. 'You're right, we shouldn't.' But she hitched her leg higher, opening to him in a way she'd never done before. The thrill of it, the *rightness* of it set her heart to soaring.

His breath stirred in her hair. A cool breeze whispered along the bare skin of her leg. But the spot where Stephen's fingers touched now was molten hot.

She jumped.

'We can't do…everything, Mae. We shouldn't even have gone this far.'

She only moved against his hand.

He moaned. It was capitulation and she rejoiced to hear it. She'd never felt closer to Stephen than she did right now, and still it wasn't enough.

Suddenly he reached down and grasped both her legs. He lifted her easily until she straddled him and carried her over to a ladder leading to a hayloft. She felt the heat and hardness of him with every step.

'There should be a clean bed of hay up there.' His words came out a statement, but Mae saw the question in his eyes.

Emphatically, she nodded.

* * *

Stephen had spent a good part of his lifetime engaged in a variety of selfish and destructive pursuits, but what he was about to do with Mae just might be the worst.

He'd tried to stop, but her insistence had won out over the creaky objections of his conscience. There was nothing left now but the heat at her core, pressing against him, and the sure, inexorable pull of desire. He shifted her to his shoulder with an ease that left her gasping and quickly ascended.

He'd been right. Here was a loft full of clean and sweet-smelling hay. Gently he laid her down and stretched out beside her. She pulled him close and the sweetness of her touch and the joy in her face erased all of his doubts, melting them into irresistible need.

He kissed her again, enjoying the taste and the scent of her. It was only moments before her skirts were lifted high once more, baring a mile of silky, slender leg. He trailed teasing fingers along the milk-white inside of her thigh. She threw her head back and laughed at the sensation.

He looked down into Mae's face, alight with happiness, and he knew that she wanted this. Hell and damnation, he wanted it too, more than he'd ever wanted anything. But nothing was settled between them.

He couldn't deny that Mae was in his blood. She was so much more than he'd ever given her credit for—not just a genius at mischief, but intelligent and full of quick wit and sly humour that called to him like the pull of a magnet. She set him aflame with her innate sensuality.

But this was a pivotal moment, one that could very well set the course for both of their lives. It was not a decision he should be making with his raging member. He had a racecourse that he'd worked hard to build and all the people associated with it counting on him. He had a reputation to build, and the undeniable need to prove himself. He could not abandon his task, not even for this.

And Mae had a mission of her own. Was she even thinking how perilous this course of action could be?

'Mae?' he asked seriously. 'Are you still practising your wiles?'

She laughed. 'Do I need practice? I'd thought it obvious they were up to the job.'

He waited. She grew serious.

'What's worrying you, Stephen?'

'I don't know. Things are different between us now.'

She smiled. 'Indeed they are. For example, I don't remember doing this.' She cupped him with her hand.

Involuntarily he pressed against her. 'Lord, Mae. We have to stop.'

She groaned and pulled away, pressing her hand to her eyes. 'Yes, Stephen,' she said in tone of utter frustration. '*This* has to stop. I can't keep doing this. You can't keep doing this! You are open, then you are closed. You push and pull me until I don't know which way is up.'

With horror he recognised the truth of her words.

She took her hand away, met his gaze without guile. 'You're making me miserable.'

Lord, but he knew what she meant. He was miserable

too. And yet somehow he was, at the same time, happier than he could ever remember.

He grabbed her fingers, held them tight to his chest. 'I know. We're caught up in the physical, now. And in the excitement of the search for Pratchett, too. But later, when we are not alone in a barn and we've either found that damned horse or failed, things might look different.'

She pulled back to look him in the eye. 'What are you saying?'

'I meant what I said earlier—I won't be like my father. I won't leave you to face the consequences of my actions. And I won't make you promises that I'm not even sure I'm capable of keeping.' He ran a caressing finger along the wonderfully stubborn length of her jaw. 'I'm saying that I'm as miserable and happy and terrified as you, but I think we should just...wait. Let's finish what we started, not only with Pratchett, but we'll carry on with your mission too.'

'And then?'

'And then, we'll see how we feel when all of this is over.'

She looked suddenly worried, and he wondered if it was because her feelings might change—or if she feared they wouldn't.

'Oh, very well,' she grumped. 'But it seems a shame to waste a perfectly good hayloft.'

He looked at her. Her hair was tousled and her lips were swollen from his kisses. Her skirts were still hiked around her thighs.

And suddenly he was tired of holding back, of keeping every damned thing out of her reach. There was one thing he could give her, one gift to symbolise the fragile new hope he felt in his heart. He leaned down, buried his fingers among her curls and sealed his lips to hers. He put everything into that kiss, all of his old loneliness and his new longings, as well as the promise of the pleasure he was going to show her.

He couldn't wait—and her eager movements beneath his hand told him he didn't have to. Searching, he found the heated heart of her.

Ahh. She was wet and ready. He slid his finger along her folds and she exhaled her approval. Back and forth he traced over her, just a little deeper with each stroke. Her breath began to come high and fast, her whole body tensed with the force of her passion.

Ever so softly he eased higher, to meet the hard centre of her desire. Gently he greeted it, circling, rubbing lightly and drinking in with pleasure all the wonderful soft sounds and swift movements of her response.

Without warning, she convulsed. Her head thrown back, and her hips jerking against his hand, she came beautifully apart. He drank in the sight even as he pressed the hot ridge of his length against her thigh.

She collapsed against him. For several agonising moments he struggled for control. But then she lolled her head back onto his shoulder and looked him in the eye.

'I had no idea,' she said in wonder.

Stephen laughed and kissed her on the nose.

'Neither did I.'

Chapter Fourteen

The race meeting opened the next morning. A stiff wind blew as the first race went off, and Mae and her mother were there to cheer the beautiful thoroughbreds on as they thundered towards the finish line.

Excitement coloured the air, along with a great many more fluttering ribbons and feathers than usual. Nearly every lady in Newmarket had come out this morning. They were not all perched in carriages or atop vehicles, either. Instead they were down among the men, debating the merits of the favourites, putting their pin money down with the legs and generally having a grand time. A few bold souls, including Lady Ryeton, even mounted up and raced to the finish along with the contenders, just as the young and unruly bucks of the *ton* did.

Mae's father was having a grand time as well—especially after Barty's Shill won her race, narrowly defeating Lord Toswick's Butterfly. She won him a solid amount of money and generated much talk of the possible private match between the two horses.

And Mae—Mae was allowing herself to feel cautiously optimistic, because...well, just because. Her body was still tingling from everything Stephen had done to her last evening. But her heart was tingling with the cautious rebirth of hope—hope for her and Stephen, hope that her instincts had been telling her the truth all along.

She brushed a stray leaf from her skirts in an effort to distract herself. She knew she looked well today, for Josette had commented knowingly on the sparkle in her eyes as she brushed the straw from Mae's riding habit. Just the recollection of it brought a flush of heat to her cheeks. Even Mr Matthew Grange commented on her high colouring as he invited her to climb up and join him for a few moments in his cabriolet.

'You must be careful, Miss Halford, or you will outshine the day,' he said gaily. His admiring glance moved from her heated cheeks and passed over her sage carriage dress. 'I can see that you are enjoying yourself this morning?'

'Tremendously, sir. I hope you are as well?'

'I am,' he returned with a smile. 'I can't tell you how happy I am to be back amongst people again.'

He didn't have to tell her, it had been obvious since she'd first seen him arrive at Lord Toswick's ball. And she rather thought his continued good cheer and unflappability had eased his way this week. His determined refusal to be ashamed of his differences or cast down by others' prejudices had paid off.

She wished her own hopes would turn out so well. If only she could collect her thoughts, review her options, and decide just what it was that she was hoping *for*.

'Convalescence is a lonely business.' He grinned to take the pathos from his words.

'And entering society—or re-entering it—can be a difficult business. Yet here you are today with a crowd of friends and a host of admirers.' She put her hand over his scarred one. 'I hope you know that I count myself first among them.'

He patted her hand. 'Then we shall form a mutual admiration society,' he said with a chuckle. 'You are an unusual young lady, Miss Halford. Those of us with differences must stick together.' He looked out over the line of horses and jockeys making their way to the start. 'I've always enjoyed racing. I hope to start up my own stables again soon.' He shot her a mischievous glance. 'But I admit that today I am finding it most enjoyable to watch the results of the ladies' experiment.'

Mae glanced about at the people happily milling along the rail. 'There does appear to be an air of female satisfaction hanging over the course today, doesn't there?'

'And an accompanying air of male interest, I would say.' His gaze drifted over her shoulder. 'Ah, here comes your friend Lady Corbet.'

Mae turned as he called a greeting. Addy had Miss Lucy Metheny in tow.

'Lady Corbet,' Mr Grange said with a nod. 'I've just finished telling Miss Halford how fine she looks, now I must comment on how very pleased with yourself you appear to be right now.'

'And why not?' Addy trilled. 'I doubled my pin money for the quarter when Mr Halford's filly won.'

Miss Lucy grinned up at them. 'And I've just heard the most titillating piece of gossip.'

'I'm all ears,' Mr Grange said.

'Go on, dear,' Addy urged her. 'Mr Grange won't mind a bit of tittle-tattle. Something like this must be of interest to any racing man, concerning Lord Ryeton as it does.'

'Lord Ryeton?' Mae asked sharply.

'Lady Ryeton, actually,' Miss Lucy said. She shot a quick glance in Mr Grange's direction. 'It's being said that Lady Ryeton left London for a reason.' She lowered her voice. 'She was dunned out!'

'By creditors,' Addy put in unnecessarily.

'I take leave to doubt this particular titbit.' With a subtle gesture Mr Grange pointed off to the right, where Lady Ryeton herself sat mounted on a splendid, restive stallion near the finish line. She was dressed in the most elegant habit Mae had ever seen, all done up in black and silver in a military style. As they watched she laughed at something one of her companions said, her eyes alight and her face carefree. 'She hasn't a worry in the world, or so one would think by her manner today.'

Or so we are all supposed to think, Mae thought darkly.

'You might be right, Mr Grange.' Miss Lucy looked thoughtful. 'Perhaps we should not repeat it again.'

'Well, it's not as if we were likely to tell anyone else, in any case,' Addy said. 'Unless we find it is true.'

Mae laughed.

'Good heavens, is that the race at Beacon course they are calling?' Addy asked. 'I promised Corbet I would meet him before it began.' She clutched Miss Lucy with one hand and waved a farewell with the other. 'Good day to you, Mr Grange! Mae, I shall see you at Lady Ryeton's.'

'I'm looking forward to it,' said Mae.

Matthew Grange watched the pair of them make their way through the crowd a moment before turning back to run a contemplative eye over Mae. 'I meant what I said earlier, Miss Halford. You are glowing quite radiantly today. Perhaps on a related note, my good friend Lord Stephen Manning is prowling about with a look of abject frustration on his face.' The wind tousled his hair and the sun highlighted the tender pink skin of his scars, but he had a smile on his face and mischief lived in his eyes. 'Judging by the way Stephen was watching you the other night, I might be inclined to think that these two might be related. Or is it presumptuous of me to mention it?' he asked with a grin.

'Not at all presumptuous—especially if I might be allowed to comment on Miss Lucy's new fascination with the past war with France.' She twinkled up at him. 'I did notice that she was particularly interested in the 13th Light Dragoons. Would it be presumptuous of me to recall that that was your company, sir?'

He held up his hands. '*Touché*, Miss Halford. Although Miss Lucy is young and flighty still, and I am too soon broke free from my sickbed to contemplate anything except my new freedoms. Perhaps it might be safer all around if we both kept our observations private.'

'Safer,' she agreed, 'but not nearly as much fun!'

They shared a comfortable laugh just as Stephen

approached the cabriolet. Mae noted that he was indeed wearing a ferocious scowl, as well as a coat of sable superfine that set off his short blond hair beautifully.

'Good morning, Stephen!' she said, intensely aware of the brightness in her expression, but unable to suppress it. She glanced at Mr Grange and then extended her hand downward. 'Will you help me down?' she asked politely. 'I see my mother is coming to fetch me.'

Her heart caught in her throat at the heated touch of his hand, but then her mother arrived, and for several moments there was no opportunity for anything other than pleasantries. Soon, though, a tumult began at the starting line and swept through the crowd toward them. Several false starts led to loud objections and cries of foul play. Everyone's attention was soon occupied with the unfolding drama, and Stephen took the opportunity to lean in close to Mae.

'This is our last chance,' he said low. 'We must find word of Pratchett today.'

Breathing deeply, she nodded. He smelled like sunshine and soap and just the faintest undertone of horse. She edged towards him and breathed in once more.

'You are going to Lady Ryeton's gathering today, are you not?'

She nodded again, keeping a wary eye on her mother.

'Good. Please, do your best to keep your eyes and ears open. And if you hear anything, even the smallest whisper, of a leg named Chester Cray, get word to me right away.'

He didn't insult her by telling her how to manage

any of it. His trust warmed her nearly as much as the quick caress he ran across her palm as he bent over her hand.

She squeezed his hand and he straightened to meet her gaze. Mae was struck by the weight of frustration on his face.

'This may be the one scheme we don't manage to pull off, Mae.' His tone was already heavy with desolation.

She scoffed. 'Ryeton is *not* going to be the one to best us.'

His expression lightened a bit.

'We'll get there, Stephen, if we don't give up. Today is our day.' She lowered her voice to a whisper. 'Did you hear the rumours circulating about Lady Ryeton?'

Eyes widening, he shook his head. She gave him a hurried explanation. The uproar at the start had been sorted out and her mother was listening as Mr Grange explained how false starts adversely affected the horses.

Stephen blinked. He looked adorably vacant for a moment. Mae wondered if she looked as distant as he did now, when all the gears in her mind started turning.

'Cray might be the key to clearing all of this up,' he said after a moment. 'I can't find him about here. I'm going to head back into town to try to search him out.' His eyes softened as his gaze met hers, and then he was taking his leave of the others.

She watched him stride away through the crowds, his hair golden in the sun and his shoulders half again as broad as any man's present.

And she grinned.

Yes, today was quite the best race day she'd had in years.

This had to be the worst race day Stephen had experienced in years.

He stalked away from Mae, only slightly mollified that he wasn't leaving her alone with Matthew Grange. He hadn't liked the look of the comfortable coze the pair of them had been sharing when first he'd found them. Shards of their companionable laughter had pierced him like steel. Here he was, still burning with unslaked lust and she sat sharing smiles and a narrow bench with one of his best friends. It was her right, of course. He'd been the one to urge her to continue her mission. Nothing they had done together had been irrevocable. Yet the sight of them had been the crowning touch on a morning filled with frustration and failure.

It wasn't all bad, of course. The fillies had generated a good bit of talk and thanks to Mr Halford and Lord Toswick; at least a mild interest in Fincote Park had begun as the setting for a private match between them.

But time was running short. He would shortly lose his chance to find Pratchett and put himself and Fincote Park square in the centre of the racing world's attention.

His brain was abuzz with possibilities. He had been dismissive of what Mae had said last night about Lord Ryeton's possible financial difficulties, but this new gossip regarding his countess forced him to think again.

He stared at the earl as he passed him by. The man sat cooped up in his carriage with a few of his cronies, ignoring his wife, gazing morosely out of the window and refusing to talk to anyone.

For the first time, Stephen considered that he might fail. But he could not give up, even if the only lead he had was a leg who hadn't even bothered to show up for the races.

Chester Cray was still not to be found, although he had heard whispers this morning that Cray was indeed in town, and perhaps ill.

Urgency grew in Stephen's breast. He was going to find that horse. One way or another, Ryeton was going to help launch Fincote Park.

He left the excitement of the races behind and returned to Newmarket proper. The streets lay quieter, the taprooms emptier than he'd seen it since he'd arrived. Good. It should make it all the easier to track down the hidden leg. He sighed. It was a damned sorry state, but the lack of distraction would make it that much harder to keep his mind off Mae Halford.

He'd told her about his mother. He still wasn't over the shock of it. It was a little uncomfortable today, walking about like normal, but knowing that she knew. Mae saw more of him, in fact—the real, flawed Stephen and not the burnished image he projected—than anyone else ever had. And with her perception and quick mind, she was likely to start putting pieces together and seeing even more. Uncomfortable? It was a ridiculously scary thing to give someone a peek at all the private, ugly bits of you. And yet, somehow, Mae's easy acceptance almost made him yearn for more.

Almost.

But he couldn't regret sharing it. Especially not if it kept her from doing anything rash. He snorted. As if there was anything more rash than nearly bedding him.

Good God, but how he'd wanted her. Wanted her still. Somehow, over the past few days, aching for Mae Halford had become a constant. The usual state of things. But he couldn't regret his restraint last night either. Things were too unsettled between them. And in any case, there were other ways to bind her to him.

He stopped short, right in the middle of the pavement. Was that what he wanted? To bind her to him?

Images crowded his mind. Shared triumph and joy. Lust and laughter. A smile of warmth and approval from her father. And the far less attractive picture of her pressed close and chortling with Matthew Grange.

Just let him find Pratchett. Then it would be the time to find things out.

Chapter Fifteen

❧

There were several radiant faces gracing Lady Ryeton's sunny parlour that afternoon, lucky ladies whose
picks had taken the field and who were going home
with extra spending money today. There were also several downcast countenances, the sad and ill-tempered
faces of those who had lost.

'Do you think that we've done them a disservice?'
Mae's mother whispered over her cup of tea.

'Of course not,' Lady Toswick insisted. 'We made
it clear—several times, at that—that no one should bet
more than they could afford to lose.'

'I'm not sure everyone took that advice,' Addy said
cautiously. 'Just look at the baroness.'

As one, the group of ladies turned to gaze at a plump,
matronly lady who stood scowling at a tray of steaming
oyster loaves.

'She's been looking like that since we arrived. And
she keeps staring at her hand.' Addy leaned forwards
and narrowed her gaze. 'Can you see a mark on her

finger? Does anyone know if she was wearing a ring earlier?'

'Oh,' breathed Miss Ward. 'Will Lord Malden be angry with her?'

'Well, it would serve her right if he was,' Lady Toswick insisted indignantly. 'We were very clear in our point that this enterprise is strategic in nature and not financial.'

'I don't believe my sister is enjoying our experiment, either.' Miss Lucy sounded resigned as she gazed across at her sister, standing alone in a corner.

'Well, I don't care,' Lady Toswick declared. 'Barring the scorn of a few old codgers, I'd call the first phase of our plan a tremendous success. Most of the gentlemen were intrigued and impressed—with our presence, of course, but, more importantly, with our knowledge.'

'Mr Grange did pronounce himself enchanted,' Miss Lucy said, brightening. 'And a chorus of other men agreed with him.'

Mae was enchanted with the invitation right into Lord Ryeton's home. The estate, located in Stetchworth, just outside of Newmarket, was ruled over by a lovely Jacobean manor house, graced with many mullioned windows, its steep roof peppered with a multitude of chimneys. There was no sign of the earl himself, but with Addy's gossip fresh in her mind, Mae was keeping her eyes open. And the tour of the stables was still to come.

'A gaggle of gentlemen wished to accompany us here this afternoon as well,' Mae's mother contributed.

'Yes, and did you not hear what Lady Ryeton told them? This celebration was for hens and chicks only, and we would meet the roosters again tonight at our soirée.' Lady Toswick laughed.

The buzz of gossip continued around them as Mae leaned closer to her mother. 'Mama, what's the first thing most people would do, should they find themselves in straitened financial circumstances?'

'Round up the valuables and start selling them off,' Elizabeth Halford answered promptly, having had some experience of such matters early in her life.

'Like paintings?' Mae directed her gaze at a small landscape on the parlour wall. It was centred in a large square of darker-coloured wallpaper, as if it had been hung in place of a much larger work of art.

Her mother followed her gaze, and then glanced about the room. After a moment she looked pointedly toward a sturdy sofa, too large for the corner nook it sat in. 'And furniture too,' she said softly.

Simultaneously they both looked at the lavish spread of food and drink, spread out across two buffet tables.

'It's a show,' Mae whispered. 'And we're the audience.'

'The signs are faint, but they are there. You have a good eye, Mae.' Her mother gave her a look of approval. 'Your father will want to know about this.'

As would Stephen. Mae could hardly wait for the stable tour to begin. Who knew what clues might be lurking there?

Stephen stepped wearily out of the gusting wind and into yet another tavern. He'd met a somewhat inebriated gentleman earlier, who had assured him that Chester Cray was indeed in town and that he liked to frequent one of the dramshops on High Street. Unfortunately, the helpful fellow didn't know which one and Stephen had underestimated just how many taprooms there were on the long stretch of road.

'Manning!' His name rang out as his eyes adjusted to the gloom. 'Come in and have a pint with us—we've good news to share!' Toswick sat at a large table with his stable manager, along with Grange, Banks, a few other assorted gentlemen and a tavern doxie or two.

Stephen sank down into the hastily pulled up chair with a heavy heart. 'I could use some good news about now.'

'Well then, brace yourself—the membership held the ballot and you are officially a member of the Jockey Club Coffee Rooms!'

'To Lord Stephen!' Matthew Grange held his mug high in a toast. 'Give him some time, gentlemen, and he'll be a full member—and soon after that, a Steward!'

A cheer broke out, warming Stephen's heart. He shook Toswick's hand in gratitude. He had made solid progress toward his goals. He had that, at least, even if he never found Pratchett and made a grand entrance into the racing world. Yet he had no desire to drop his fruitless quest for the damned horse. He felt driven to find the animal, by the weight of expectations that awaited him at home, and now, by the unwise wish to impress Mae.

And that was the thought that had been making him more uncomfortable as the afternoon wore on. He'd been painfully honest with Mae last evening. Perhaps it was time he was brutally honest with himself, now.

Because what he feared was that this adventure was slowly becoming more about her than it was about Ryeton or Pratchett or even Fincote.

He sighed and ordered a pint.

Toswick did too, although it was clear that he was having a much better day. 'Ah, it was a great day all around, was it not?' the earl reflected. 'Even though Butterfly lost—but by a nose only!' He shook his head. 'Now there's a horse that hates to lose.'

His manager agreed. 'You've called that one right. She's like a lady with the megrims tonight. Her groom will have his hands full, trying to console her.'

'Further good news for you, though, Manning,' Grange said. 'There's a good bit of talk about that private match we're putting together.'

Stephen summoned a smile. 'I'm looking forward to it.'

'You don't look it,' Toswick said bluntly. 'You look like a lad who has lost his best friend.'

'No, I've only lost a leg,' sighed Stephen.

'That makes two of us,' quipped Matthew Grange.

A moment of stunned silence held sway, and then there was a roar of laughter. Stephen laughed until he cried and then he laughed a little more. It took a good five minutes for order to be restored around their table and then Stephen called for a round of drinks and toasted his friend.

'Ah, me, but that was a good one.' Toswick chuckled and wiped his eyes. 'Are you still looking for Cray, then?' he asked.

'Yes, the man's a magician, I swear, for every time I think I've got a bead on him, he disappears.'

'Not a magician, but an invalid,' Toswick's manager said. He glanced Matthew's way. 'Cray took a bad spill off his horse and broke his leg. He's holed up in town, recuperating.'

Stephen nearly dropped his pint. 'Where?'

'At the Two Crowns, I believe?' The man sounded uncertain. 'I heard the stable lads gossiping about it. They all think Cray hit his head in the fall.'

'Why?'

'He's gone daft. He's holed up in the taproom, sitting on his chair like a throne and holding court like a prince. He's still making his book, but only with the stable lads and grooms that frequent the place.' He shook his head. 'And they say he's keeping Pratchett on his book for the Guineas. He's still taking bets on the horse.' He took a long swig. 'Daft indeed.'

'Unless he knows something about Pratchett's disappearance,' said Stephen, sitting up straight. 'Perhaps Ryeton was right about him all along.'

'Can't be,' the manager disagreed. 'Cray's been holed up at the Crowns for over a fortnight. And believe me, if he'd used some of the Newmarket lads to do the job, word would have got around.'

But the man was taking bets on the horse? In all likelihood, if Cray didn't take Pratchett, he might know who did.

This was it then, Stephen's moment of decision. Did he follow this lead and try again to chase that damned horse down? It was clear now that he didn't have to. He could drop this quest and be content with the progress that he'd already made on his goals. He had a race that would launch Fincote, even if it wasn't meteoric. He had a foot in, a measure of respect from the men of racing.

But it wasn't enough. Fincote's launch had to be as spectacular as he could possibly contrive, the sort that could still happen, if only he found Pratchett. And what of Mae? Even if he succeeded, there were still obstacles standing in their way. His secrets, her father, perhaps even her own inclination. He wasn't sure he could ever find a way to have both her and the sort of success that Fincote needed.

But he had to try.

Stephen stood. 'Thank you for the information,' he said sincerely. 'And for the company,' he said to the table at large. 'And for the laugh,' he told Matthew. 'You've replaced your leg with a beauty, now I'm going to go and find mine.'

Mae had thought that Miss Hague had only been engaging in so much hyperbole when she complained that Lord Ryeton's horses lived better than his women, but now she had cause to agree.

The earl's stables were magnificent. A line of yews and white gravel led the way to the grouped buildings. Long rows of box stalls sat open to fresh air and the gentle south-facing sun. Grassy paddocks were shaded and inviting, and the ladies cooed over the mares and foals. Small outbuildings held tack and supplies.

The tour for the ladies was to be given by Mr Walker, Lord Ryeton's head groom. Lady Ryeton hung on his arm as he emerged from the stable office.

'I'm sure that I cannot speak for all of you ladies,' she

said with a wink. 'But I'm also sure that my favourite part of racing is all the delicious men.'

Mae couldn't help but feel uncomfortable for the man. Surely he'd laboured for years to earn his elevated position among the earl's servants, likely since he was a boy. He might not appreciate being ogled for his manly frame. But Mr Walker did not seem to mind the countess at all. He patted her hand and, bending at the waist, swept an arm to welcome the rest of the ladies to his domain.

Several of the women around Mae sighed. Walker was a grand specimen of a man, finely moulded and in possession of a beautifully chiselled chin. 'An honour it is, to have so many fine ladies in our stables,' he pronounced with a broad Irish brogue. 'I'm happy to be of service, if ye will tell me what it is that ye're wishin' to know.'

'Anything,' breathed Miss Lucy. 'Anything at all that you wish to tell us.'

Her sister nudged her.

'Everything,' Lady Toswick said firmly. 'We would love to see how you keep Lord Ryeton's fine animals, sir, and to see and hear how they are trained. We want to know all the things that go into forming a good racehorse.'

'Well, now. The truth is that good racehorses are bred as much as trained, but explaining the Stud Book and all the, uh, intricacies of breeding, are beyond my skills.' He cast a glance in Miss Lucy's direction and grinned. 'But even the best-bred animals do need training and care. I'll be happy to show you how all of Lord Ryeton's lovelies spend their days.'

'And nights,' whispered Miss Lucy.

This time her sister poked her with her parasol.

It truly was an interesting hour as Mr Walker took them through all the various outbuildings and barns. He spoke of purges and sweats and training schedules and bran mashes. He let them inspect the stalls where the horses slept.

'But why are there cots along the walls of the stalls?' Miss Lucy asked.

'The grooms sleep in with the horses in their care,' Mr Walker explained. 'Since Pratchett's disappearance, they have been locked in for the night.'

'All night?' Miss Lucy was aghast.

'Well, we do let them out for morning chores.' He grinned at the girl.

The long line of spacious stalls was impressive, with at least twenty animals in residence this week and room for ten more. Mae's only disappointment was that she saw no sign of anything that might help her and Stephen.

'Where was Pratchett's stall, Mr Walker?' she asked as the tour began to wind down.

A pained look crossed the man's face. He led them down the centre aisle, past the last occupied stall and stopped at a large and spacious box, still being kept in readiness for its missing occupant.

'The horse was stolen from here?' Mae's mother looked about her with a frown. It might have been doubt in her expression as she noted the busy and public nature of the spot.

'Right out from under our noses,' Walker answered grimly.

'But don't you have dogs about the stables?' Lady Toswick asked. 'Surely they would have raised an alarm.'

'No dogs.' Lady Ryeton spoke firmly and gave a shudder. 'I can't abide dogs. I won't have them on any of our estates.'

'Likely they would have been drugged, in any case.' Mr Walker's sigh was heavy.

'The whole thing must have been terribly distressing.' The incorrigible Miss Lucy was definitely batting her eyelashes at him.

'What has happened to Pratchett's groom—the man found unconscious after the horse's disappearance?' Mae asked.

'He's recovered, but he's still fair upset,' Walker admitted. 'I've given another horse into his care, but his heart is not in it.' Clearly finished with the topic, he gestured back down the direction they'd come. He set out, heading for the stable office, and all the ladies began to trail behind.

Except for Mae. She stayed, staring into the empty stall. Quiet settled over the spot as the ladies and their chattering grew farther away. *Where are you?* She sent the silent question out to the missing horse.

Her mind and her stomach were churning. This hunt for Pratchett had unexpectedly given her a second chance with Stephen. She felt closer to him than ever before. Perhaps it didn't matter if they never found Pratchett.

Except that it did, for it was important to him. They

were so close to finally unravelling this puzzle. She wanted to solve it for him and set Stephen's feet firmly on whichever path he wished to follow. Whatever happened between them from here, she didn't want it to be by default.

Mmmrph.

Mae jumped, but it was just a barn cat rubbing affectionately against her ankles.

'Well, and a good afternoon to you, too.' She was forgivably and immediately reminded of Pratchett's cat companion, for this animal was black, but had a white chest that almost looked like a cravat, two creamy boots on her back feet and a matching tip to her tail. She butted Mae imperiously with her head until she bent down to stroke her. 'You certainly are a bossy one,' she said with a smile. 'But such a pretty girl, too.'

The cat purred in response, but then darted swiftly away, heading along the row of unoccupied stalls.

'Oh, do you have a nest of kittens back there?' Mae asked. Perhaps it was foolish to talk to a cat, but suddenly she longed for the warm and simple pleasure that only soft and cuddly kittens could give. Lady Ryeton's and Miss Lucy's opinion notwithstanding, but Mae would much rather admire a litter of new babies than ogle Mr Walker. Handsome though he might be, he couldn't warm her heart with his smile as Stephen could, nor could he set her pulse a-quiver as Stephen could with just a look from his clear blue eyes.

Hopeful, she followed the cat until she stopped at the last stall in the long row. An obvious coquette, she glanced at Mae before she jumped lightly up on to the open half-door. With another little call she disappeared inside.

The light shone dimmer at this end and the quiet lay heavier in the air. Instinctively, Mae lightened her step. 'Do you have your darlings hidden in there?' she asked in a crooning, sing-song voice.

Her answer, as she stepped closer, came in the form of an angry squeal. Mae let out a corresponding scream and jumped back as an equine head shot out from the stall, teeth bared and aimed for her arm with vicious intent.

Gasping, she backed away. Thick mucous sprayed as the horse squealed again. The drainage coated the sides of its mouth and around the tender skin of its nostrils. The animal's eyes rolled in its pique, and it thumped its displeasure in a deafening boom as it kicked the barn wall.

'Miss!' Mr Walker had reached her side. He gripped her arms and tried to pull her away. 'Miss! Are you all right?'

'Wot's this?' A burly, heavily scowling man came around the corner of the building, a heavy bucket in one hand. He took one look at the horse, still snorting his displeasure and indulging in little hops off his front feet before dropping the bucket and turning to glare at Mae. 'What in bleedin' hell is she doin' down here, Walker? You was supposed to keep the *liedies* away!'

Mae stared at him. He sounded like a Seven-Dials cracksman, not a Suffolk-bred groom. He didn't look like any stable lad she'd ever seen before, either. He glared and took a threatening step towards her.

She held her ground, long enough to glance past

him and get a good look at the horse. A bay with four white feet.

'Come along, miss. Let's get you back to the stable office with the other ladies.'

'What is wrong with that animal, Mr Walker?' Mae was still stubbornly standing her ground.

'He's suffering from an equine malady. He'll be fine in a couple of days, but he's skittish in the meantime.'

'He's *sick,* is wot's wrong wit' 'im,' the other man growled. 'It makes him cranky, jest like interferin' liedies make me cranky.' He laughed. 'The difference is, he gets oats and molasses and yer lucky ye got away with all yer fingers.'

Mae stepped back, ready to go with Mr Walker just in order to get away from the unpleasant man. The horse didn't appear to like him any better than he liked her. Lightning quick, he tried to take a chunk out of the hands that held the upturned bucket over his feed box. The burly man cursed and jumped back just as she had.

Mae turned away, but before she could take a step, the cat jumped from her perch in the corner of the stall. The animal leapt lightly and landed on the horse's rump.

Mae gasped in alarm.

Before she could get a protest past her lips, the horse stopped half-rearing. Daintily the cat walked down his rump and settled into the dip of the stallion's back, curling up contentedly like the spot had been made for her. The bay nickered and bent to nose at the sticky mass in its box.

Numb, Mae let herself be led away. She and Mr

Walker were met halfway down the row of stalls by the group of twittering ladies.

'Mae, are you all right?' Her mother looked pale with worry.

'I'm fine, Mama.' More truthfully, her brain was nearly rattling in her skull, so busily was it working.

'Good heavens, who knew horses could be so vicious?' Miss Lucy simpered up at the groom. 'Mr Walker, your job must be quite dangerous.'

'Just look at your skirts, Miss Halford.' Miss Metheny said, nearly scolding. 'You'll be lucky if they are not ruined.'

Mae glanced down, expecting to see a spray of horse mucous across her skirts. Instead, she found a smear of white marring her hems.

'It is all over your hands, as well!' Miss Metheny could not hide her disgust.

Mae looked down at the white streaks across her palm.

'Come along to the office,' Walker urged. 'We'll find a cloth and get you cleaned up.'

She didn't look him in the eye. Couldn't. Because voices were echoing in her head and broken images were sliding together to form an unbelievable whole. A bay with four white feet boarded alone in the middle of nowhere. Another here in Lord Ryeton's stables. A black cat and white streaks on her hands.

She had to find Stephen. Now.

She had to tell him that she'd found Pratchett. That he'd never really been lost at all.

Actually, Stephen had to disagree with Lord Toswick's stable manager. Chester Cray did not look so much like a king on a throne as a broody hen on her nest.

The Two Crowns was roaring with life. Racing men from every aspect of the sport filled the room, from the group of jockeys singing at the bar to the wealthy owners playing at cards at a corner table. Stephen even thought he saw a few disreputable-looking men suspected to be hired touts sitting with their heads together at a table. The taproom was doing a booming business and all about men were celebrating, commiserating or making plans for tomorrow's even bigger day of racing.

Except for Cray. He sat alone in a corner, comfortably ensconced on a padded chair, his broken leg propped up on a pillow and stool before him. He was surrounded by bits of paper. Ragged pieces, covered with scribbles, spread out across his lap and filled his chair. Layers of crumpled sheets lay deep on the floor all about him. He had his chin propped on a fist and sat quiet, apart from all the others. One look at the distance in his eyes and Stephen could see that the man was far away—and likely had no desire to be brought back to reality. He sat down near him, ordered a pint and waited.

It took a while for Cray to come back. Stephen rejected the eager offers of two tavern girls and made it clear to a couple of hard-eyed gamblers that he had no wish to join a game of any sort.

Finally, Cray moved. His chin came down, he looked around and started a little as he spied Stephen.

He grunted.

Stephen just waited.

'Manning, isn't it?' The leg's voice sounded creaky, as if it hadn't seen much use lately.

Stephen nodded. 'Cray.'

'I knew your father. You've the look of him.'

Another nod.

That look of distant reflection came over the man's face again. 'A good man, your father. He could scheme and manoeuvre with the best of them. Ruthless at it, too.'

Stephen suppressed a smile. That did sound like his father.

'Heard you were following in his rakish footsteps a while back. Thought you were going to turn out as wild as he. But now I hear you've gone respectable.'

'Sad, but true.' This time the grin did break out.

Cray did not look amused. 'Jockey Club's changing things. The whole damned sport has gone respectable.' He narrowed his eyes. 'At least on the surface. Or for a while.'

Stephen shrugged. 'Perhaps it is time. Racing might flourish even more if it goes respectable.'

Cray frowned. 'It'll take all the shine out o' it.' He sat silent for a moment, perhaps contemplating such a thing. 'Heard about your course,' he said at last. 'I'd likely visit it myself, were I not retiring.'

'Retiring?' Stephen was surprised.

'Yes.' The other man laid a hand on his thigh, above the splint on his broken leg. 'Something like this happens and suddenly you find yourself at a stop. With plenty of time to think.' He glanced about the crowded, noisy room. 'I think I'm done. This is my last book.'

He shot Stephen a sly glance. 'I contemplated going respectable myself.'

'I can highly recommend it.' Stephen laughed.

'I meant to retire in style.' His face bitter, he waved for a serving wench to bring him a drink. 'I thought I'd finally played out the one scheme guaranteed to get me a fortune as big as any of these titled toffs.' Worry appeared to settle over him like a blanket. 'Now I begin to think I been outplayed.'

Stephen gazed at the man steadily for a moment. Sudden understanding flashed between them. 'Ryeton,' was all he said.

Cray stared a bit longer, measuring Stephen like it was his own life hanging in the balance. As perhaps it was. At last he gave a slow nod.

'I mean to find that horse.' Stephen allowed all the earnestness and conviction he felt to colour his tone.

Cray still looked hard. 'Why?'

Stephen thought for a minute, and in the end, he decided to tell the man the truth. 'At first I wanted to find him because I thought if I returned him, I could convince the earl to race him at my track. I had a spectacular private match in mind to start us off right.'

'It's sound thinking.'

'But then I began to look into the matter. And no one knows anything. There are a million foolish conjectures and not one whiff of anything solid. That's significant in and of itself.'

Cray only nodded.

'You know this world as well as I do. Everybody talks. Endlessly. I should have been able to find some nuggets of truth behind the gossip. But there were none.

Why not? And then other things began to come to light and I began to come up with some very odd ideas, myself. And now I find that they make me even more determined.'

'Why?' Cray asked again.

'Because if what I've begun to suspect is correct, then Ryeton is the worst sort of hypocrite—spouting one set of principles while practising another. Because if he is perpetrating this fraud on all of us in the racing world, then it would do me and my track a world of good were I to expose him. Because he mortally insulted a friend of mine.' He breathed deep. 'Because I'm hoping to impress a lady.'

A crack of laughter exploded out of Cray. 'Now that sounds like your father's son!'

He continued to chuckle, but Stephen leaned forwards. 'Tell me why you are still taking bets on Pratchett for the Guineas.'

Silence reigned in their corner for several long moments. Stephen began to fear that Cray had offered as much co-operation as he was going to get.

'Bet,' the leg creaked at last. 'Bet. Not bets.'

Stephen thought about that for a moment. 'Only Ryeton?'

'Aye. I think I've begun to have the same inkling as you have—an idea of what he must be up to.' He swallowed. 'And if it's true, then that earl is an actor worthy of a place on Drury Lane. He had me that fooled, earlier this week.'

'You saw him after Pratchett's disappearance?'

Cray nodded. 'He came in here, cast down in his

cups. Sat at the bar drinking, pretending not to see me.'
He spat into a corner. 'Damn me for a fool.'

'You spoke to him?'

'Aye. The blighter owes me money, has done for
months. I admit I come on strong, asking after it.
But I never poisoned his horses.' He saw the reserve
in Stephen's eyes and grew vehement. 'Nor any other
man's, either! But my business has sorely suffered since
Ryeton began bandying my name about as a cheat.'

'So he came in here and you couldn't resist rubbing
his nose in his misery. How did he respond?'

'He was drunk and defiant. Or so I thought. He
swore he was going to find that horse in time to race
him in the Guineas. Now, I'd already heard several wild
theories as to what happened to that thoroughbred. I
heard an American stole him to strengthen the bloodlines over there. I heard one of Ryeton's enemies took
him and had him gelded to extract revenge and prevent
the earl from making a fortune in stud fees. And those
were the milder ideas. We all thought that no matter
which of them turned out to be true, there was no way
Pratchett was coming back to run that race.'

'You were so convinced that you gambled on it.'

Cray sighed. 'Aye. We bet all that the earl already
owed me and a king's ransom on top o' that. I thought
he must ha' been dead drunk to agree to such terms,
but I didn't feel guilty about it. I spent the last couple o'
days anticipatin' the rich life I was goin' to retire to.'

'But something has changed your mind?'

Cray looked at him out of the corner of his eye.
'Have you heard the stories about his countess? Run
out of town by her London creditors?'

Stephen nodded.

'It started me thinkin'. Then I heard a name.' He sighed. 'And I knew.'

Puzzled, Stephen frowned. 'A name?'

'A name that can only mean bad news. A man who goes by the handle o' Peck.' Cray was watching closely for Stephen's reaction. 'Heard o' him?'

'No. Should I have?'

'Depends. He's an ugly sort. The worst. Peck is short for Pecked to Death, which is what he done to the first toff what he killed—killed him slow with his knife, bit by bit.'

'Charming.' Stephen grimaced. And then he stilled. 'You heard this man's name in connection with Pratchett?'

'In connection with Ryeton. You should understand, Peck's name is not well known. The man's practically a trade secret for unsavory sorts. He keeps his head low and his hands dirty. The men who hire him are usually desperate enough to agree to his outrageous terms.'

'And now Ryeton's hired him?'

'That's what I heard. And I asks myself, why would the earl need a man like Peck on his payroll? And in his stables, no less?'

Stephen's heart rate ratcheted. 'I think we can both make a good guess why, can't we?'

'He'll ruin me.' Cray's shoulders drooped. 'I've won and lost fortunes in this business, but if that horse races and wins—it will finish me. I won't have a *sou* left to my name.' His expression hardened. 'And somehow I doubt that I'm the only fool he's convinced with his play-actin'. He's goin' to bring that horse out in the morning—miraculously rescued! Back from the dead! Ryeton will be swimming in sovereigns by night's fall tomorrow.'

Stephen sat, silently marvelling. It was a brilliant plan. He could scarce believe Ryeton had nearly pulled it off.

Cray growled low in his throat. 'It's no more than I deserve, lettin' a dastard like Ryeton get one over on me like that.'

Stephen stood. 'You won't be ruined if I stop him.'

'And how do you propose to do that?' The leg sounded amused at his presumption.

'Simple. I'm going to search the earl's stables. And I'm going to steal Pratchett back.'

Cray laughed. 'You've got spirit, boy, but Peck is dead skilled with a knife. You wouldn't make it within three feet of him without his blade piercin' yer heart.'

His mind was racing. 'Then I won't go alone.'

'Damn me if I wouldn't join you—were it not for this blasted leg.'

'Maybe next time.' Stephen turned to go. 'Thank you for sharing your information.'

Cray watched him go. Stephen was nearly to the door when he barked out his name. 'Manning?'

Stephen stopped at the urgent tone in the leg's voice.

'Come here and pick up one of those damned pieces of paper from the floor.'

Impatient to be off, Stephen nearly refused. But then he thought better of it. He did as the man asked.

'I'm making up a plan of Ryeton's stables for you.' Cray had pulled a pencil from his pocket and started scribbling. 'You fetch the satchel out from under this chair.'

Stephen did.

'Outside pocket. Small leather bag. It's yours.'

'What is it?' He held the bag up.

'Opium balls. What?' Cray barked at the expression on Stephen's face. 'I told ye I never poisoned a horse, not that I never drugged one.' He cocked an eyebrow at him. 'And be thankful that I did, for you won't be getting Pratchett to go anywhere with you without one o' them.' He paused thoughtfully. 'Wait a minute. Hand it back.' He took the bag and hefted it. 'Let me think. Too little and it will act as a stimulant. Too much and he'll be passed out on the stable floor. Let me…' He fetched out a few of the pellets inside and stuffed them in his pocket. 'There. That should be good to make sure he's only drowsy and docile.'

Stephen rubbed his brow. 'I can't believe I'm even thinking about doing this.'

Cray grinned. 'Yer father would be proud.' He handed over the map. 'One more thing. Peck's a right fearsome opponent. But he does got a weakness for fine French brandy.'

A slow smile spread over Stephen's face.

'Excellent.' A plan was already formulating in his head. 'I know just the person to serve it to him.'

Chapter Sixteen

Lady Toswick had planned a small soirée for the evening. What she got was a genuine crush—practically unheard of in Suffolk. But all the signs were there. Too many people stuffed into rooms too small to hold them? Stifling heat from hundreds of candles and a similar number of bodies? A riot of colour from flashing jewels, elaborate gowns and embroidered waistcoats? The list was complete.

It was to her great good fortune that nearly everyone was in a jovial mood. The first day of racing had been accounted a huge success. The races went off as scheduled, many of the favourites had won, but there had been enough surprises to give everyone something to talk about. Not to mention the fact that there was still all of the excitement of the Guineas to look forward to tomorrow.

Mae, for one, was glad of all the excitement and anticipation in the atmosphere, mainly because it masked her own agitation so well. She stood with her mother and several other ladies near the door to Lady Toswick's largest parlour, watching people enter. She took her gaze off of the entrance long enough to glance at her mother. No matter what else might happen, there was one reason why she would always remember this week fondly—her mother's new-found confidence in her circle of friends.

Her father approached, towing yet another eligible young gentleman in his wake. Mae suppressed a sigh. This one held a partnership in a bank and part-ownership of a four-year-old that had won his heat today. But Mae held absolutely no interest in him. She kept half an ear on the conversation and kept watch on the new arrivals. After a few minutes of mundane chit-chat, the gentleman retreated. Her father shot her a look of disgust.

She glanced back towards the door, watching for Stephen, but so far there had been no sign of him.

'Good heavens, but I recognise that look,' her mother said. The wistfulness in her tone caused Mae to look back. Her father had departed, no doubt in search of another candidate to offer up.

'I'm sorry, Mama. What was that you said?'

'Perhaps I should say that I recognise the feeling behind that look. I'm sure my face held just the same expression every day—as I waited for your father to pass by *my* father's shop on his way home from the dockyards.'

Embarrassed heat rose upwards from her chest. Mae was sure her cheeks must have gone red, but she didn't deny the implication behind her mother's words.

'Your father and I have worried for you, Mae. It seems like for a very long time.'

'I'm fine, Mama.'

'You certainly seem happier since we returned to England.' A frown marred her mother's still smooth brow. 'Did we do the wrong thing, taking you away?'

Mae reached out to grasp her mother's hand. 'Absolutely not. I needed to get away. To grow up, I suppose. You did what you thought was right and I never thanked you for it. But I will now.' She leaned down and kissed her mother's cheek. 'Thank you.'

'I love you, Mae.' It came out in a whisper.

'As I do you. I'm sorry if it was a hardship for you—all the travel, I mean.'

'I would do anything for you, dear.' Her mother smiled. 'But I am glad to be home.' The smile faded and Mae could see that nerves still lurked. 'Tell me just one thing, please. He is a good man, isn't he?'

'Who?'

'The one you are watching and waiting for.'

'I'm not…' Mae started to protest, but she stopped herself. 'He is, Mama,' she said softly. 'He's not perfect. He's flippant and can be horrendously bossy, and sometimes he does things that don't seem to make a bit of sense. He hasn't a clue what he wants, and he makes me insane, so that I don't either.' She sighed. 'But I know he's a good man. With all my heart.'

'Your father and I only want you to be safe and happy, dear.'

'I'm trying.' She took her mother's hand again and squeezed. 'But it may not be easy.'

Her mother's chuckle held a definite ring of irony. 'It never is with you, Mae.'

Impatient, Stephen pushed his way through the crowd gathered at Titchley. Who knew that there were even this many people *in* Newmarket?

He forced his way into the largest parlour. The air was close and warm in here, despite the energetic waving of many fans. Frustration loomed, but he swatted it away. At first he had planned on missing this gathering entirely. But it would be hours before he could do anything about Peck, and he didn't plan on doing it alone, in any case. He craned his neck to look for the real reason he had taken the time to suit himself out in evening dress.

Mae. He couldn't wait to share with her what he'd discovered. Very privately, he admitted to himself that he was hoping to inspire a particular look upon her face—that old expression of pleasure and admiration that used to grate on his nerves, but now he found he longed to see again.

A space opened up to the right. Stephen wormed his way along the wall. Nearly halfway in, he paused to scan the crowd again. Now at last he caught a glimpse of Mae. She stood across the room, speaking with her mother. Stephen pulled up short, stunned just a little. How beautiful she looked. He needed a moment just to savour it. My God. When had he begun catching his breath at the sight of her?

She was dressed in a gorgeous, cream-coloured gown, cut tight and clinging about the bodice and on to the tiny, cropped sleeves. Rich, scarlet brocade sashed her small waist and trimmed her skirts. Matching creamy kid gloves encased her arms, fingertip to elbow, but above and beyond lay a gleaming expanse of soft, glowing skin.

Everything tightened at the sight of her. He felt he might drown under a great wave of pure *want*.

His view was blocked, suddenly. Her father had stepped up next to her and brought another man along with him. Stephen craned to see. He waited, fists clenched as the introductions were made and the small talk began. Stephen's blood began to sing, a dark song of impatient possession. He took a step towards them.

And the gentleman turned in profile and Stephen realised just whom it was. Barnett, a horse breeder of some renown and heir to the Marquess of Badesworth.

Silent and eloquent, Stephen began to swear. Damn and blast her mission and his own doubts. Deep down, though, he knew that wasn't really what was bothering him. Mae was not the sort of woman to be swayed by a title.

But he was beginning to wonder just what would sway her. She'd said she was searching for a husband. Yet to his eyes she appeared to be more vested in the search for Pratchett. She hadn't shown any marked interest in any gentleman he knew of, save perhaps for Matthew Grange.

Stephen ignored the surge of irritation that rose up at the thought. *He* was the one she'd been kissing, rolling about in the hay with, tempting beyond all reason. And yet he had the sinking fear that Mae had only been exploring passion with the same zest and zeal with which she pursued everything else in life. After all, in her eyes, who could be safer than the man who had never wanted her?

But it was becoming clear he did want her, and not just for a roll in the hay. He was also beginning to wonder if the unthinkable had happened, and for the first time, *Mae* did not know what she truly wanted.

She had said she only wished to be happy. If he was certain of anything it was that she deserved no less. She deserved to fall in love and spend her life using those prodigious skills of hers to drive her husband to distraction—and spoil him rotten and make him blissfully happy. He wanted to be that man. He felt better for making the admission to himself. But could he do it without making her miserable, as she said, for the rest of her life? He just didn't know.

Mae glanced up just then and caught sight of him. He relaxed a little as her face lit up. She bent and said something to her mother, excused herself from the group and started towards him.

He moved forwards as well, but they found themselves caught, with the crowd working against them. The countess's musicians had begun to play and footmen were clearing a space for dancing. Mae was caught in the flow of those wishing to dance as they filed eagerly in. Stephen was stuck behind the column of others moving to escape.

He craned his neck and met her gaze. Heat sprang to life between them, tangling through the throng, connecting them in some elemental and deeply satisfying way. Doubt receded. She smiled. He shrugged, then cocked his head towards the back of the room and pointed to a bank of potted trees.

They were moving then, following invisible strands and angling toward each other. Suddenly he'd arrived and she was pushing past a group of spectators. Eyes dancing, she reached for his hands.

'Stephen,' she gasped.

At the same time he began, 'Mae—'

'It's Ryeton!'

Their words emerged in unison, and so did their shocked laughs. Stephen, rueful, shook his head. Trust Mae to steal his thunder! But that thought faded as he took her in. There it was, the look he'd been waiting for, but altered slightly. She radiated surprise and delight, but that edge of anxiety that he remembered from long ago was gone. It made him glad. It was so much better, more fulfilling, to meet as equals.

'We're a pair, aren't we?' He didn't give her a chance to answer. Instead he tugged and pulled her a little farther into the corner. Suddenly conscious of the many eyes in the room, he dropped her hands.

'Listen, Mae,' he said urgently. 'You were right all along. Ryeton is financially strapped.'

'Yes, all the signs were there at the Ryetons' estate today. It looks as if they've been selling off valuables.'

'Probably to raise mercenary fees,' Stephen replied sourly. 'I would have never have suspected the earl of such a nasty piece of business. He hired a thug to do the dirty work, kidnap the horse and keep his secrets. I have to admit, it's brilliant in its own way. The price has long since gone out on that thoroughbred to win the Guineas. But Ryeton is betting on him, and if he produces Pratchett and wins—he could collect a fortune several times over.'

'So that's it!' There was wonder in her voice and a grudging respect. 'I'd worked out it was Ryeton, but I couldn't make out how he was going to profit on his scheme.'

'I'm going to need help dealing with this man he's hired.' He narrowed his eyes. 'But we have to do it. This is suddenly about more than trying to coerce Ryeton to race at Fincote Park. That part of our plan is dead now.' He felt a fleeting regret for the loss of that perfect opportunity. 'But he's trying to perpetrate a fraud on the entire racing world. We have to stop him—which means we have to get Peck to tell us where Pratchett is.'

She started. 'Stephen—I already know where Pratchett is! That horse in the barn—with Miss Hague's Minna—he's nothing but a decoy! Ryeton switched the horses. Pratchett was never kidnapped—they only painted white feet on him and moved him to a different stall. And moved the other horse out into the country.'

'What?' He listened, stunned as she told her tale. When she had finished, he simply gazed at her a moment. He scrubbed a hand in his hair and it stuck there a minute, while he stood frozen. No one else could have pieced so many disparate clues together to come up with the frighteningly simple truth. 'I'm speechless,' he finally admitted. 'I hesitate to damn you with faint praise, but quite simply, you amaze me.'

'Thank you.' He'd pleased her with the compliment. He'd also awakened a hunger in her eyes. And unless he was mistaken, a vivid memory of their last encounter had caused the sudden twisting and clasping of her hands.

He knew exactly how she felt. Excitement coursed through his veins just from the thought of what they had done—and all that they had yet to do. It fought for space along with gratitude and determination and the nearly irresistible desire to touch that glorious expanse of skin. He took a step to close the space between them.

And stopped as his foot was crushed beneath the blunt end of an elaborately carved wooden peg.

'Do excuse me, Stephen!' Matthew Grange's eyes were sparkling with repressed laughter. 'Clearly I am still learning my way with this thing.' He bent to lovingly thump his wooden leg. At the same time he lowered his voice and addressed the both of them. 'I do believe it is time to break up this little tête-à-tête. People begin to talk and the lady's parents are growing concerned.'

Stephen glanced up. Across the room Barty Halford frowned in their direction while his wife whispered furiously in his ear. He wanted to groan. They still had so much to accomplish and he had to find a way to do it without alienating her father and ruining his chances with Mae and with Fincote.

But nearer to hand, couples formed and swept on to the dance floor as the first strains of a waltz began. He looked back to Mae and held out his hand. 'Shall we dance, then?'

She nodded. Her hand eased into his and the fire banked inside of him blazed suddenly high. Without another word he swept her into the dance.

Later, if asked, Mae would vow that it was the dance that changed her life. Stephen's arms closed solid and warm about her. More than anything she wished she could let go and just melt against him. Her body sighed. It was the only word for the complete release of tension and the longing she felt to mould herself against his hard form.

It was impossible. So she looked up instead, into his eyes. And that proved to be even more dangerous.

There was a light there that she'd never seen before. She imagined that it was triumph, of course. Perhaps a thrill at the challenge that lay ahead. And desire. The knowledge of how incredible passion could be between them—and the sweet anticipation that it might be yet again. But it was also more than that.

Stephen was happy. She felt his contentment flow into her, warming her blood, crawling into her very sinews and bones. It was beautiful. It made her *feel* beautiful, and whole.

Her eyes slid closed. For long minutes she lost herself to the glory of the music and the moment. Stephen gave in to it as well; she could feel his surrender in the grip of his hands, in the intimate press of his legs to hers, and in the graceful, floating ease with which he guided them about the dance floor.

And that was when she knew she'd come full circle. Her campaign was forgotten, her plans and strategies left behind. Here she was, right back where she'd started, two years ago, wanting Stephen Manning with all of her heart.

Yet, thankfully, not everything remained the same. There were new levels to their friendship, their partnership. So easily had he come to share his victory with her tonight. So naturally had he assumed she would take part in the next step. He was the one who had gifted her with appreciation and acceptance and passion and all the things she'd vowed to have in a husband.

Perhaps she needed a new campaign, with new strategies designed to win his heart. Because she longed for it, and for his unfathomable blue eyes and his maddening imperious ways and his warm acceptance and his heated kisses.

But there was one other thing that was different now, too. She wasn't that young girl any more, happy to accept whatever part of himself Stephen was willing or able to give. She wanted all of him. And no campaign of hers was going to be successful in flushing it out. She sighed. He had to choose to give it.

The music wound to a finish and she opened her eyes—to find Stephen's brief instant of joy had fled. The mirrors were back up and over his eyes and serenity had been replaced with grim determination.

She felt the loss of his elation almost as a physical pain. And she knew then, that it didn't matter what had eased his soul for those brief, shining moments. She would do anything to bring such peace to his eyes again.

'Ryeton,' he said, breaking the spell completely. 'The earl put it about that his horse was kidnapped—and we're going to do him the favour of turning the lie into truth. Tonight, Mae.'

She nodded, not quite ready to fall all the way back into the real world.

'First, I'm going to take you back to Matthew. We are going to need his help. Can you fill him in on the whole insane story?'

'Of course.'

'I want to thank you, Mae. None of this would have come together, if not for you.'

She blinked, and then scowled ferociously. 'That sounded remarkably final. I hope you don't think you are going to do this without me.'

'And have you sneaking out of the house to follow me?' He grinned down at her and squeezed her hand where it lay on his arm. 'I wouldn't dream of it. In any case, I fear this is a job too big for even the two of us.'

They had arrived back to where Matthew Grange stood at the edge of the dancing. He handed her over to him in a formal manner. 'Mae has a story to tell you, Matthew. I hope you will listen carefully.'

Mr Grange spared a smile for her. 'I should be delighted to do so.' He shot a curious glance between the two of them. 'Something tells me it will be a fascinating tale.'

Stephen didn't respond. His focus had remained on her. 'This isn't going to be easy. Are you sure?'

She gave a quiet nod.

'Explain everything to Matthew. Afterwards, I'm afraid you'll need to develop a headache and retire early.' He glanced across the room. 'Will your parents worry overmuch?'

She shook her head.

'Two o'clock, then. Behind the clapboard barn beyond the stables. There's a narrow lane behind it. You and Josette meet us there. Wear dark clothes. And be careful.'

'Us?' Matthew said hopefully. 'I'm not sure what the

two of you are up to, but it sounds like too much fun to be missed.'

'Oh, we definitely need you,' Stephen assured him.

Mae felt Matthew straighten a little, under her arm. Perhaps he had not expected to hear such a thing again.

Stephen bowed and turned to go. After a single step, though, he paused. 'Mae?'

'Yes?'

'Thank you. You can't know, but I find that this is even more important to me than I had thought.'

'You're welcome,' she whispered. But he was wrong. She knew it was important to him. She only wished she knew why.

Chapter Seventeen

Had they been in London, the hour would have been too early and society would just have hit its stride. This was Newmarket, though, and aside from a few dedicated gamblers tucked into taverns, most of the town was anticipating an early morning at the course and had gone to bed.

Stephen's leg bounced impatiently as he and Matthew made their way through the darkened streets and headed north towards Titchley. He'd done what he could. They were perhaps a few minutes late, but he judged that they were thoroughly prepared.

The ladies were waiting as Matthew manoeuvred their farm cart down the narrow lane. Swathed in dark cloaks, they emerged from the shadows of the barn.

'Don't stop, just slow to a roll,' Stephen said low to Matthew. He clambered to the back edge of the cart and pulled the women in one by one.

'A farm cart?' Mae asked as he hauled her in.

'We are in disguise,' Stephen told her.

'Addy's going to be so angry that she missed this,' she muttered.

Stephen laughed. He held her a tad too close, for just a little too long, considering their situation. His blood immediately heated, but her huge grin only broadcast her delight in the adventure.

He found he couldn't let her go. For just a moment he wanted to hold her tight. Ridiculously, in the midst of all this, he actually had the urge to take the risk and lay bare his heart. Mae made herself vulnerable every day. How could he do less?

But he could not. He still had to secure Fincote Park's success before he could worry about his happiness.

And they had work to do before any of that could happen. So he contented himself with a sly grin and a quick, clandestine caress to her backside before he settled her safely towards the front of the cart, between two casks of oats. Josette he perched comfortably on a saddle. He paused for a moment, swaying with the cart's slow and steady motion, and had to laugh at his incongruous cargo.

An heiress. A French maid. Oats, carrots and sugar. Loaded pistols, assorted tack and a special basket with a latch. All of the implements needed for stealing a not-truly-kidnapped thoroughbred currently masquerading as a sick hack.

He met Mae's eye and grinned. 'Of all of the rigs we've got up to, all of the pranks we've pulled in the past, this must be the oddest.'

Her answer came back unexpectedly fierce. 'But the one with the biggest pay-off.'

Stephen silently seconded that as he moved to return to the bench with Matthew. 'Keep your heads down, ladies. We're going to stop to formulate our strategy after we leave the town.'

'Dead.' Mae whispered in answer. 'Addy's going to kill me quite dead.'

They pulled the wagon to a halt in a stand of trees somewhere between Newmarket and Stetchworth. Matthew pulled a covered lantern from beneath the bench seat and climbed awkwardly down. Nimble as goats, Mae and Josette hopped out of the back of the cart before Stephen could make it back to assist them.

The night was warm and clear. Through the treetops, starlight twinkled like a spill of diamonds across the sky. When Matthew slid back the cover of the lantern, however, the four of them found themselves isolated in a bubble of warm light.

Stephen cleared his throat. 'I wish to be clear about a few things. Despite my earlier remark, this is no childish prank.' He cast a wry glance around the group. 'I don't think anyone here has ever shied away from a chance at mischief, but this man we are facing tonight is dangerous. We have to approach this in a serious and thoughtful manner. And I need to know now if anyone wishes to abstain from participating.' He sighed. 'God knows I wouldn't blame you.'

He was met with silence. And a snort from Mae.

'Then I will assume that we are all united in this by choice.' He pulled the map Cray had drawn from his pocket. 'Let's start with the layout of the stables.'

Everyone leaned forwards over the open back of the cart. Josette flipped her cloak back and out of the way.

Stephen forgot what he was going to say next. Beside him, Matthew gulped audibly.

'What?' The silence had gone on too long for Mae. She followed the direction of their gazes. 'Oh.' She lifted a shoulder. 'Josette knows what she is doing.'

The French girl was dressed in a skirt with a high waist and a higher hem. Her ankles and section of calf showed below—and above... Stephen swallowed.

'I thought you told them to wear dark clothes?' Matthew choked out.

Josette rolled her eyes. 'Dark clothes?' she asked. 'Bah. A situation like this—it calls for violence or seduction, *non*?' The disparaging look she cast in his and Matthew's shared direction might have shattered a lesser man's confidence.

'We assumed it would be seduction,' Mae put in.

'And since I would never in a hundred years allow *mademoiselle* to do such a thing—'

Not in a million years.

'—I dressed appropriately,' the maid finished. She ran a hand over the blouse made of the lightest linen. It lay low across her shoulders and practically non-existent next to her bosom. It was clear—abundantly—that she wore nothing underneath.

'This shirt, it is made for seduction. It starts high—'

That was *high*?

Josette shrugged a shoulder and the whole thing slipped even lower on the right side. 'And it goes lower with each—'

'No need for a demonstration,' Stephen objected quickly.

'Shut up, man, and let the lady finish.' Matthew's eyes were firmly fixed on the maid's widening expanse of skin.

Mae frowned at Matthew. 'Stop teasing them, Josette,' she ordered. 'We have work to do.'

The maid muttered something in French. Something about what Mae was wearing. He eyed her cloak and looked away. Stephen didn't want to know. Or perhaps he just didn't want Matthew to see.

He shook his head to clear it. 'This is a rendering of the stables. Mae, if you can add anything, let me know.' He pointed. 'The gates are here. Ryeton is either worse off than we thought, or he is arrogantly confident—'

'I vote for the latter,' Mae said, low.

'—because they appear to be neither locked nor guarded.'

'There was no one attending them when the ladies came through.'

'I checked it out earlier this evening, as well. I circled around and found the back gate, where the deliveries are made. We'll enter there.'

'How did you get onto the estate?' Matthew asked.

'Before I attended Lady Toswick's soirée as an invited guest, I stopped by Lord Ryeton's stables as a hired messenger.' Stephen laughed at the look on their faces. 'I dressed in old clothes and went to speak with Pratchett's old groom.'

'Patrick,' Josette spoke up suddenly. 'I spoke with him.'

'Yes, Patrick. Mae said you didn't believe he was involved. I'd hoped for his co-operation.'

'He has no part in this hoax. I would swear to it.'

'That is what he maintained this evening when I spoke with him.'

'I believe him,' she insisted.

'I did too. He was genuinely angry when he thought about that blow to his head.'

'He has suffered headaches,' Josette said sadly.

'Well, no one else is likely to believe that he had nothing to do with this great mess,' Matthew asserted. 'I hope you told him so.'

'I did. I advised him to pretend I had brought a message regarding a family emergency and make himself scarce. I also gave him enough blunt to head back home to Dublin and perhaps on to the Americas.' Stephen watched Josette, but she didn't appear to have anything to say to that. 'In return, I asked him to make a couple of arrangements regarding the box stalls. What that means for us is that Pratchett's old stall is still empty, of course, but now the one next to it will be as well.' He pointed out the spot on the map.

'All the rest of these,' Mae said with a sweep of her hand, 'will have grooms sleeping inside. But they are locked in and not let out until morning.'

'Yes, but still, we are going to have to keep this quiet if we don't want to raise an alarm.' Stephen pointed again. 'Pratchett is currently here—at the end of the row, away from the others.'

'Yes, because of his illness.' Mae's sarcasm was cut short when she blinked and straightened. 'You don't think he's really ill, do you?'

'I doubt it. It just gave them a good excuse to keep everyone away.'

'Pratchett's groom doesn't sleep in with him,' Mae said. 'I got a good look in his stall, after he tried to bite me. There was no cot.'

'His groom is no groom at all, but the thug Ryeton

hired to see all this through. And if he's not in the stall, then you can be sure that he's somewhere nearby.' Stephen looked very seriously at the French girl. 'He's a bad man, Josette. Are you sure you'll be fine? That you can handle him?'

She threw her shoulders back. 'Of course.'

'Of course,' echoed Matthew.

Mae shot him another discomforted look.

'We're not bawds and pimps, here,' Stephen protested. 'There is no need for you to actually seduce him, Josette. Cray says he has a weakness for expensive French brandy. I've got some and I've doctored it with a bit of laudanum. There's a decanter and a couple of mugs in the cart. If you can get him to drink enough of it, even we should be able to handle him.' He laughed.

Matthew didn't.

'But, Josette, will you be able to fend him off, if he wishes to…you know.' Blushing furiously, Mae refused to look at anyone but her maid.

'But of course. This I know how to do.' Josette patted Mae's hand in reassurance.

'I thought you might pretend that you had planned to meet Pratchett's groom.'

'Patrick.'

'Patrick. And that you were dejected to find him gone.'

'Ah, yes. First I sprinkle a little of this brandy about me.' The maid was warming to her role. 'Then I will be sobbing a little—quietly and very prettily.'

'Outside Pratchett's stall, so he is sure to find you.'

'Yes. I shall offer him a drink and I shall begin to tell him of my life. It is a very interesting story I tell, you see, with just enough spicy bits to keep any man listening. And drinking.'

'Perfect,' Stephen told her. 'It would be best if you could lure him down the row of empty stalls a bit. Get him all the way to Pratchett's old box if you can. Tell him you need a little privacy.' He glanced at that blouse she wore, once more. 'He won't object. Trust me. Once you are in a stall, then I will sneak in and dose Pratchett with one of these.' He held up a small leather bag.

'What is it?' asked Mae.

'Opium balls.'

Matthew shook his head.

'Don't ask,' Stephen answered his friend's silent question. 'Just be happy that while Peck is getting inebriated, so will Pratchett. It's the only way we'll get that horse out of there without a colossal fuss.'

'You have oats in the cart?' asked Mae. She pulled a thick bottle from her cloak. 'Mix them with this. Molasses. Pratchett likes it and it's likely the only way you'll get the drug in him without getting your fingers taken off.'

'You're an angel,' Stephen told her as he took the bottle. 'After we dose the horse, Mae and I will wait in an empty stall next to Josette. If you need help, or once you are ready for me to come in and take him out, all you'll have to do is rap on the wall.'

'Why, exactly, am I here?' Matthew asked plaintively.

'Who else can drive the wagon half so well?' Mae asked him.

Stephen wished she'd stop paying his friend so damned much attention. If she was going to show anyone a preference, he damned well wanted it to be him.

'I need you to keep watch,' he told Matthew. 'I'll need you to park here.' He showed his friend the spot on the map. 'Once Peck is taken care of and Pratchett is ready, then bring the cart around so we can hitch the horse to the back.'

'But then what shall we do with him?' asked Mae.

'We'll take him to my estate,' Matthew told her. 'It's not far, just a few miles away, in Mildenhall. I'll keep him safe there until the stewards and the magistrate can decide what to do with Ryeton.' He took on a malicious cast. 'It'll be my pleasure to do it, too.'

The admiring look Josette cast at Stephen had him nearly blushing. 'You are an accomplished schemer,' she said with approval. 'You have thought of all the things we need. Let us hope you have also thought of all the things that might go wrong.'

'Good Lord, everyone cross your fingers and pray nothing goes wrong.' Stephen couldn't help glancing in Mae's direction. *Look at me.* That compliment would have sounded much sweeter had it come from her.

She was staring at the map, seemingly completely absorbed in the plan. Watching her, his heart sank a little.

'It's going to take all of us to bring this off,' he said with a sigh. 'Does everybody understand the plan?'

A chorus of affirmatives answered him.

'Then let's get moving.'

Chapter Eighteen

Mae crouched low in the farm cart as they approached the back gates to Lord Ryeton's estate. This was it—the last push to rescue Pratchett. The last chance to push Stephen into seeing that they had a future together beyond Ryeton's exposure.

She had indulged in such rich fantasies as she prepared for this. She'd imagined the intimacy as she and Stephen worked in tandem, how they would think and act in synchronicity. She had to laugh at herself a little, now. This was dangerous business. And they were caught up in a fellowship, not a partnership. She understood the necessity. But she could still mourn the lost opportunity.

It was not in Mae's nature to leave anything to chance—especially not something as important as her future. Yet, she had determined that in this battle between them, the ball was firmly in Stephen's court. If they were to move ahead together, then Stephen was going to have to make some difficult decisions.

She looked down and adjusted her cloak. Of course, that didn't mean that she couldn't give him a little *incentive*.

They made it to the designated spot. Mae quieted the carthorse with a feeding bag while Stephen mixed the drugged oats for Pratchett and Josette collected her brandy and mugs.

Mae prepared to deploy her secret weapon. She waited until Stephen was gathering pistols to hand out. Once he was behind her, she removed her cloak. She tossed it into the cart with a small flourish.

She'd chosen her ensemble carefully tonight. A glance over her shoulder at Stephen's eye-popping, stuttering response told her that she had chosen well.

'Is something wrong, Stephen?' She turned to take a pistol from his lifeless hand and casually tucked it into her waistband.

'What are you wearing?' he demanded in a harsh whisper.

'It's only a divided skirt. I had it made when we were crossing into Italy. The riding was rough and these provided so much more freedom of movement.' And so much gratifying male attention. She ran a hand over her derriere, where the soft fabric fit snugly; hugging her bottom like no other garment had ever done before.

'But...your back...behind your...' Stephen couldn't finish his sentence.

'Well, I am usually astride when I'm wearing them,' she explained.

'You aren't astride now!' he protested.

Matthew twisted about in his seat, trying to see what

the fuss was about. He blinked. 'Thank you, Stephen, for bringing me along tonight,' he breathed.

With a strangled cry, Stephen stepped to block his view. 'Stay here,' he snarled at his friend. 'Keep watch. Whistle if you have any trouble.'

Keeping Mae in front of him, he jerked his head at Josette and led them both to the row of box stables. He positioned the maid along the outer stable wall—also the outer side of Pratchett's box. Pressing a finger to his mouth to signal silence, he tugged Mae with him to the small shed and tack room across the way. This was to be their vantage point.

It was locked. Stephen cursed the air blue under his breath while he jiggled the knob again. Helpless, he looked at his pistol, and then stood back, preparing to try to kick the door in.

'No.' Mae put a staying hand on his arm. 'I'll do it.' She dropped to her knees in front of the lock and pulled out two hairpins.

'How?' Stephen dropped beside her and mouthed the question.

Mae grinned and jerked her head back toward Josette.

It took several minutes, another hairpin and Stephen's help, but she got the thing unlocked. Stephen tugged her into the darkness of the shed. He set his bucket down and left the door open the smallest crack. Poking a finger through, he signalled Josette to begin.

Silence settled in around them. The air in the shed was close and warm.

'Keep still,' Stephen breathed. 'We don't want to set the tack to jingling.'

Mae turned carefully and crouched at the door. She peered out. Josette had slumped against the stable wall, a picture of abject misery.

Seeking a vantage point, Stephen moved into position above her. And around her. She closed her eyes and let the picture linger in her mind. She was encased in the strong, solid shell of Stephen's strength.

She breathed in. And wished she had not. The musky scent of him was a treacherous thing, filling her up with sweet recollection: her face buried in his neck, her hand burrowed into his hair, his hand burning between her thighs.

Oh, God, but she hoped the scent of her was driving him similarly insane.

Outside, Josette had begun to cry. The sound of her delicate, despairing sobs barely reached their hideaway. If someone were to hear they would have to be very close to her location. Or listening very closely.

Stephen shifted slightly and Mae jumped. Oh, but that was his pistol pressed against her hip. She suffered a level of disappointment that must be a severe character flaw.

How tempted she was to move—just a little—until her thinly clad bottom was pressed right up against his front. Then she would feel for herself if he were as uninterested as he was feigning to be.

He stiffened suddenly and grasped her arm. Mae froze.

The burly, surly man from earlier today—no, it was yesterday—edged around the corner of the stable. Mae caught the glint of moonlight shining off of the blade in his hand. She gasped.

Stephen drew his pistol. His hand gripped the door.

Peck drew to a halt several feet away from Josette. 'What in hell's half-acre is going on here?' Obviously he wasn't eager for attention either. He pitched his voice low and gruff so it wouldn't carry.

Josette only continued to sob.

He took a step closer. Roughly he grabbed the maid's arm. 'Who are you? Why are you here?'

With a soft wail Josette threw herself into his arms and proceeded to bawl down the front of him.

Miraculously, this seemed to take all the bluster out of the man. He cursed quietly. 'I never saw a stable overrun with so many blasted womenfolk,' he complained. But he still held a wicked-looking blade in his hand. It made him awkward as he reached up to try to pry Josette off him. But his free hand encountered a sample of her curves and the anger almost visibly drained out of him. 'Come on now, stop yer blubbering. You don't belong here, in any case. What are ye doin' out here?' The knife disappeared and he held her farther out, so he could get a good look at her. 'A pretty girl like ye? Why aren't ye inside, warming his lordship's bed?'

Josette accepted this for the compliment it was meant to be. 'Oh, no.' She wiped her eye. 'I've a man already. Never would I serve him so.'

'Who is your man?' Peck demanded. 'Someone here?'

'P-P-Patrick!' she cried with another quiet wail. 'They said in the taverns that he was gone, but I knew he would never leave me without a word. I came to meet him tonight as we'd planned, but he...he is not here!' She collapsed in a spate of fresh sobs.

'Aye, he is gone, and so must ye go. Ye cannot stay here.' It came out reluctantly.

'Oh—and after I stole away a decanter of my employer's best brandy, too,' Josette said forlornly. She gave a heavy sigh. 'Its cost was that dear, I'll be sacked in the morning, and for what?' Her brow furrowed and her lip trembled and even from so far away Mae marvelled at her skill. Josette's misery was a thing of beauty.

'Wait, now. What is it that you've got, there?'

With a visible hiccup, she reached into her bag and pulled out the decanter. Peck removed the stopper, took a sniff and then a taste.

'Bleedin' 'ell, that's some fine stuff! Nary an excise label ever to touch it, either, if I made a guess.' He took another swig.

Josette let out a little sigh and leaned her head against him. 'We could share it. If I am to be sacked, I might as well get a little pleasure out of it.'

Peck's eyes lit up at the idea of Josette's pleasure. 'I shouldn't,' he said reluctantly. 'I got to stay alert.'

'For what?' Josette straightened and scoffed. 'Someone must listen for the snoring of these fine horses and their grooms?' She pulled away with a sniff. 'I do not understand these Englishmen,' she muttered. 'To throw away a willing woman and a bottle of fine spirits?' She kept grumbling as she snatched the bottle back and returned it to her sack. 'Goodnight, *monsieur*,' she said with her nose in the air. 'I shall try to sneak this back where it belongs. Then I am for France, where I belong.' She turned to go.

Peck wavered. He let her go a few steps before the brandy, or the sight of her calves, won him over. 'Wait.'

She turned her head over her shoulder. 'You will help me forget Patrick?' she asked plaintively.

He nodded.

'Come,' she beckoned with a finger. 'You will drink with me in the same place that he meant to.' She slid her gaze up and down the man. 'This will be very good,' she said in a rough whisper. 'You will wipe my mind clean of that treacherous man.'

He took a step towards her.

She held out a hand. 'I will tell you of the first man who broke my heart. I was very young and had only just blossomed into my womanhood.' She ran a hand across her bosom and Peck, his eyes glued to her fingers, followed her like a lamb around the corner.

Mae straightened a little. Stephen sagged against her in his relief. For a moment they stayed where they were, barely touching, but Mae drew strength and comfort from him anyway. Then he stood and eased the shed door open. Taking the bucket with them, they crossed to the stable wall.

Stephen peered around the corner. 'Okay, let's go,' he whispered.

They slid around the corner and Stephen swung open the top half of Pratchett's stall door. There was no reaction from within.

'Perhaps this won't be so bad,' Stephen said, hopeful.

'He prefers a sneak attack,' Mae whispered wryly.

'And you aren't quite close enough yet. Listen—his feed box is there, on the left. He already knows he wants a bite out of me, so I'll approach from the right. When he lunges for me, you dump the pottage in.'

It worked like a charm. Pratchett's first feint was silent and quick. He let out an angry snort when he missed, but Stephen was already swinging the top door shut again, which helped to muffle the sound. They slid quickly back around the corner.

Peck must have heard something. Mae heard Josette's soft voice calling him to come back to her. The words were unintelligible, but the tone was clear. She and Stephen froze where they were.

Nothing. No steps. No response. Neither of them moved. After several minutes, Stephen peered around the corner again. He motioned for her to follow and very carefully they made their way to the box next to where Josette had taken Peck.

The empty stalls all stood open at the top. Stephen took great pains and several long seconds to silently open the bottom half of the door and the two of them slid in. He stopped her hand when she would have closed it after them.

'We may need to get over there quickly,' he whispered.

She nodded and left it where it was.

From here they could hear the sing-song rhythm of Josette's voice. There came the sound of pottery clacking together.

Stephen tugged her along to the opposite wall of the stall. 'Now, we wait.' He breathed the words in her ear.

A shiver started everywhere his hot breath touched

her skin, then raced up and down her spine. Insolent with need, unmindful of their circumstances, her nipples tightened up and poked through her linen shirt.

He didn't notice. He settled against the far wall and beckoned for her to join him.

She did, but she positioned herself far enough away from him to be safe.

Time stretched out. Their breathing settled into a comfortable rhythm. *He breathes out. I breathe in.* Over and again. Perhaps it was the nearness of him, perhaps it was the very precarious nature of their situation, but the tension in the air held a decidedly sensual tinge. Mae's nipples were still peaked and tight.

More murmuring next door. More clinking of cups. Stephen suddenly shifted and moved closer to her.

Good heavens. Was he not beset with images of everything they had got up to the last time they settled into the straw together? Mae remembered it vividly. The images—and her consuming wish to do it all again—were setting her blood to boiling. Her skin flushed. Her whole body was awake and tingling, hanging breathless while it waited for his to catch up.

'By my count, Peck has got to be on his fourth or fifth glass,' he whispered. 'If he's got any awareness left right now, I guarantee it is all fastened firmly on Josette. I'd say we've got a few glasses to go before he's done with the decanter.' His gaze lowered to her knees, propped up and clearly delineated in her divided skirt. 'Tell me a story,' he asked. 'Distract me.'

The look mollified her. A little. Slowly, she raised her eyes to his.

* * *

Stephen leaned away as Mae looked up to meet his gaze. His ears were tuned to the low murmur of conversation next door, his body tense with anticipation of the action to come. And yet—perhaps it was the straw and the unavoidable memories it invoked, perhaps it was that damned split skirt—but his head was filled with the sight and the scent and the incredible uniqueness that was Mae.

He needed to stay alert, but what he wanted was to sit her down and start enumerating all the ways in which his feelings for her had changed in the last week. He longed to tell her how much he enjoyed her quick wit, and admired her indefatigable spirit. How he'd caught himself a hundred times over the last days, filing away odd thoughts and funny incidents and serious observations until he could share them with her. How he adored her quirky need to streamline everything around her as much as her ready laughter and her tempting curves.

And if that didn't work, then he thought he'd rather enjoy laying her down and binding her to him with soft murmurings and softer caresses. Playing with her and intriguing her and making her achingly curious for what came next. With tenderness and laughter and fierce, hard passion he wanted to make her forget she'd ever held any aspiration other than to be his.

She was staring at him. Oh, Lord, but he recognised that steady, unrelenting expression.

'No, Stephen,' her voice pitched low, she replied to his request. 'I rather think that it is your turn to talk.'

He bowed his head. That was his Mae. She was not going to come easily, or without cost. She was never going to accept the flashy, shallow view he fobbed off on the rest of the world.

'I agree completely that we had to forge ahead tonight and stop Ryeton from perpetrating a fraud upon the entire world of racing. Heaven knows, I would not have missed this for the world.' He caught the flash of her grin in the dim light. 'But you've lost your chance at a match between Pratchett and Ornithopter.'

He groaned. 'Don't remind me.'

'Are you hoping to gain something further from this?'

He shrugged. 'The notoriety that would have come from returning Pratchett will double with the exposure of Ryeton's duplicity. I can hope to use it to help Fincote.'

'All of this…' and her gesture took in more than just the incredible adventure they found themselves in at the moment '…it's all been for Fincote Park.'

'I owe—'

'Yes, Stephen,' she interrupted him. 'Of course you owe your best to the people who look to you. But there is more to it, isn't there? My father said that he and Toswick agreed to race their fillies at your track. So there's an opening match for you.'

'It's not enough…' He turned from her, his voice trailing away. God, he'd known it was going to come to this. It didn't matter that they were in the middle of a horse theft, or that every event and emotion that they had set in motion was careening out of control. He was going to have to strip his soul bare before her.

'Why isn't it enough?' she demanded in a harsh whisper. 'Why is it so important that Fincote's launch be grand and spectacular? What is it that you are not telling me, Stephen?'

'I…' He was going to do it. Every instinct screamed for him to evade, escape, push back or take flight, but he was going to force the words past the fist of fear squeezing his throat. 'I'm not sure if I can explain,' he began.

He was interrupted when a loud rapping sounded on the other side of the stall.

Chapter Nineteen

It all happened so quickly after Josette summoned them. Stephen was up and gone from the stall like he'd been shot out. Mae followed, and found him standing bemused over Peck's form, prostrate across the stable floor.

'I didn't even get to hit him,' Stephen protested.

'I could not wait,' Josette said calmly. 'He was drunk, and he started to get restless when I was telling him about my last great *affaire*. So I accidentally dropped my mug. He stumbled, trying to fetch it for me, and I thought it best to hit him over the head with the decanter.'

Stephen pursed his lips. In a sudden explosive movement he reached out, swung Josette about and gave her a smacking kiss on the cheek.

Just as a great flare of jealousy surged inside Mae, he set her maid down and treated her to the same bit of handling.

'It's all downhill from here, ladies,' he said in a ferocious whisper.

And it was. Mae ran to fetch Matthew and the cart while Stephen bound and gagged Peck. They left him sleeping off his brandy in the stall.

The opium had begun to work on Pratchett. He stood fixed when Stephen slipped into his stall, and his head had begun to droop. He did snap at Stephen when he placed the bridle on him, but his movements were slow and half-hearted.

Stephen touched the viscous coating gathered at the horse's nose. He sniffed his gloved fingers and rubbed them together. Looking about the stall, he strode suddenly to the front corner and snatched up a bowl from the floor. It was coated inside with the same thick stuff. 'Flour and water, if I don't miss my guess.'

He bent down to touch a white foreleg. His glove came away smeared. Grimly, he met Mae's eye, but he didn't speak again.

Pratchett didn't protest when he was hitched on a leading rein to the back of the farm cart, but when they had gathered everything and everyone and Matthew picked up the reins to set out, the thoroughbred planted his feet and refused to move. No amount of tugging, encouragement or bribery worked.

They all gazed at each other in despair.

'The cat!' The thought struck Mae suddenly.

'Oh, I forgot,' said Stephen with relief. 'Will she come to you?'

'I think so.'

'Then use this.' He handed her a large basket with a latch.

'You really do think of everything,' Josette said with admiration.

Mae collected the cat from her nest in the straw. Moving to where Pratchett could see her, she placed the cat in, latched it closed and set the basket in the cart right before the horse's nose. When they started off again, Pratchett followed docilely along.

It was a quiet journey back to Newmarket. Stephen and Matthew were in high spirits. Josette was as unflappable as ever. Mae, on the hand, felt nearly as subdued as the stallion, despite the evening's successes. She'd missed her opportunity. Stephen was hiding something, something to do with Fincote, true, but it was more than that. Just a little more time, and she thought she could have coaxed him into sharing.

They entered Newmarket proper without incident and plodded right down High Street with their ill-gotten stallion. They made their way slightly north and when they reached Titchley's border, Matthew paused to let the rest of them scramble out.

'I'll see Pratchett and his friend settled tonight.' He jerked his head toward the back of the cart. 'But I will be back to take part in the fireworks in the morning!' With a cheeky grin, he called to his horse to walk on.

Stephen looked tired, but happy as he escorted Mae and Josette along the lane they had traversed earlier. 'Let's get you ladies home,' he said. 'You two can lie abed, but I've got several more stops to make, if we are to confront Ryeton in the morning.'

Mae's feet were dragging. She could not get those unspoken words out of her mind. He'd escaped and his relief was obvious. She glanced over at him. 'Stephen, will you be happy, do you think? After tomorrow's revelations?' In her mind she could see the attention he was bound to attract, the success he was going to bring to his people and to his enterprise.

They trudged along a moment in silence. Stephen never took his gaze from her. She wondered if he saw her, or if he was imagining the same sorts of scenes she was.

'Yes,' he answered at last. 'I intend to be happy.'

The air practically crawled with all of the things that were being left unsaid between them. The silence continued, leaving her upset and unsatisfied. Then they were at her back gate and Stephen was bending over her hand, and over Josette's as well.

'I cannot express my thanks, ladies.'

Mae didn't wish to hear him try, because she feared that was all that he would ever have the courage to express. Already her mind was awhirl with possibilities, conjuring ways that she could draw him out, but firmly she put a stop to it.

How she hated to leave her fate in anyone else's, even Stephen's, hands. But it had to be done. If there was to be a victory here, then he was going to have to make the choice and mount his own campaign.

The tension was tight about her shoulders again as she turned away and left him.

The faintest light had just appeared on the horizon the next morning, when Lord Ryeton crunched along the walkway to his stables. He must have been expecting a flurry of activity in the last box in his stable row, but what he found was Lord Stephen Manning, waiting

along with Lord Toswick, a grinning Matthew Grange
and Sir Charles Bunbury, Steward and unofficial presi-
dent of the Jockey Club.

The earl promptly broke down into tears at the
sight.

His countess, on the other hand, promptly broke
out of the house and fled the country. With his head
groom.

Several hours later, the trumpets summoned one and
all, and the racing began. A line of beautiful horses and
brightly coloured jockeys came together at the Rowley
Mile. The tape fell and the 2,000 Guineas went off
without a hitch, *sans* Pratchett, of course. Ornithopter
easily beat the others to the finish post, finishing far
ahead of the field and looking as if he could have run
another race besides.

The crowds cheered him wildly. The unknown,
unattractive horse was a sensation. No one could speak
of anything else.

Until the news of Ryeton's disgrace, Pratchett's
rescue and Lord Stephen Manning's part in all of it
broke. Even in Newmarket there had never been seen
anything like the fury of cheering, jeering and gossip
that resulted.

Stephen's arm grew sore from being pumped in congratulations. His back grew tender from the many slaps
of congratulations. His name, and Fincote Park's, featured in conversations all over town, and in the notes of
newspapermen from across the kingdom. Racing men
were approaching him, congratulating him, asking
questions about Fincote and enquiring about scheduling

private matches at his course. It was nearly everything he'd ever wanted. But unfortunately not everything he wanted now.

He could barely enjoy his triumph, so anxious was he to see Mae. His victory felt hollow, somehow, with her not there to share in it. His chance came in the late afternoon, after the racing was done. Lord Toswick threw an impromptu gathering to celebrate the day's incredible successes. All of his houseguests were present, of course, and much of Newmarket's population, besides. The rooms and passageways of Titchley were filled with racing fans recounting the day's events, toasting Stephen's insight, Matthew's bravery and Ryeton's downfall.

Stephen only wanted to find Mae. They had to settle things between them. He'd been on the verge of opening himself to her. But she'd closed herself off on the ride back into Newmarket, become distant and withdrawn.

Now he finally caught a glimpse of her in the yellow salon—Good God, had it really only been days ago when he'd kissed her against that wall? She looked sober, almost listless—a marked contrast to the carefree people celebrating all around her.

Stephen's anxiety grew as the evening wore on. All of his pleasure in the day and anticipation for the future began to fade. Mae, his vibrant and energetic Mae, slunk through the party, quiet and subdued. She was obviously avoiding him. Stephen's heart sank. It struck him suddenly, that this is how she must have felt, all those years ago, as she had followed him with hope in her heart and he had slid continuously away. What had happened to their new companionship? Where were the heat and the joy that had lately sprung up between them? When had they reverted to the mirror opposite of their old relationship?

His nerves were balancing on a knife's edge by the time Barty Halford drew him aside into a corner. It was a touch quieter here, but Stephen was not yet ready to speak to the man. He needed to resolve things with his daughter before he was forced to figure in Halford's perspective.

'Damn, but I'm proud of you, my boy.' Halford glanced at him, then turned his gaze once more to the seething, celebratory throng. 'You've done the sport proud, and done all of us a favour, exposing Ryeton's deceit like that.'

'Matthew said that the earl is being confined to the magistrate's house.'

Halford sighed. 'That won't last, I'm afraid. He hadn't actually done anything wrong, as of yet.' He chuckled. 'I don't suppose the magistrate will be able to charge him with painting socks on his prized stallion.' Sobering, he took a deep draw on his own cigar. 'But he's finished in racing. No gentleman will ever stand a horse against him again. And word's out now about his financial losses.' His head shook in disapproval. 'It was the gambling that did him in. There's nothing left, except the title, it seems. Not even his wife. Seems she discovered how bad things were and tried to help him cover it. She'll not likely return.' He blew another cloud of smoke. 'No, Ryeton won't be having an easy time of it.'

Something in the air told Stephen that the same might be said of him.

'Well, you are getting more than a few accolades for your bit in this débâcle. Your friend Grange, too. That's all well and good. And well deserved, I'm sure.' Halford raised a brow. 'But something tells me that it wasn't your hand alone stirring this pot of scandalbroth.'

Stephen didn't comment, but apparently he didn't have to.

'I know that Mae was in this with you, thick as thieves. But I have to thank you for keeping her name out of the limelight. All this attention will only help your cause, but it isn't the sort she needs right now.'

If only Stephen knew *what* she needed right now! Damn her for becoming suddenly enigmatic.

'My girl does appear to be happy since our return to England's fair shores, and as I've said before, I know I've you to thank for much of that. You've been a good influence on her these past days, Lord Stephen, and for that I thank you.'

'And as I've said before, it is my pleasure, sir.'

Halford smiled, but the expression noticeably did not make it to his eyes. 'Now that Ornithopter is a sensation I'll be happy to thank you by racing him at your Fincote Park.' He shrugged. 'I would have liked to race him against Pratchett.' He sighed. 'That would have been something to see.'

Stephen winced. Seeing Pratchett run now would have been something that anybody remotely connected to racing would have paid to see. But as expected, the Stewards had declared that the horse was not to race again—at least until recent events were thoroughly investigated.

'The Stewards have that horse in hand, now. They'll

keep him in custody until the situation with Ryeton is settled, but the earl's stables will be sold off, likely, to pay his debts. Might get to race against that horse afterwards, but it won't be the same.'

Another glance in Stephen's direction. 'Still and all, you did the right thing. We'll find another horse to lose to mine.' Halford chuckled. 'And though it is a bit too soon to think of it now, once all of this commotion dies down, I'll be pleased and proud to stand as your sponsor as a full member in the Jockey Club.'

It was ridiculous, really. The man was handing him a platter full of his fondest dreams. All the best things that could result from this infernal situation—except the most important one. A week ago he would have been ecstatic. Five days ago he would have given anything to hear those exact words. But Barty Halford had not risen to his exalted financial status by granting wishes and getting nothing in return. Stephen feared the price was going to be very high indeed.

The older man eyed him knowingly. 'Of course, there is something you can do for me in return.'

Of course. 'What would that be, sir?'

'It concerns Mae.'

Of course.

'And your friend, Mr Matthew Grange.'

Stephen closed his eyes. That was just the opening blow and it hurt like hell. It made him wonder if he was going to make it intact to the end of this cordial battle.

'You did agree to help in her search for prospective husbands. Perhaps Grange is not what most fathers would want in a match for their daughters,' Halford mused. 'But then, most fathers don't have to contend with a daughter such as Mae.' He chuckled. 'But the man has been a war hero. And as far as I'm concerned he proved his mettle and his courage over again when he faced down society's wolves here this week.'

'I couldn't agree more.'

'Grange has spent a fair amount of time with Mae in the last days and they seem to get on quite well.' Carefully, Halford sipped at his drink. 'The thing is, the man is going to need a solid helpmate to go on, what with his difficulties and all. And my Mae, she needs to be needed. If she weds him, she'll have no time for restlessness. She'll be busy looking after him, and helping him look after his interests. It's just the sort of thing to keep her occupied until the children start to come along—and then she'll be busy managing them, won't she?' He laughed.

It was perhaps the lowest blow. It rocked him from his gut right down to the soles of his feet.

'Mae seems to value your opinion,' Halford said. 'I don't need her to make up her mind today. Plenty of time. But if you talk to your friend and find him willing—well, then, I'd appreciate it if you would steer her in that direction.'

The old man waited for an answer, calm and expectant. Did he know what he was doing? What choice he was forcing Stephen to make?

Of course he knew. Mae had learned strategy and manipulation at his knee.

Stephen's chest heaved like a bellows. He wanted to shout a denial; to inform Halford unequivocally that no one would ever wed his daughter but him. He resisted the urge to cover his eyes with a hand. He'd done this to himself. He'd worried that it might come down to such a choice. He couldn't regret opening his eyes at last to all the beauty, generosity and exasperating perfection that was Mae, but what could compare to the pain of losing her, of seeing her spend her life with another man?

Only one thing—and the weight of it had already begun to crush the air from his lungs. The burden of guilt he would be taking on along with her hand. The heavy load of disappointment and sorrow from scores of people back home if he angered Halford and allowed him to withdraw his support and his patronage, if Fincote Park continued to sit empty, its people idle, their hope slipping away once more with each passing day. And, worst of all, the incalculably oppressive weight of his own failure, of the knowledge that his mother had been right, and that all of his struggles had been for naught.

Tiny slivers were running all along the shiny, reflective surface that Stephen showed to the world. It was an internal battle to hold them all together now.

'I'll be happy to talk to Grange, sir.' It was all he managed to get out.

'And Mae?' The man was ruthless.

Stephen nodded.

With a satisfied expression, Halford crushed the cigar. He held out a hand and wrung Stephen's nearly as hard as he'd just wrung his heart. Somehow, Stephen forced out the usual parting pleasantries. He left the corner, staggering a little. He felt, suddenly, as if he were an old man. He couldn't go back to the raucous party. He turned instead for the back of the house, and headed for the back door, wondering, as he went, just how many glittering pieces of himself he was leaving behind.

Chapter Twenty

Mae knew her father. That meant that she had a pretty good idea what that little meeting he'd held with Stephen had been all about. From across the room she watched Stephen gingerly step away from their somewhat isolated corner—and then she was certain. Silent, she followed and watched him head for the back of the house and she wondered if he meant to escape or if he only needed a moment to compose himself. She gave him a few minutes to accomplish either one or the other, and then she went after him.

He wasn't in the back passageways. Nor was he in the yellow salon. She felt a twang as she went past, the echo of that first kiss. She reached the kitchen, swung through the door and into organised chaos. Most of the busy kitchen maids didn't even look up from their flying fingers. Mae raised an eyebrow to the cook. The stout woman merely kept whipping her cream and cocked her head towards the back door.

This part of the grounds held no formal garden, just

a plot of land for the kitchen's use. There was a crude bench in the corner, for the cook's assistants to rest on as they cleaned carrots and snapped beans. Stephen sat there. Mae breathed in the fresh scent of spring onions and thyme and went to join him.

He looked pale. Lost. Like he had on that first night, after Ryeton had insulted his friend and dashed his hopes. She sat beside him. It was a small bench, but she pushed herself in and up against him. His dejection was telling her volumes and breaking her heart. Surely he deserved to hurt right along with her. She was not going to make this easy on him. She never had been one to play fair.

'So, what did he offer you?'

He heaved a sigh. 'Ornithopter at Fincote Park, as well as his filly. And full membership in the Jockey Club.'

Mae nodded. 'He usually knows his man.'

'I am supposed to push you into considering Matthew Grange as a prime candidate for marriage.'

She snorted. 'My father is not blind. You can bet that he knows what Matthew needs right now is freedom.'

His eyebrows rose. She decided to look at them and not at the incredibly clear blue of his eyes. Apparently *he* had not been considering Matthew Grange's needs. Well, she could forgive him that, as it was likely her fault. She had been keeping him busy, after all.

'You know he was just warning you off. From me.' She said it bluntly. If he was going to ruin her life, she'd rather it be done with swiftly.

He nodded.

'Is it so difficult, then?'

He didn't answer, just asked a question of his own. 'Did you send him to do it?'

Swift tears arose. Impatient, she blinked them back and shook her head.

'There's that, at least,' he muttered.

They sat together in the quiet evening for several minutes. It should be raining, she thought irritably. Why wasn't it raining? If it rained she could postpone this—the worst moment of her life—the one she was entirely to blame for. If it rained, then the noise of the falling droplets would mask the slow drip, drop of sorrow leaking from her broken heart.

Still silence. Mae was reminded suddenly of the old adage. *You can lead a horse to water, but you can't make him drink.*

'Excuse me?'

Had she said it out loud? She turned to look at him. This time she made the mistake of looking into those clear eyes, the ones that took in everything and showed nothing of the real Stephen inside. For the last time, she looked—and she fell, far and long and down, while he stole her breath, her future and her happiness.

Wordless, she waited. *Now,* she silently urged him. Now was the time for him to come out, or to let her in. Everything—their entire lives—hung in the balance.

'I wish this were easier,' he said miserably. 'Part of me knows that there is only one answer—that you are everything to me.'

'Bring out the other part, then, and let me deal with it.' She tried to laugh. And failed miserably.

'It's about more than just me.' He sounded

stricken. 'You can't know. No one knows—not even Nicky—everything I feel about Fincote Park.'

Mae drew a breath. Tried to think. 'I know how much you want it to succeed.' Enough to trade her— and their happiness—to ensure it?

'I told you about my mother. About how she was unable to deal with the dissolution of her marriage. She let it destroy her life.'

She nodded. Waited.

'That's not the worst of it. She let it destroy everyone's lives. Everyone at Fincote. She couldn't look outside her own sorrow long enough to notice anything. Not me. Not Nicky. Not even the rack and ruin that grew up around her.' He swallowed, and she wondered if he was going to be able to go on.

'She wanted to be invisible, I think. And she didn't want to see. I couldn't get through to her. I let it hurt me. I let her neglect define me, in so many ways. But worse, I let her blindness hurt others.'

'What happened?' Mae was losing him. She felt it. But she had to know why.

'It was the steward. My fault, though. I simply stopped visiting. What was the use? My visits grew shorter, with greater lengths between them, and finally, I could barely make myself go. Mother certainly didn't care what he did, so he was unchecked. There was no one to stop him from taking what he wanted. From whomever he wanted. He bled them all dry, Mae.'

She made an inarticulate sound.

'There's worse. When she died, she left Fincote to me. It was my inheritance, my responsibility, but I didn't want to go back. I was kicking up my heels in town—why should I return there and confront all the anger and inadequacy roiling inside of me? So I stayed away, and the villain was left free to do as he wished. He stole everything, even their hope. Until the land became as desolate and the people became as listless as my mother.'

He paused for a moment, and then he whispered, 'I didn't tell anyone. I couldn't. I didn't even discover it until long after she died.'

'Right before Charlotte's wedding.' She was whispering too. Suddenly his pain, his frustration and short temper all those years ago made sense. She'd known something was wrong. She'd pushed the matter and set all of these events in motion.

'I found…a wasteland. It was shocking. The soil was drained, every building and tenant house derelict, the livestock and equipment gone. They'd lost all hope.'

'But you helped them.'

'I just jumped in and did what I could. I'd always wanted to start up my own racecourse. I fell back on the idea and convinced them to go along with it. Two long years I've invested what money I have and worked at their side and promised them a better future. I have to deliver it.'

He looked up at her in anguish. 'I could have stopped it. Saved them years of despair. But I was selfish and thoughtless. And they suffered. How can I make the same choice now? Put my own happiness above theirs? I owe them, Mae.'

This was it, then. The end of her dream. Her heart was breaking. It shouldn't be allowed, such pain. She knew Stephen suffered too. But not as much, she suspected. For she had given this last attempt her all, and he had been hiding this secret away, balancing his feelings for her against the guilt that still racked him.

And suddenly, she was angry. He was not going to fight! She could scarcely believe it. Damn him—he was just going to give up and let her go. And she was going to drown in waves of pain.

'I should have known,' he said hollowly, 'I'm my father's son, after all. Someone is going to pay the price for my folly.' His eyes closed. 'I don't want to live without you, Mae, but I can't live with myself if I choose selfishly again.' Even his voice sounded bruised.

She stared at him. Everything that had happened, and still he was unwilling to take that last step. He looked like he had already been damned, standing there and waiting for her to answer.

This time, though, she wasn't going to push. She wasn't going to give chase. She wasn't that girl anymore. She'd let him break her heart again, but she'd changed. She'd gained a little wisdom and learned about pride, but most importantly—she'd learned to *truly* love.

She remembered the promise that she had made to him, as they lay entwined in the hay in that barn—she wouldn't add to his burdens. And she remembered their dance. She recalled the peace in his eyes and the lightness in his step. They had echoed, for a moment, the tranquillity in his soul.

'All I want is for you to be happy, Stephen.'

It was the truth. They had ended that dance and she had thought that she'd do anything to give him peace and happiness back. Somewhere in the last few days her marriage campaign had ceased to be about her happiness and become about his.

All of her tears were falling on the inside. Unending, they fell, yet still they could not fill the hollow spaces inside of her. 'I want you to make the choice that you must.'

He sucked in a breath.

From somewhere she dredged up a smile, though she doubted it was convincing. 'I want you to go home and be happy, Stephen. Pay your debt and be free. Open your course to fanfare and acclaim. Be safe knowing that everyone sees you, and respects you and the work you've done. Make it a success.'

She stepped close to him. Took his hand. 'And some day, when you are free to do it, I want you to open yourself up and let someone in. Show her all the wonderful parts of you—and the less stellar bits too. And then, at last, you will really be happy.'

She kissed his cheek. And left him there. And as she stepped carefully down the kitchen stairs, her tears started to fall on the outside, too. And at last, too late, so did the rain.

Chapter Twenty-One

It was good to be home.

Stephen rode slowly along the route of Fincote's course. As he rode, he paid close attention, checking for the evenness of the ground, the springiness of the turf and the padding on the course posts. Fincote Park's inaugural meet loomed, mere days away. He had been busy and productive nearly every hour since he'd returned from Newmarket, a fortnight past.

It was good to be home. He didn't know why he had to keep repeating it to himself. Perhaps because he kept forgetting that it was true.

This is what you wanted. He reminded himself of it daily. He was busy. Happy.

He was a damned fool. And a coward, to boot.

He'd come home braced to meet his people's disappointment, steeled to find sorrow and fear for the future in their eyes. He'd done his best, given more than he'd ever thought he'd have to; yet he worried it still hadn't been enough. He hadn't delivered Pratchett as he'd promised. Or a substitute on Pratchett's level, even. Though they worked now in preparation for the match between Halford's and Toswick's fillies, it was not the irresistible, not-to-be-missed event that they had all been hoping for, the sort to bring the racing community to them in droves.

And yet, to his utter amazement, he had seen only pleasure and anticipation in the people's faces. Even now, gardeners, track men, grooms, housemaids, even the merchants and innkeepers in the village, were working to make sure that all was in perfect readiness. They all bustled about, seemingly happy. Seemingly content.

It had felt unreal. A lie. Stephen had walked about on eggshells for several days. Carefully, he had watched for some sign of blame, resentment or accusation. But it had not come. And he'd been forced, at last, to a conclusion.

All of the disappointment and fear—and all the other negative emotions that went with them—came from inside him.

It was an ugly, humbling, life-altering realisation—one that had shaken him to his foundation and sent him reeling about like a drunkard for more than a few days. Unseeing, he had wandered all about the estate, berating himself for a fool.

Nothing would come completely into focus until, at last, he'd stood in the threshold of the one room of the main house that he'd always avoided. His mother's sitting room. Her tomb, to be truthful, the place where she had retreated, physically and mentally, away from him and the rest of the world.

He hated and despised that room. But he entered. Closed the door. Sat in her chair and inhaled the fading scent of her. And as he stared at the walls that had been less of a prison than the ramparts she had built in her own mind, the anger that he'd carried inside of him for so long rose up, ripping its savage way to the surface.

God, how it hurt! He'd been just a boy when all of this rage and anguish had begun to gather inside of him. But he did it—he relived each terrifying and infuriating moment, and he finally examined how he'd let it shape his life. All day he spent inside that horrid place and of all the painful revelations that he suffered during those long hours, the worst was the realisation that he had allowed himself to become just like her.

He'd spent his life defying the notion that his mother didn't love him enough to fight, trying to disprove his fear that he wasn't worthy of the effort to rid herself of her despondency. And then he'd been rocked by the knowledge of what his neglect and irresponsibility had done to Fincote and he'd known she'd been right all along.

It had been an insupportable notion. So he'd worked hard to prove himself, laboured endlessly to finally become a man who was worthy of love—and then he had thrown it away. He'd betrayed Mae, just as his mother had betrayed him. He'd allowed her to believe that she was not as important as his obsession.

Impossible to endure, such torment. Nearly mad with the pain of it, Stephen had grasped the high back of her chair, dragged it to the window and flung it through. With a crash the window shattered. Servants came running. Footmen muttered, maids whispered tearfully behind him, but Stephen stood unmoving, staring at the wreckage below, feeling the wind rush into the room. A cleansing wind. He let it blow through him, allowed it to carry away grief and rage, all the aching sorrow and hurt.

At last he'd turned, strode through the gaggle of staring servants and ordered that the room be emptied and stripped down to the bare walls and floors.

Now, the room had already been transformed, converted into a small parlour and given over for the housekeeper's use. But Stephen was still empty. Hollow.

But he was ready, now, to do something about it—and it started today.

He followed the course through until the end. Taking his time about it, he returned his mount to the stables and strolled back to the main house. Barty Halford was due in today. A message had come in last night from Horsham, telling him that Halford had stopped there for the night. He should have had plenty of time to arrive by now.

Stephen slapped his gloves casually against his thigh as he mounted the steps to the house. What he was about to do was going to put their entire project in jeopardy. But he trusted his instincts. And he was done living his life by the dictates of guilt and fear. His people had taught him well.

His housekeeper informed him that Halford had indeed arrived. The man had asked to await his host's pleasure in the bookroom. Every accommodation had been made to please him.

Stephen thanked the woman. He made his way there, only to find Halford had indeed made himself at home.

The older man had settled into Stephen's favourite plush reading chair. He had his feet up, a cheroot at hand and a stack of papers before him on a portable writing desk. Well, Stephen supposed that one didn't become as rich as Croesus by idling one's time away.

'Good afternoon, Mr Halford.' He strode across to meet his guest as Halford set the desk aside. 'Welcome to Fincote Park.'

'Lord Stephen! Thank you. A wonderful set-up you've got here.' Halford glanced out of the bank of windows and nodded his head. 'Your staff told me of all the work you've done and about some of the improvements you've made. It shows.'

'Thank you.'

Halford rubbed his hands together. 'I brought the filly along with me. Ornithopter is on his way as we speak. His trainer is walking him from Newmarket. I'm particularly looking forward to touring your stables and seeing your course.'

Stephen crossed to a cabinet and took out a decanter. He held it up as an invitation. 'Would you care to chase off the road dust, first?'

Halford was a man who knew how to read the currents in a room. He eyed Stephen carefully. 'Aye, don't mind if I do.'

'And how is your family, Mr Halford?'

'Well enough, thank you.'

'And Mae?'

There was the slightest pause. 'As challenging as usual, I would say.'

Stephen handed the man his glass of port. He tossed one back himself. 'The stables await your string of horses, sir. My staff is prepared. We've arranged for extra horse-boys to help with their care.' He allowed a note of satisfaction to creep into his voice. 'The course is immaculate and a pleasure to behold, if I do say so myself.'

'I don't doubt a word of it.' Halford still watched him closely.

'It is possible that you may change your mind completely about racing here—after I have had my say.'

Now Halford looked interested. 'Go ahead and say it, then.'

'I'm going to marry your daughter.'

For the briefest moment, Halford's gaze grew hard. There it was, then, a glimpse of the iron and the hot, gritty intensity that had brought the man so far from his humble origins. 'Are you now?' The question was mild. Deceptive.

'Yes.' Stephen was implacable. 'I am.' He poured himself another drink. 'That was a hell of a test you put me through.'

'Do you think I want her to marry a man not willing to fight for her?' Halford gave a little laugh. 'You should have seen what Mae's grandfather put me through.' He sighed. 'Aye, it was a test, and you didn't do so well. Are you sure she'll have you?'

'I'm sure. She's mine.' Stephen knew a bit about being hard, too. 'And she knows it.'

Halford shook his head. 'Give me leave to doubt that one, will you?' He sighed. 'I hope you're ready to fight now. There is no one like my Mae. She is absolutely the brightest young lady in the kingdom.' He took a drink. 'Except when it comes to you.'

'Yes, well, I can understand and forgive that small fault, since it goes both ways.'

'I don't know, Manning. You might have missed your chance. My girl is right put out.' He frowned. 'And I don't know that I want her to wed a chap that would let me run him off.'

Stephen shook his head. 'At first I thought that was exactly what had happened.' He was incredulous. 'But the truth is even worse.'

Halford raised a questioning brow.

Stephen let out a short bark of laughter. 'I'm not afraid of *you*. I'm afraid of *her*.'

Halford nodded. 'Well, that's only sensible.'

They both drank to that.

'Truly, though. You might have left it too late. Mae's got it in her head to go back abroad. She's packing as we speak.'

Stephen set down his glass. 'Then I'm sorry, sir—'

Halford waved a hand. 'Go on. Get it over with and all settled, finally, will you?' He looked about him with satisfaction. 'If you don't mind, I'll stay on here. I can oversee the preparations for the match and enjoy the hospitality of your fine estate.'

He shook the man's hand. 'Thank you, sir. If you don't mind…?'

'Go on with you.'

Stephen obeyed.

The Halford's London butler took Stephen's calling card. Without glancing at it, he informed Stephen that Miss Mae Halford was not at home to visitors.

Self-consciously, Stephen brushed a bit of straw

from his shoulder. 'Packing, is she?' Even from the front steps Stephen could see a footman racing up the stairs with an empty trunk and maids scurrying to and fro on the upstairs landing. He stepped brazenly inside and right past the man, heading for the stairs.

'But…sir! Wait! You cannot just…' The butler was frantically waving for someone to come and help him stop the madman invading his entry hall.

'Don't worry!' Stephen called out. 'Everything is fine.' He had already started up the stairs. 'I've just come from the lady's father. I have something that must be put straight into her hands.'

He followed the stream of frantic activity. It led him to a sitting room, obviously part of a suite of bedroom apartments. What he saw inside made him stall on the threshold. His jaw dropped.

Mae stood in the centre of the room, one hand absently massaging a shoulder, directing a whirlwind of activity around her. For the first time in his life, he saw that she was creating chaos around her, instead of taming it.

'Lace and other trimmings go in that one, Mama,' she directed her mother, standing patiently with her arms full of scraps of femininity, to an open trunk in the corner. 'No!' she cried as her mother obediently crossed the room. 'That one is medicinals.' She turned in a circle, gazing at the mounds of tissue, piles of clothing, stacks of books and various anonymous packages with dismay and a helplessness that Stephen had never seen in her before. 'Where are the trimmings? Oh!' She slapped a hand to her forehead. 'Why can I not *think*?'

She completed her circle and ended facing the door. She caught sight of him. Her hand fell to her side. 'Stephen! What are you doing here?' She frowned.

Her mother turned.

In the corner, Josette looked up from her folding. 'Thank God. You have come at last,' she said calmly. Standing and stretching, she frowned at him. 'I thought I would go insane.'

Mrs Halford clapped her hands. 'Everybody out!'

Sighs of relief came from the maids in the room and from the ones in the passage behind him.

'Except for you, dear.' Mrs Halford placed a restraining hand on Mae when she would have stepped forwards. 'You stay here.' Her mother paused in front of Stephen. She reached up and patted his cheek. 'It took you long enough,' she said.

He bent and whispered in her ear.

Her eyes widened, and she frowned. But then she glanced back at her daughter and a slow smile broke out across her face. She nodded. Shooing the last of the maids out, she closed the door behind her and they were alone.

Stephen faced Mae. 'I would ask how you are doing, except that I can see the answer for myself.' He gestured at their cluttered surroundings.

Her chin came up. 'I would ask you the same, except that I don't really care to know the answer.'

'Ouch.' He winced. 'Such hostility.'

'What did you expect to get from me, Stephen?'

'A welcome would be welcome. Especially when I've come to tell you a story.'

'I don't care to hear any of your stories, either,' she said wearily. 'Just go. I have quite a lot of work to do.'

'You don't want to hear? Not even if the story is about me?'

'*Especially* if the story is about you.' She folded her arms.

'Would you change your mind if I promised to end it with the admission that I am an idiot as well as a blind fool?'

Her arms uncrossed. 'I might be interested in that part,' she admitted. 'Could you skip straight to the end?'

'I'm afraid not.' He strode into the centre of the room and hefted her into his arms.

She shrieked.

He ignored her and crossed to the door. It was difficult, but he managed to get it open. Her mother and all the women stood there, in the passage.

There came another chorus of sighs from the maids. Without breaking his stride, he strode through them and carried her to the stairs.

'Stephen! What are you doing?'

'You'll have to forgive me. It took me nearly the whole of the past two weeks to work it all out. Who I am. Who I'm not. What I need. And, I hope, what it is that you want.'

'Ha!' She bounced in his arms at the force of her exclamation. 'I don't think that you have the faintest idea what I want.' But her arms tightened around his neck.

'I'm here, am I not? Please forgive my tardiness.

Perhaps it will help if you recall that I am but a man, and thus incapable of thinking as fast as a woman.'

She pursed her lips. 'I suppose I will have to take that into consideration.'

They had reached the entry hall now. The butler, in the corner talking sternly to a couple of footmen, turned several alarming shades of red. Stephen grinned at him as he passed by, heading for the back of the house.

'Back door?' he asked Mae.

'Next to the kitchens,' she answered. 'Stephen?'

'Mmm-hmm?'

'Where is it that you are taking me?'

'You'll see in a moment.' They shocked a maid into silence as she emerged from the kitchen. She stared, and then obligingly held the outer door for him.

'Some day I'm going to walk out the front door with you on my arm, like a normal suitor,' he said.

'Suitor?' she sniffed. 'We have yet to see about that.'

Through the back garden he carried her, across the alley and into the cobbled yard of the mews. The largest door was closed, but he'd left the smaller, inset door open a crack. He kicked it in and carried her inside.

'Where is everyone?' she asked, looking about.

'I gave them the afternoon off.'

'Stephen!' she gasped. 'They are not even your staff!'

He raised a brow at her. 'Out of all of this, that is the part that shocks you?' He shook his head. 'Well, perhaps I can do better.' He heaved and tossed her over his shoulder, head down and bottom up.

'That's enough of this now!' she protested. 'I want to know what is going on!'

He grunted as he started up the ladder to the loft over the tack room. 'I told you. I finally worked it out. For a time I couldn't think, what with all the flirting and kissing, horse stealing and husband hunting. It took me a while, but I finally understand.'

'I wouldn't be so sure of that.' Even upside down she oozed sarcasm.

He climbed higher. 'I took a leaf out of your book and started up a scheme of my own.' They were at the top now. He set her down and turned her to look.

'Oh!'

'It's small, but cosy.' He'd transformed the utilitarian space, draping it with fine linen, covering it with fresh hay, flowers, piles of the softest blankets and well-stuffed pillows. 'It seems fitting that we do this in a place like this, doesn't it?'

'Do this?' There was still a bit of resentment in her. 'Do what?'

'I did finally come to my senses, Mae. I realised any number of truths, one of which was that it was important that I make the choice for myself. That's what this is all about.'

He stepped in front of her and took her hands. 'I choose you, Mae. I can't live alone, cut off from everyone any more. I can't live without you—every challenging, exasperating and wonderful thing about you.' He looked sternly down at her. 'So I am going to finish what I started back in that barn in Suffolk.'

He pulled her close and nuzzled her. 'That's the first bit of my grand scheme. I am going to seduce you, soft and slow and sweet.' He whispered it in her ear. 'And then I am going to marry you.' He buried his face in the warm and fragrant curve of her neck. 'And then I am going to spend the rest of my life making you happy.'

The last came out slightly muffled. He pulled back. 'I know I cannot hold a candle to you, when it comes to intrigue, but I thought it a sound plan. What do you think?'

She pulled away from him, raised her hands in a helpless gesture. 'I say it's lovely—but it's not enough. What's changed, Stephen? What is different from a fortnight ago?' She swallowed. 'What about your people at Fincote?'

'My people?' He blinked at her, filled with a sudden sense of wonder. 'Do you know, I've never phrased it that way before. *My* people. They've always been Fincote's people, even in my head.'

He shook his head to clear it. 'That's the funny thing, Mae. My people, they're happy.' He scrubbed a hand against his brow. 'At first, I couldn't countenance it. I came home with no Pratchett. No spectacular début race. We've got a respectable match, to be sure, thanks to your father and Lord Toswick, but it wasn't what we had planned for. I thought that they must be disappointed. But they are not.'

He dropped his hand. 'All this time, I thought the choice had to be between my happiness and theirs—but they've been happy all along.'

Her mouth formed a circle of surprise and he shrugged. 'I left them, busy and content. I finally realised that they didn't need the spectacle and the drama—they just needed a purpose, something to work towards. The knowledge that someone cared, and was looking out for the future.'

Her eyes brimmed with tears and sudden understanding. 'All they needed was you.'

Solemn, he nodded. 'It scared me spitless. How can I be responsible for their happiness? I've never even had the courage to be responsible for my own.'

She made a sound of protest.

'It's true—and it started at Fincote, with my mother.' He sighed. 'That's the story I meant to tell you. I need to tell you.' He looked closely at her. 'Will you listen?'

She bit her lip. Nodded.

Stephen breathed deep and forged ahead. 'When I was a boy, I used to pretend that my mother was a sad princess, locked in a tower. Just like in the old stories.'

He shifted. 'There was a problem with this pretend, though. If she truly were a princess in a story, then surely she would fight off her melancholy, find a way to a happy ending. At the very least, she would have kept the sadness at bay long enough to enjoy the visits of her sons, wouldn't she?'

Clearly she didn't know what to say.

'But she did not. Or could not. I was so angry, Mae.' He had to pause a moment. 'Except that I didn't know what to do with it. How could I be angry with her? Neither was it easy to be angry with my father, who had brought on all of this sadness. So it all simmered, and I was left to watch helplessly while my mother faded away from the world. Eventually she was forgotten. Every time I visited, she grew quieter and more alone. Though I might be standing in the same room with her, still she was alone. Gradually the anger and helplessness mixed and spawned fear. I was afraid for her, but also for myself.'

She moved closer and he welcomed her into his arms. Her warmth made it easier to continue. 'I grew afraid that I would begin to disappear too. Fade away into nothingness, like her. Even when I returned to Welbourne Manor, with all the children and chaos and love, I was still afraid. I thought I might get lost in the crowd, and that would be the beginning of it.' He tightened his grip on her. 'I began to do everything I could to make myself stand out. I was loud and mischievous and I learned to make people laugh.' He allowed some of the self-recrimination he felt to leak into his voice. 'It didn't matter that the attention I received might be negative, it made me feel safe.'

'You were just a boy,' she protested.

'Yes, and the pattern was set—and so was the ugly truth hiding behind it. I *was* afraid of fading away. Worse—I was afraid that the reason my mother couldn't see me or love me, was my own fault. That I wasn't worth loving.'

'Oh, Stephen,' she breathed out a sob. 'So many burdens for such a little boy.'

But he couldn't stop now. She deserved all of the truth. 'I became accustomed to deflecting and redirecting emotion—both others' and my own. I never faced the anger and fear that I felt, until the situation at Fincote forced me to. And then I began to believe that she had been right all along.'

'You were both wrong,' Mae said fiercely.

'I diverted all of my resources to proving that. I

thought that if I made Fincote a smashing success, only then would I know that I was worthy. I would restore their lives, their futures and it would become clear to myself, my people, even to the ghost of my mother's voice inside of me, that I deserved love.'

Her eyes filled again and she pulled him close. 'You should have listened to me. I knew it all along.'

He shook his head. 'It seemed impossible. How could I ask you to love me, believe in me, if I didn't believe in myself?' He ran a finger along the side of her face. Cupping her jaw, he met her gaze and tried to convey the wealth of sorrow that he felt. 'I'm sorry I hurt you, Mae,' he whispered. 'The choice was mine and I chose badly. I knew it as soon as it was done, and it only grew worse as the days passed, until I was forced to confront the awful truth. I did what I've never before had the courage to do. I took a good, long look at myself.'

His mouth twisted. 'It wasn't easy. Or particularly pretty. I saw how badly I'd hurt you, after everything you had done for me, and I was ashamed. I knew I had to come here to apologise, if nothing else.'

She sighed.

'And I had to tell you, too, that I'm done closing myself off. I am ready to share all that I am with you, if you'll have me. There is nothing I want more than the chance to love you—and to accept your love in return.'

He could feel the intensity with which she examined him, but he didn't flinch. Love and happiness and relief were written in her eyes. She smiled. 'Now, was that so hard?'

He snorted. 'Excruciating.'

'Then I think we should get on with it,' she said. 'The loving part, I mean.'

He was nothing if not obedient. He slid his hands up from the curve of her waist, over the bountiful arc of her glorious breasts. For a moment he lingered there, distracted, but his fingers had a job to do. *Soon,* he promised himself.

He buried his hands in the golden sunset of her hair and began to pull out pins as quick as he could find them. Locks tumbled down and over her shoulders like rays of light. He hid his face in them, breathing deeply.

Sunshine. She was heat and warmth and love and sunshine. He could never survive without her.

Her hair fell across her bosom in waves, caressing her there. Jealous, he swept the locks aside. *Now.*

She wore a simple day dress of sprigged muslin. It was but a matter of moments to have her bodice down and her stays off. And then she was his to worship.

He laid her back on the softest of the blankets and filled his hands with her. Taking his time, he made love to her breasts with his fingers and tongue and teeth. Her own restlessly caressing hands gradually stilled. Her eyes closed. Soon she was bracing herself upon their bed of straw with her back arched, wordlessly offering herself up for more and more and more.

With his tongue he gave one last teasing flick of her nipple before he pulled back. 'I forgot. I have something for you.'

She gazed up at him, drugged with lust. 'Something more?'

'Here.' He took her hand and guided it to the heavy bulge in his breeches. 'A package I promised to deliver straight into your hands.' He laughed.

She ran her hands along the hard ridge of him, exploring, and the laugh descended into a moan.

'I do love surprises,' she said. 'Shall I unwrap it? Or will you?'

Soon they were both unwrapped...undressed. Stephen knelt between Mae's thighs and put a hand to the centre of her. Beautiful, wet heat. She sighed at his touch and opened her legs wider.

He looked up, caught her eye and grinned. 'Hold on,' he warned. 'There is another bit of strategy I have to implement.' He bent to taste her. Her shocked gasp died away. Moans of pleasure filled the void. His mouth and tongue caressed, her body trembled.

He couldn't wait any longer. He poised himself between her thighs and eased his way home. She encouraged him with words and hands and adorably awkward hip movements. He didn't need encouragement. She was tight and irresistible. He breathed deeply and plunged home.

Mae tensed. She muttered an unladylike expletive in his ear.

'I'm sorry, so sorry,' he murmured, stroking her hair. 'Let's just be still a moment. It will get better. I hope.'

It did. She relaxed, shifted, gave way and he was sinking again into heaven. And then they were moving, rocking, climbing higher together. Heat intensified, pleasure strengthened, and incredibly, he lengthened. He slipped a hand between them and stroked where his tongue lately had, where she needed it most.

She cried out and flew over, into the abyss. Another thrust and he followed. They floated, at peace with the endless emptiness about them because they drifted together, bodies and souls entwined.

Slowly, they came to earth, with contented sighs and happy murmurings. Gradually Stephen came back to his senses. They were curled on their sides, Mae's body tucked into his. Their sated breathing was the only sound in the small space.

A long curl of her hair lay across her shoulder. He began to trace his way along its fiery path. She grasped his arm, pulled it across her bosom and hugged it tight.

Stephen was grateful. Peace, contentment and caring flowed into him along with the warmth of her touch. It made him feel strong.

'You saved me, Mae. I had turned all that anger into a mirrored wall, invisible, but strong enough to protect the helpless boy still inside. And no one had a clue. Except you.'

She smiled ruefully. 'That wall has made me insane for years.'

'I know. It scared the hell out me that you even knew it existed. I might never have turned the mirror inwards, if not for you.'

Her fingers were back, caressing their way through his hair. 'I tried my best, in Newmarket, to knock it down for good.' Her smile was wry. 'I tried every trick I knew and most of Josette's, too.'

'You put a damned good dent in it,' he said. He couldn't quite summon a laugh. 'I was cracking apart in a hundred different directions. You had me in a frenzy. I wanted to tell you how badly I wanted you. I nearly found the courage, that night in Ryeton's stables. I swore I was going to be as valiant as you and lay myself bare.' He sighed. 'I knew if you wanted me, then I wouldn't be able to have you and to stay tucked away safe as well. I'm just sorry it took me so long.'

Mae's eyes grew sad. 'I'm afraid I am a horrible nuisance. I know this about myself. Everything is neck or nothing. Full measure. It is just the way I am made. I understand that not everyone can live with this.' Tears welled and her eyes sparkled like diamonds. 'It is a lot to ask of a person.'

'You should absolutely ask it, Mae. You deserve no less. Listen to me.' He sat up, took her hands and pulled her gently up as well. 'I had to choose it. If that wall was going to come down, then it had to be my doing. My choice.' He kissed both of her hands. 'I don't need the world's attention any longer. Not as long as you look at me with love in your eyes. Not as long as I have you to remind me of the man I am and the one I want to be. I don't need that damned wall, because I have you to keep my heart safe.'

She gripped his arms, but didn't respond. Stephen felt a flash of alarm.

'Shall I prove it?' He held her shoulders tight. 'I will. Anything.' He said it with all the fierceness of his conviction. 'Shall I give up racing? Sell Fincote?' He glanced back towards the house and smiled. 'Shall we go abroad? If you feel you will be happiest in Europe, it is fine with me. I'll embark on any adventure, as long as I have you by my side.'

She only gazed at him, intent.

'Mae?'

She reached up and held his face with both hands. Her gaze met his and held it.

'Mae?'

She blinked back sudden tears once more. 'It's you,' she whispered. 'You truly are in there. I can see you.'

He smiled through his own suddenly watery eyes. 'Yes. I'm here. Out here. In the open. Thanks to you.'

She started to cry in earnest, then. He wrapped himself around her and held her tight. Tears were fitting, he thought, after everything they had put each other through. Tears of happiness at the start of their new life.

Eventually, the storm died away. She raised tearful eyes to his. 'I promise, I will keep your heart safe. Always,' she said in a whisper.

'I know you will,' he said tenderly. And then he grinned. 'And I promise to keep you busy.' He jerked his head towards the house and the mounds of half-packed trunks. 'Well, what of it, Mae? Are we for Plymouth and points beyond?'

'I don't know,' she mused. 'There must be a great many things to keep track of, when you are operating a racecourse. I wouldn't mind trying my hand at it.'

He laughed. 'Well, perhaps we can accomplish all of it. Make a mental note, my beauty, so we don't forget. First, be safe,' he began.

'And be happy,' she reminded him.

'Next, run England's most organised racecourse,' he continued.

'And *then* go to visit Europe,' she finished.

'Well, that should keep us occupied for quite a while.' He bent to kiss her.

And so it did.

* * * * *

HISTORICAL

 Regency

MISS IN A MAN'S WORLD
by Anne Ashley

With her beloved godfather's death shrouded in scandal, the impetuous Miss Georgiana Grey disguises herself as a boy and heads to London to discover the truth. Being hired as the notorious Viscount Fincham's page helps Georgie's investigations, but plays havoc with her heart...

Regency

CAPTAIN CORCORAN'S HOYDEN BRIDE
by Annie Burrows

After her father scandalously auctions off her virginity, Miss Aimée Peters flees London to become a governess in remote Yorkshire. But her new employer, the piratical Captain Corcoran, never sought a governess—he wants a bride!

Regency

HIS COUNTERFEIT CONDESA
by Joanna Fulford

Major Robert Falconbridge and English rose Sabrina Huntley must pose as the Conde and Condesa de Ordoñez on a perilous mission. Soon Falconbridge doesn't know what is more dangerous—his enemies or the torment of sharing a room with this tantalising beauty...

On sale from 1st April 2011
Don't miss out!

0311/04a

HISTORICAL

Regency

REBELLIOUS RAKE, INNOCENT GOVERNESS
by Elizabeth Beacon

Notorious rake Benedict Shaw can have his pick of *ton* heiresses, but one woman has caught his experienced eye... governess Miss Charlotte Wells! And he isn't used to taking no for an answer...

WANTED IN ALASKA
by Kate Bridges

Outlaw Quinn can't risk doctor's visits—kidnapping a nurse is the only answer. But Autumn MacNeil is only dressed as a nurse for a costume ball, Still, there's no way he can let her go now...

TAMING HER IRISH WARRIOR
by Michelle Willingham

Widow Honora St Leger knows there is little pleasure in the marriage bed, so why should she care that the disturbingly sexy Ewan MacEgan is to wed her sister? Ewan finds himself drawn to the forbidden Honora—one touch and he is longing to awaken her sensuality...

On sale from 1st April 2011
Don't miss out!

She was his last chance for a
future of happiness

Fortune-teller Jenny can make even the greatest
sceptic believe her predictions just by batting
her eyelashes. Until she meets her match in
Gareth Carhart, the Marquess of Blakely, a
sworn bachelor and scientist.

Broodingly handsome Gareth vows to prove
Jenny a fraud. But his unexpected attraction to the
enchantress defies logic. Engaging in a passionate
battle of wills, they must choose between everything
they know…and the endless possibilities of love.

Available 18th March 2011

www.millsandboon.co.uk